"Please, Mr. Wallin? I don't think I could be so bold as to ask a stranger. I know I can trust you."

Nora trusted in him on the thinnest of connections. And how was he to know she wouldn't abuse his trust? She wouldn't be the first to disappoint him.

But she may be the first to truly understand you.

Where had that thought come from? He'd yet to find anyone who shared his views on life. His was the lone voice of reason some days at Wallin Landing. Therefore, he should evaluate this proposal on logic, not emotion.

She was offering one hundred and sixty acres he badly needed and could get no other way. He was offering protection from an overbearing brother. They didn't have to live together.

It was all strictly platonic. They both achieved their goals with relatively little effort. What was wrong with that?

"Very well, Miss Underhill," he said. "I'll make the arrangements for us to wed."

She offered him her hand. "To our bargain."

Simon took it, felt the tremor in her fingers. She wasn't any more sure of this marriage of convenience than he was.

Had he just agreed to something they'd both live to regret?

Regina Scott has always wanted to be a writer. Since her first book was published in 1998, her stories have traveled the globe, with translations in many languages. Fascinated by history, she learned to fence and sail a tall ship. She and her husband reside in Washington state with their overactive Irish terrier. You can find her online blogging at nineteenteen.com. Learn more about her at reginascott.com or connect with her on Facebook at Facebook.com/authorreginascott.

REGINA SCOTT

*A Convenient
Christmas Wedding*

HARLEQUIN® LOVE INSPIRED® HISTORICAL

Recycling programs for this product may not exist in your area.

LOVE INSPIRED BOOKS

ISBN-13: 978-0-373-28382-8

A Convenient Christmas Wedding

Copyright © 2016 by Regina Lundgren

www.Harlequin.com

Printed in U.S.A.

Chapter One

Seattle, Washington Territory
December 1866

What better time than a wedding to ask a man to marry you?

Nora Underhill stood in the corner of the Occidental Hotel's fine restaurant, watching as toasts were raised. Behind the head table draped in white, her friend Maddie O'Rourke looked beautiful in the embroidered spruce-colored wool gown Nora had sewn for her. The other ladies wore their church clothes, soft wools and a few velvets in rich colors that glowed like jewels in the golden lamplight.

Everyone seemed so happy, particularly Michael Haggerty as he gazed down at his bride, whose blush was nearly as red as her hair. Nora liked seeing people happy. She liked making people happy. A shame she'd never managed that with her parents or her brother and sister-in-law. If her brother's socially astute wife were here, Nora could imagine what Meredith would say.

You are quite right to hide in the shadows, Nora.

These people will only judge you and find you lacking. I can't imagine what your friend was thinking to name you maid of honor. No doubt she was only being kind.

And Maddie was kind. Nora knew that. The outspoken Irishwoman had befriended her, trusted Nora to teach her little sister, Ciara, how to sew. Maddie had even complimented Nora on her dress today—lavender crepe with a scalloped overskirt, fitted bodice and embroidered amethyst-colored hearts along every edge. Quite fitting for a wedding, she'd thought when she'd finished it. And she'd managed to tame her unruly black hair back behind her head in a bun that was at least a trifle fashionable. Even Meredith would find her satisfactory today. But then, it wasn't Meredith she was trying to please.

Let him look with favor on my proposal, Father.

Immediately, guilt gnawed at her. She tried never to ask for things for herself. When her parents had sickened, she'd prayed for them as she'd nursed them. The Lord had seen fit to bring them home to heaven.

When her brother, Charles, and his wife, Meredith, had taken her in, she'd prayed at first for their strength. They'd always seemed terribly burdened by her presence.

When she'd decided to leave home and venture to Seattle with the Mercer Expedition, she'd prayed for its success, for the health and safety of the ladies sailing all the way around the continent to make a new life. God had delivered them to Seattle, where nearly all her traveling companions, including Maddie, had found employment and husbands.

Surely, just this once, He'd consider it appropriate for her to pray for herself.

And she certainly needed His help. She wasn't brave or bold like Maddie, but today she would ask the bravest, boldest question a lady might utter. Her entire future depended on how Simon Wallin answered. She couldn't return to the life she'd led back in Lowell, Massachusetts. She'd thought she'd escaped by coming to Seattle with Asa Mercer last May. She'd fallen in love with the wide sweeps of fir, the massive mountains in the distance, the gentle call of the waves on Puget Sound. Even the cool, damp air smelled like freedom here!

And then her brother, Charles, had written that he and Meredith were also coming to Seattle. It seemed they'd suffered a financial setback and thought to reestablish themselves here. Charles had instructed her to secure a home for them and furnish it, the costs to be paid with his remaining funds. Of course, he didn't ask her to find a cook or a maid. She knew who would be cooking and cleaning and helping his wife dress.

Her.

She shuddered and had to paste a smile back on her face as more of Maddie's friends rose to cheer her good fortune. Maddie and Michael made a fine couple, and the way Maddie's little brother and sister beamed, the four were already on the way to becoming a loving family.

That was not her experience of family. Family clutched at you, pecked at you, bared each of your faults and made you feel small, stupid and vulnerable. Neither her parents nor her brother had ever loved her. Perhaps the only love she'd have was that of her Heavenly Father. There was a certain contentment in that. No one could steal it from her.

But Charles and Meredith could certainly try to steal her happiness, her prosperity. She could attempt to stand up to them, but they were like a stream running down a mountain. The mountain could stand as tall and proud as it liked. The water was still going to cut a canyon.

Like her parents, her brother felt it his duty to protect her from a world that was unkind, condemning a lady who lacked fortune, figure and face. What he saw as protection, she felt as a swaddling blanket, tight, smothering. Meredith had, surprisingly, been the one to encourage her to leave Lowell. Why couldn't Charles understand that Nora had done well for herself here, with no help from him? There wasn't a man or woman in the room who hadn't come to her to either repair or create clothing.

Except one.

She could see him now, standing against the opposite wall as if he too had other matters on his mind. Though his strong arms were crossed over his chest, tightening the wool of his plain brown suit, there was nothing hesitant or shy about Simon Wallin. He burned with the intensity of an oil lamp's flame, barely contained by the glass. He alone was as tall as his older brother Drew, who had married Catherine Stanway of the Mercer Expedition, and Simon held himself with his head high, his gaze firm as he watched his family nearby.

They too seemed terribly happy together, enough so that a sigh came out of her. Mrs. Wallin, the matriarch of the family, her graying red hair curling, had linked arms with her blond-haired daughter, Beth, who smiled up at her. Towering over them, Drew exchanged glances with his pretty wife, Catherine, as if remembering their own wedding day, as did the regal Alexandrina and her dapper husband, James Wallin. Younger brothers John and Levi jostled each other good-naturedly as if they couldn't wait to get out of the suits and into the more comfortable clothes they likely wore when logging.

She supposed she might have approached John. He was by all accounts studious and kind, even if he was a few years her junior. But Simon, she thought, held greater possibilities when it came to strengths. Surely that high forehead was testimony to intelligence. The long, lanky body certainly spoke of hard labor, and the firm fingers told of days wielding an ax and nights cradling his father's violin. She'd heard him play at Catherine's and Rina's weddings. A man capable of bringing such joy must have the capacity to understand her hopes.

But there was another reason she'd chosen Simon. Maddie had confided that he was a man who could be utterly fixed on a course of action, and he was focused now on a goal to help his family. With two new brides and babies on the horizon, the Wallins needed more farmland.

And that was something Nora could offer.

She raised her head, determination stiffening her spine and forcing her feet across the room to his side as the other guests came forward to accept pieces of the wedding cake Maddie had created in her bakery. Nora felt Simon's gaze shift to her and nearly wilted under the considering look. She reminded herself that whatever he thought of her, whatever he said, it could be no worse than what she would endure once Charles and Meredith arrived.

"Mr. Wallin," she said, the sound of her thundering heart nearly eclipsing her voice in her ears. "I'm Nora Underhill, and I have a proposal for you."

He frowned. His brows were a shade darker than his

short, light brown hair. They made a firm slash across his tanned skin. Those green eyes were like chips of jade as he gazed down at her. "A proposal?"

"Yes," she said, amazed at her own audacity. "An actual proposal. Simon Wallin, I want you to marry me."

Simon blinked. Even in primitive Seattle, even at a reception where weddings were on everyone's mind, a lady didn't ask a gentleman to marry. She had no reason, for Seattle boasted ten men for every lady of marriageable age. Instead of offering, a lady generally had to fend off too many offers.

And it wasn't as if he was well acquainted with the woman. He had met her only once or twice. He might not have remembered her name if she hadn't reminded him now.

Besides, she certainly didn't seem the forward type. He'd noticed her, standing against the far wall, one hand hugging her waist, her face first brightening in a smile, then darkening. Now her gray eyes were growing misty in her expressive face, and her generous lips were trembling.

He could not imagine what would have driven her to make such a bold request, but he wasn't about to grant it.

"I think," he said, keeping his voice kind and respectful, "that you are talking to the wrong man. Any number of fellows would no doubt be delighted to pay you court, Miss Underhill."

She shook her head so strongly her hair flew out of the bun in which she'd attempted to bind it, thick black tendrils curling like smoke around her broad cheeks. "No. It must be you. You see, I don't want a husband,

and from what I gather, you don't want a wife. We'd be perfect for each other."

He could not follow her logic, but that was nothing new. He struggled to understand even his brothers' choices.

Drew was myopic, so focused on raising their brothers and sister after their father's logging accident that his oldest brother sometimes forgot most of them were grown now and able to make their own way. His younger brother James was too spontaneous, leaping into action without considering the consequences. John had his head in the clouds, always dreaming, and Levi was young enough that he tended to think only of himself. They all saw the world as they wanted it to be. He saw what it could be. Was it any wonder none of them realized the problems looming over the farm?

"I appreciate your faith in me," Simon told the woman in front of him as the rest of his family headed to accept a piece of Maddie's no-doubt delicious spice cake. "But I must decline."

He pushed off the wall to follow them, and she darted in front of him once more. She was short; the top of her head came below his collarbone. But her figure in the lavender gown was sturdy, solid.

"Please," she said, her gaze turned up to his and her face pinched. "Hear me out. You need land. As your wife, I can bring you one hundred and sixty acres."

About to brush past her again, Simon paused. She was right, of course. He'd already tried to convince Drew and James to file for their wives, to no avail. With Catherine four months pregnant, Drew didn't want to chance making her travel to Olympia to claim the land the law allowed her as his wife. And James, the only other one of them besides Drew and Simon to have earned his patent, was determined to claim the bluff overlooking the lake for the town site they had planned to honor their father's memory. That land was no good for farming.

So it was all up to Simon to find a way to gain the much-needed farmland, even if the family budget would not extend that far. He had even identified the property—a good stretch of flat acreage running above his claim, his mother's and Drew's. He'd prayed for guidance, but as usual, he'd heard no answer.

But to marry a stranger? He'd never planned to marry, despite the fact that he'd threatened Drew with courting Catherine when his brother had proven reticent to add the pretty nurse to the family. Simon tended to bump heads with anyone close to him, no matter how hard he tried. Perhaps that was why God so often remained silent. It seemed Simon's role in life to spot the flaw in any plan, to point out the error in misconceived ideas. Love, and faith, did not grow in that environment.

Yet here stood Nora Underhill, biting her lower lip, gazing up at him as if he alone had the capacity to make her dreams come true. If it had been one of his brothers or Beth suggesting that he marry for the land, he would have told them they were being idiotic. But she had obviously taken a risk by approaching him, and he could only respect her for that.

"I'm not the most patient and tolerant of fellows," he admitted instead. "You might call me a cynic. I doubt I'd make a good husband. I like things just so, and I can't abide senseless frivolity."

"I am not the least bit frivolous," she assured him, waving both hands so that he caught a glimpse of the entirely frivolous hearts embroidered along her equally frivolous scalloped cuffs. "This would be a simple bargain. You would continue to live as you always have. I intend to stay in my room at the boardinghouse in Seattle. I'm a seamstress, and I should like to keep working."

A practical consideration, he'd give her that. But any number of things troubled him about this bride bargain, the largest being her motivation. Why would a woman surrounded by bachelors need to approach him?

"And what do you gain from this marriage?" he challenged.

She drew in a breath as if for fortification. "Protection."

Simon stiffened. "Protection? If someone is threatening you, Miss Underhill, tell me his name, and I'll put a stop to it. And if you don't wish to confide in me, I know a dozen men in Seattle who would be happy to oblige. You have no need to sell yourself in marriage to escape unwanted attentions."

Color sprang to her cheeks, making them as red and round as the apples on the tree Ma had planted their first spring at Wallin Landing. He had to fist his hands to keep from reaching out to touch the no-doubt warm skin.

"That is very kind of you, Mr. Wallin," she said. "But it isn't a would-be suitor, I fear. It's my brother."

The concept of a brother harming a sister was so far from his reality that he could only stare at her.

"He doesn't strike me, if that's what you're thinking," she hurried to assure him. "He merely feels strongly that I should be sheltered from the world. And he has the law on his side. You see, my father's will names my brother, Charles, my guardian until I turn five and twenty, which is nearly a year away. I believe Washington territorial law will allow me to wed without his permission."

"So you're running away," he said, not sure why the thought disappointed him.

"I prefer to think of it as a strategic retreat," she told him. Her little chin jutted out as if to prove she had some spirit. "Please believe me when I say that only a man of character and conviction can fend off my brother." She glanced up at him. "You might say I'm buying courage for those one hundred and sixty acres."

"And at the price of your future," Simon pointed out, his mind still trying to grapple with the concept. "Even here, divorces aren't easy to come by. They have to be approved by the territorial legislature. If you marry me, Miss Underhill, you'll most likely be stuck with me. What if you find another fellow you truly love?"

She rubbed at the fancy embroidery on her cuff. "That's not likely to happen," she murmured. "I don't seem the sort men fall in love with."

And why not? She had a certain intelligence—she'd certainly thought through her surprising plan. She was industrious—look at her work as a seamstress. She might not be the prettiest member of the Mercer Expedition, but there was something sweet about that round face, those wide gray eyes. Surely any number of loggers and miners would cherish such a wife.

Of course, they didn't need one hundred and sixty acres.

And soon. By his calculation, if his family was careful, they would just scrape through this winter with enough food for themselves and the animals. By next winter, Catherine and likely Rina would each have a baby. The members of their extended family would only increase from there. He needed time to clear the land and prepare it for spring planting. Winter was coming, and with it the Christmas celebrations. Every day counted. He'd been racking his brain trying to find a way to secure the claim.

Here was Nora, offering it to him. All he had to do was fend off her brother. If the man was half as controlling as she claimed, Simon looked forward to the confrontation. Any brother who denied his sister love deserved to be put in his place.

Still, marriage? Out here, a man took a wife to continue his line and raise children to help in taming the wilderness. It certainly seemed to him that's what his father had done. But it didn't fall to Simon to continue the Wallin name. He had four brothers to take care of that.

And it wasn't exactly convenient to marry in Seattle. Even with Asa Mercer bringing his brides, there were still too many lonesome bachelors for every lady. He'd watched Drew fret over courting Catherine, seen James turn himself inside out to please his bride. But Simon wasn't a man who changed easily. Just ask his family. They'd called him proud, stubborn and downright fussy on occasion.

She must have sensed his vacillation, for she laid a hand on his arm. "Please, Mr. Wallin? I don't think I could be so bold as to ask a stranger. I know I can trust you. Maddie speaks so highly of all your family."

Did she? Certainly he admired the feisty redhead who had achieved her dream of opening a bakery. But surely even she would not condone this marriage of convenience.

"Did you ask her about this?" he replied.

She shook her head, eyes solemn. "No. Never. She'd try to talk me out of it."

He should do the same. Nora trusted in him on the

thinnest of connections. And how was he to know she wouldn't abuse his trust? She wouldn't be the first to disappoint him.

But she may be the first to truly understand you.

Where had that thought come from? He'd yet to find anyone who shared his views on life. His was the lone voice of reason some days at Wallin Landing. Therefore, he should evaluate this proposal on logic, not emotion.

She was offering one hundred and sixty acres he badly needed and could get no other way. He was offering protection from an overbearing brother. They didn't have to live together, make a family. He had enough problems with the family he had.

It was all strictly platonic. They both achieved their goals with relatively little effort. What was wrong with that?

Glancing up, he saw that nearly everyone else was busy eating. Not a one realized that two more lives were about to change forever, if Simon could bring himself to agree.

His oldest brother laughed then, his deep voice like the toll of a bell. It had been a long time since Drew had laughed so freely. He'd sacrificed years of his life to raise his brothers and sister. Could Simon do less for his family?

"Very well, Miss Underhill," he said. "I'll make the arrangements for us to wed. A lumber schooner is scheduled to arrive in Seattle on Tuesday. Meet me at the Brown Church that morning at ten, and we can travel to Olympia after the ceremony to file the claim."

She offered him her hand. "To our bargain."

Simon took it, felt the tremor in her fingers. She

wasn't any more sure of this marriage of convenience than he was.

Had he just agreed to something they'd both live to regret?

Chapter Two

"Are you sure about this?" Levi demanded Tuesday morning. "From where I sit, girls are nothing but trouble."

Simon glanced at his youngest brother, whom he'd brought to stand as one of the witnesses to his wedding and then the land claim. Levi's curly blond hair framed a face that could look remarkably innocent when Simon was sure his brother was plotting mischief. Now his dark blue eyes were narrowed, his hands shoved deep in the pockets of his gray wool trousers.

"I'm sure," Simon said, shifting on his feet as they stood in the vestibule of the church. John, his closest brother, had gone to fetch the minister while they waited for Nora to arrive. "We need the land. She needs a protector."

"If she won't stand up to her own brother, she can't have much spunk," Levi declared. "Maybe that's good. We had enough trouble with Ma and Beth, even before we added Catherine and Rina to the family."

Until the last year, his mother and younger sister had been the only females at the northern end of Lake Union, where his family had staked their claims. If Simon brought Nora home, the number of women and men would at last be even. That is, until Catherine gave birth.

Still, Simon couldn't deny that Nora's confidence seemed to lag where her brother was concerned. Once again he looked forward to putting the fellow in his place. That was his side of their bargain, after all. He knew from experience that his height and angular features could serve to intimidate.

A door to one side of the altar opened to admit John. His red hair flashed in the dim light as he loped down the dark box pews under the arches soaring overhead.

"Mr. Bagley will be here shortly," he reported as he came to a stop beside Simon and Levi and paused to adjust the starched collar of his dress shirt. "He seemed a little surprised you were in such a hurry. I told him why you needed to get to Olympia."

"If we don't make the sailing of the *Merry Maid*," Simon replied, "there may not be another ship for a week or more. I don't want to wait. That's why I didn't tell Ma or the others."

Levi wrinkled his nose. "You'll have to pay for that."

"I'll survive," Simon predicted.

John, always the peacemaker, held up his hands. "We'll help you explain the situation to her. She'll have to admit your intentions were good."

Simon had confided his and Nora's unusual bargain to his two youngest brothers. John in particular had put up a fight at first, but Simon had convinced him of the necessity. He wasn't sure his mother and sister would be so easily swayed. He was only glad Nora would remain in Seattle and not have to face them.

The main door to the church opened then, and sunlight pierced the shaded vestibule. A vision of loveliness floated in on the light, bountiful curves outlined in a green as bright as spring. Simon blinked, bemused.

The door closed, shutting off the light. Standing beside him was the woman who'd asked him to marry her. Nora's thick hair was carefully bound in a coil at the nape of her neck, and a cloth hat of lavender silk sat on her head, a white feather pinned on it with a green glass broach. Gone was the embroidered dress from yesterday. Today's creation boasted a sleeveless green overcoat embroidered with darker green leaves and scalloped along all the edges over a white wool bodice fitted to her form. It was as impractical as it was beautiful. Simon found himself staring.

"Everything ready?" she asked, setting a carpetbag on the floor by the door and draping a gray wool cloak over it.

He managed a nod. "Yes. The minister will be here shortly, and the ship arrived right on schedule."

Beside him, John cleared his throat, then nudged Levi aside to take Nora's hand. "Let me be the first to wish you happy. I'll soon be your brother John."

"Nora Underhill," she said with a curtsy that made her skirts poof out around her. "We've met before. I attended the weddings when Miss Stanway married your oldest brother, when Miss Fosgrave married your brother James and when my friend Maddie married Michael Haggerty. You were all there."

"Funny," John said with a charming smile. "I thought I'd danced with every pretty girl at the receptions."

"You did," Levi said, earning him an elbow to the gut from John.

Nora's cheeks brightened in a blush, and Simon fought the urge to scold his brother. The youngest boy in the family, at eighteen, Levi had been spoiled by their doting mother and was only starting to realize he needed to take responsibility for his words and actions.

"I didn't mean anything by that," he muttered now, rubbing his ribs. He nodded to Nora. "I'm Levi. Thank you for marrying Simon. Somebody should."

Simon shook his head, but her blush deepened. "Your brother is doing me a favor," she murmured.

Simon was just glad to see Mr. Bagley hurrying through the door at the back of the church. A slight man with a head of bushy hair and an equally bushy beard over his chin, he nonetheless managed to exude a certain sense of propriety as he stopped before the altar and motioned them forward.

"Mr. Wallin, Miss Underhill," he greeted with a look over his spectacles. "I know you are both of age. Are there any legal impediments to this marriage?"

"None," Simon said with a look to Nora, who shook her head.

Mr. Bagley nodded. "And are you both in agreement to wed?" His look shot to Nora too.

Simon held himself still. If she had any reservations, now would be the time to state them. "Yes, Mr. Bagley," she murmured, her face paling.

The minister nodded again. "And are you certain you must marry now? I believe I heard your brother and his wife will be arriving soon. Surely you'd prefer that he give you away."

He made it sound as if Simon was dragging her to the altar. She positively squirmed; Simon could see her finery quivering. He was going to lose her, and while that might not have seemed such a bad thing when she had first made her bold proposal, now he was determined to win his family those acres.

He took her cold hand in his. "Nora has agreed to be my wife, Mr. Bagley. I don't care who gives her away or who attends this wedding."

The minister positively glowered over the top of his spectacles. "This is highly irregular, Mr. Wallin. I see your own mother and sister declined to attend. Is there some reason this wedding must be so rushed?"

Nora flamed, pulling her hand from Simon's. "No, no reason. Really. I..." She glanced at Simon, her eyes pools of misery.

Simon had too much experience with people arguing with him to quail before the minister's annoyance. He drew himself up to his full height, dwarfing everyone else in the room. "You have the information for our marriage certificate, Mr. Bagley. We are both of age and willing to wed. If that's not enough for you, I'll go to the justice of the peace. Assuming Doc Maynard is still in the law's good graces, he can marry us."

Nora gasped, John took a step back and Levi grinned as if applauding Simon's boldness at challenging the renowned minister.

Mr. Bagley tugged on the bottom of his plain blue waistcoat. "See here, sir. I will not have the members of my congregation married by that charlatan. Besides, you should know that it will do you no good to claim land in Olympia for your wife if the state does not consider you legally wed."

"So," Simon returned, "marry us."

For a moment, the minister met his gaze, his eyes narrowed as if he would see inside Simon. He could look all he liked. Ma always said Simon had been born with an iron rod for a spine. He did not bow, and he did not bend. If the minister thought he could cow him, he had better think again.

Mr. Bagley shook his head as he lowered his gaze to his book of prayer. "Very well. But this is highly irregular." He shook out his arms and began reading the ceremony. Her hands still visibly trembling, Nora bowed her head and clasped her fingers together.

Simon only half listened. He was too relieved to have won. His mind immediately began working out crop yields, considering directions to draw the furrows, determining which crops to plant depending on when he cleared the acreage. Once he dealt with Nora's brother, there would be no impediments to his work, except the cold winter weather and Christmas.

"Simon Wallin." His name as well as the tone of Mr. Bagley's voice made Simon meet the clergyman's gaze. The minister's eyes could have been arrows over the silver of his spectacles.

"Wilt thou have this woman to be thy wedded wife," he demanded, "to live together under God's ordinance in the Holy Estate of Matrimony? Wilt thou love her, comfort her, honor and keep her, in sickness and in health, and forsaking all others, keep thee only unto her as long as you both shall live?"

Love and comfort her? Live together, forever? That wasn't what Simon had intended. He wasn't offering Nora a home or a place in his life.

"Mr. Wallin?" Mr. Bagley prompted sternly.

Nora dropped her gaze, shrinking in on herself as if she'd been struck. She must be wondering why he didn't speak. She'd just heard him declare he'd be married or else. She'd laid out the terms of their bargain. She wasn't expecting undying devotion. He wasn't offering anything more than to protect her from her brother. And he gained the land his family needed.

"I will," he said. But the twist in his gut belied the confident words.

Nora nearly collapsed in relief. For a moment there, she'd feared it was all a horrid joke. He'd turn and shout, *April Fools'!* even though it was early December. Her life had been like that.

But this marriage would put an end to that life. No more must she please her brother and Meredith. She drew in a deep breath as the minister asked her the same question, then she firmly said, "I will."

Mr. Bagley took both their hands and held them together. She could feel Simon's calluses rubbing against her skin. Could he feel the nicks and scratches from her sewing? Did he care?

The minister gave them more vows to say, all about plighting and giving troth. She wasn't entirely sure what troth was. Then Mr. Bagley released them to hold out his hand, gaze on Simon.

Simon frowned at him.

"The ring?" he prompted.

Nora glanced at Simon. Her groom shook his head. "No ring. That isn't required for a legal marriage."

Mr. Bagley's mouth thinned a moment before he drew back his hand and continued with the ceremony. She supposed if she had been terribly in love she might have minded that she would carry no ring on her finger. But as it was, she just wanted to get this over with.

Finally Mr. Bagley came to the end.

"I now pronounce you husband and wife," he declared, his voice ringing in the nearly empty church. Nora sucked in a breath. It was done. She was married. Charles had lost his hold on her. Forever. She was her own person at last.

Then she noticed Simon's brothers waiting, watching.

Had she forgotten something?

"Is there more?" she asked the minister.

Mr. Bagley glanced between them. "I believe it is customary for the husband to offer his wife a kiss."

Nora swallowed, her stomach fluttering. She'd never been kissed, but all the girls in the boardinghouse floated in with bemused smiles after saying good-night to their chosen beaus. Still, Simon wasn't a suitor. She hardly knew him. Did she want him to kiss her?

Those firm lips looked rather unforgiving at the moment. He gazed down at her, unmoving, as if he were studying her face. It was the same face she'd worn when she'd asked him to marry her. She wasn't sure why it was so important to him now. He wasn't in love with her. And physical intimacy, of any kind, was not part of their bargain.

But then he bent closer, and she found herself closing her eyes, pursing her lips, her heart thundering once more as she drew in the cool, clean scent of him.

She felt a gentle pressure on her cheek, the faintest brush of skin. Then she opened her eyes to find him pulling back, his face still solemn. That was it? Somehow she'd thought a kiss would be more momentous.

"Congratulations, Mrs. Wallin," Mr. Bagley said.

"Welcome to the family, Nora," said Simon's brother John.

Simon put a hand to her back, the touch so proprietary, a shiver ran through her. "We should be going."

"Yes, of course," she agreed, chiding herself for her reaction. He wasn't Charles. He wasn't ordering her about. He was merely being practical. They had a ship to catch, after all.

She preceded him down the aisle, paused only long enough to pick up the carpetbag of her overnight things and slip on her cloak, then started with him and his brothers down the hill for the pier, where Puget Sound glistened gray.

Simon reached out his hand. Nora frowned at it a moment, then realized he was offering to carry her bag. Blinking in surprise, she gave it to him.

How nice to have someone else do some of the carrying.

He had stamina too. His long legs ate up the muddy ground. He moved with such purpose, such determination. Charles would like him. He always said there was nothing worse than an aimless fellow.

Nora shuddered, scurrying to keep up. No, no. She didn't want Charles to like Simon. She wanted Charles to respect him, fear him and leave her alone. She was looking forward to the day when Simon and Charles locked horns. She was fairly certain who would win.

She wasn't sure what ship Simon had found to take them on the journey, but she couldn't help smiling at the long, lean lumber schooner that lay at anchor near Yesler's pier. It wasn't nearly as large as the *Continental*, which had carried her away from New York, but she would always have a special place in her heart for this ship. The *Merry Maid* had rescued her and some of the others in San Francisco and brought them the rest of the way to Seattle.

"You're just in time," the burly mate told Simon as they reached the ship. "Get aboard and stow your things." He glanced toward Nora. Eyes widening, he tugged off his cap in respect. "Miss Underhill, an honor to be traveling with you again."

"Good to see you, Mr. Chorizon," she said. "I noticed the jib sail is holding up."

He grinned at her. "Those stitches you took were just the thing, ma'am. The sailmaker in San Francisco claimed he couldn't have done better. Captain Collings says you're welcome to travel with us anytime." He nodded to Simon. "No charge for you, seeing as you're friends with Miss Underhill."

"Mrs. Wallin," John corrected him with a look to his brother.

Mr. Chorizon grabbed Simon's hand and shook it. "Good for you, Mr. Wallin. She's a fine lady. I wish you both happy."

Simon inclined his head, but he retrieved his hand and reached for Nora's to help her up the gangplank and onto the ship.

"What did he mean?" Levi asked as they settled themselves along the bulwark, where they'd be out of the crew's way.

"The *Merry Maid* brought us up from San Francisco," Nora explained. "They had a little trouble with that front sail there." She nodded toward the triangular canvas at the front of the schooner. "I was able to patch it up."

"She's a sailmaker?" Levi demanded with an accusatory look to Simon as if annoyed he hadn't been told his new sister-in-law had skills few men boasted.

"I'm a seamstress," she told him.

"And she's obviously a good one, if she could fix a sail," Simon added with a look that made his brother move down the rail a little ways. With an apologetic nod, John went to join him.

"Thank you," Nora murmured, leaning against the polished rail.

Simon frowned. "For what? It was only the truth. My mother sews quilts and made most of our clothes when we were younger. I know how hard she worked. She would never have attempted something as detailed as what you're wearing, and I doubt it would have dawned on her to use her skills to fix a sail."

Her cheeks were warming again, despite the chill winter breeze that blew across Puget Sound, tugging at the canvas above them. "Thank you nonetheless. I'm not used to people defending me."

He put a hand over hers on the rail. "I'm your husband. It's my duty to defend you. That was the bargain."

The bargain. Of course. He was only doing his part. She should not read more into the matter.

The crew cast off a short time later, maneuvering the schooner out of Elliott Bay and sending her south along the shores of Puget Sound. She skimmed the choppy gray waters as gracefully as a gull, spray rising to dampen Nora's cheeks. One hand holding her hat to her head, she breathed deep of the cool salty air, eyeing the clouds that crowded out any view of the mountains on either side of the water.

"The captain said we could wait in his cabin," Simon offered, turning up his collar.

Nora waved to the vistas. "And miss all this? No, thank you. But if you want to go inside, please don't mind me."

He didn't move.

Nora drew in another breath. She wasn't sure why he stayed. Was he too marveling that his life had changed?

"Do you feel different?" she asked.

He frowned as if considering the idea. "No," he said with a shake of his head that sent the breeze fingering through his light brown hair. "You?"

She wiggled a little, trying to sense any change in her bones, her muscles. "No. But I never thought to marry. Well, there was a young man from church who showed interest, a Mr. Winnower. He used to talk to me after services, and once he even walked me home. My brother, Charles, took him aside to discuss his intentions. He only ever looked at me from across the room after that. If I approached him, he'd dash out the door. I always wondered whether Charles might have told him I had some dread disease that would infect him."

"I'm going to enjoy talking with your brother," Simon said with such a dark tone that Nora could only smile.

"And perhaps my sister-in-law?" she suggested. "Meredith always claimed I was destined to die an old maid. If she could have picked a husband for me, I'm certain it would have been some elderly widower who needed comfort in his final hours and wasn't overly particular in his bride. I'm having the most delightful time imagining the look on her face when I walk in on your arm." She couldn't help the giggle that bubbled up.

"Her as well," Simon agreed.

Nora smiled. "Oh, and perhaps a few of the ladies in town? There has been a distressing rumor that I'm destined to be the last Mercer Belle to wed."

He shifted away from her. "I'll win your freedom from your family, Nora, as I promised. But don't expect to parade me all over Seattle like one of your fancy gowns. I have work to do, and the sooner I get to it, the better."

She almost acquiesced. It was on the tip of her tongue to say, "Yes, of course." To bow her head contritely for impinging on his precious time. To crawl back into her corner and lick her wounds.

Not again. Not with him. Not ever.

She raised her head and met his gaze. "I understand you have work ahead of you, Mr. Wallin. But know one thing—I may owe my brother a debt for taking me in after my parents died, but you and I have a bargain. You are getting one hundred and sixty acres from our marriage. I am getting a husband who helps and supports me. If you cannot abide by that agreement, then I will take the first ship back to Seattle, and you can argue with the registrar over whether you have earned those acres."

Chapter Three

Who was this woman he'd married?

Nora had quaked at stern words from Mr. Bagley. She claimed she could not stand up against her brother. Now her face was set, her fists planted on her ample hips. He felt as if a tabby had turned into a mountain lion right before his eyes.

But he'd never run from a mountain lion, and he didn't intend to now.

"I'll honor our bargain," he told her. "You'll be free to live as you like. All I ask is the right to do the same."

She relaxed with a brisk nod. "Very well. You can go and wait in the captain's quarters. I'll be fine. I'm used to being alone." She turned her gaze once more to the water.

He could not find his equilibrium with her. Feeling as if he'd been dismissed, he went to join John and Levi farther down the rail.

"I like her," Levi said. "She seems nice."

Simon was no longer so sure. Where had that surge of confidence come from? Had she overstated her fears about her brother? Did something more lay behind her proposal to wed?

He kept his distance the rest of the trip.

They arrived in Olympia late in the afternoon. Unlike Seattle, the territorial capital afforded several docks, and more than one ship crowded the harbor at the base of Budd Inlet, the terminus of Puget Sound. The entire town was built on a spit of land, with water on three sides and mountains on two. Simon much preferred the more solid footing of Wallin Landing, with the hill at his back and the lake in front.

But as he walked down the pier toward the town proper, Nora's case in his hand, he couldn't help noticing that they were causing a stir. Sailors glanced at Nora as she passed; longshoremen paused in their work to watch. Even here, where the territorial legislature met, women were rare. Though Nora seemed unaware of the interest, Simon put his other hand to her back and stayed close. She favored him with a frown but did not resist him.

"Busy place," John commented behind them as they made their way south along the boardwalk past all manner of businesses.

"I like it here," Levi declared, glancing at a hall where banners proclaimed the upcoming performance of a dance troupe. "A fellow could find a lot more to do than farm and log."

"There's the land office," Simon said, nodding to a whitewashed building ahead. He strode to it, shifted Nora's case under one arm and held the door open for her, then followed her inside with his brothers in his wake.

The long, narrow office was bisected by a counter. Chairs against the white-paneled walls told of lengthy waits, but today the only person in the room was a slender man behind the counter. He was shrugging into a coat as if getting ready to close up for the day.

Handing Nora's case to John, Simon hurried forward. "I need to file a claim."

The fellow paused, eyed him and then glanced at Nora, who came to stand beside Simon. The clerk smoothed down his lank brown hair and stepped up to the counter. "Do you have the necessary application and fee?"

Simon drew out the ten-dollar fee, then pulled the papers from his coat and laid them on the counter. The clerk took his time reading them, glancing now and then at Nora, who bowed her head as if looking at the shoes peeping out from under her scalloped hem.

"And this is your wife?" he asked at last.

Simon nodded. "I brought witnesses to the fact, as required."

John and Levi stepped closer. The clerk's gaze returned to Nora. "Are you Mrs. Wallin?"

She glanced at Simon as if wondering the same thing, and for a moment he thought they were all doomed. Had she decided he wasn't the man she'd thought him? Had he married for nothing?

Nora turned and held out her hand to the clerk. "Yes, I'm Mrs. Simon Wallin. No need to wish me happy, for I find I have happiness to spare."

The clerk's smile appeared, brightening his lean face. "Mr. Wallin is one fortunate fellow." He turned to pull a heavy, leather-bound book from his desk, thumped it down on the counter and opened it to a page to begin recording the claim.

Simon knew he ought to feel blessed indeed as he accepted the receipt from the clerk. He had just earned his family the farmland they so badly needed. The acreage would serve the Wallins for years to come and support the town that had been his father's dream. Yet something nagged at him, warned him that he had miscalculated.

He never miscalculated.

"What now?" Nora asked him as they left the land office.

"The tide's against us," Simon told her, pushing away his troublesome emotions. "We won't be able to return north until early tomorrow morning."

"I expected as much," she replied, taking her case from John. "Where should we wait?"

John cleared his throat. "I'm sure you and your bride would like some privacy. Levi and I can make our own way."

Nora glanced between him and Simon. "There's no need."

"None at all," Simon agreed.

John and Levi exchanged glances. "But you just married," John pointed out.

"I know this is you, Simon," Levi added, "but Drew and Catherine and James and Rina were pretty lovey-dovey when they married."

Nora flamed. "I never intended— That is I never supposed— I mean, really, I—" She appeared to run out of steam like a poorly tended engine.

Simon pulled a coin from his pocket and tossed it to John. "McClendon's, on Main. Request three rooms. We'll join you shortly."

With a nod toward Nora, his brothers took off up the street.

Nora had her feet planted so firmly on the boardwalk

she might have been part of its construction. "I can see we should have discussed the details of our convenient wedding more fully."

He might on occasion have a difficult time following other people's logic, but he thought he knew what was troubling Nora. "Then let's discuss them now." He started up the boardwalk, careful to slow his stride to allow her to keep up. She paced him, head down and case close. The feather in her hat bobbed with her movements.

"We're not really married, you know," she said.

Simon raised a brow. "I distinctly remember a ceremony just a few hours ago."

She nodded. "Yes, yes. But that's the extent of it. Nothing need change. We are agreed on that."

She didn't sound convinced of the fact. "I'll do my duty," Simon told her.

She stopped on the boardwalk. "Please don't use that word with me. I am not a duty, Mr. Wallin. I am your partner in this bargain." She glanced at him under her lashes. "And partners do not share sleeping accommodations."

He couldn't help chuckling. "I thought that might be your concern. I have no intentions of claiming my husbandly rights."

She clutched her case closer. "You requested three rooms. There are four of us."

"One room is for me, one is for you," Simon replied. "The last is for John and Levi. I saw no reason they couldn't share."

She took a deep breath, setting her green overskirt to fluttering under the edge of her cloak. "I see. Forgive me. I suppose that's settled, then."

She had a way of overlooking things. Was it inexperience or blind trust? Neither boded well for the future.

"That's not the only detail we should discuss," Simon told her, starting forward again and allowing her to fall into step beside him. "There will be no mingling of finances. What you earn from your sewing is yours. What I earn from my logging is mine."

"Agreed," she said. "And very wise of you."

For some reason, that made his head come up a little higher. Silly reaction. He didn't need her praise. "You will call me Simon, and I will call you Nora," he continued. "People will expect that."

"My father always called my mother Mrs. Underhill," she said. "But very well. What else?"

This was the toughest part. "We will tell our families that we entered into this arrangement for stability. I will not lie and claim it a love match."

He thought she might take umbrage. Beth was forever prosing on about romance, for all she claimed she would never want a husband hanging about.

Instead, Nora shrugged. "My family will never believe it's a love match. I intend to tell them we decided we'd suit well enough, and you are too busy with the farm to come into town on a regular basis but were willing to allow me to continue to ply my trade. I don't intend to inflict them on you any more than absolutely necessary."

He still struggled to imagine any family that cruel. "Are they truly so bad?" he asked.

"That," Nora replied, "you'll soon see for yourself."

Charles and Meredith arrived on a rainy day exactly a week after Nora and Simon returned from Olympia. The harbormaster had sent word to Nora at the Kellogg brothers' store, where her sewing customers met her, so she was standing on the pier, umbrella over her head, when the longboat bumped the pilings. She smiled as the sailors helped Charles and Meredith to the wide wood planks of the pier and hoped they would attribute her shiver to the cool weather. She was only glad she'd had an opportunity to send a note to Simon through a miner headed north. Her husband should be able to reach her by dinnertime. She only had to survive until then.

"Wretched trip," Charles greeted her as if it were somehow her fault. No one who did not know them well would ever have taken Charles for her brother. Though he wasn't a tall man, he was certainly taller and thinner than she was. His hair was lighter than hers, a fine chestnut, and it was pomaded back from his square-jawed face. His well-tailored coats were always crisp and clean, and his trousers always held a crease.

"Do tell me you brought the carriage," Meredith said, her feathered hat taking a beating from the rain. She plucked the umbrella from Nora's grip and huddled under it. Meredith was the very epitome of a grand lady, her gown with its top cape festooned with lace and ribbons and tucks that had fairly worn out Nora's fingers and patience to arrange to her sister-in-law's liking. Everyone in Lowell had talked about how the fair-haired, blue-eyed beauty had married above herself when she'd snagged noted accountant Charles Underhill, but Meredith always acted as if she were the one born to privilege.

"There isn't a single carriage in the city and precious few horses," Nora told her sister-in-law. "Most people either travel by wagon or walk."

Meredith gasped. "Walk! I cannot be expected to walk all the way into town from the harbor."

"It isn't so far," Nora assured her. She waved toward the hillside rising above them. "That's all there is."

Charles and Meredith exchanged looks of dismay. Perhaps they would be concerned enough to turn tail and leave on the first ship out. Hiding the hope that thought engendered, Nora motioned to the waiting teamster to come take her family's belongings.

"Mr. Mercer will carry your things up to the house," she explained as the fellow pushed past them with a nod. "He's the older brother of the Mr. Mercer who escorted us here. You remember him."

"Indeed," Charles assured her, giving Asa's brother a sharp look. "He was quite persuasive about the opportunities to be found in Seattle." He returned his gaze to the hillside, clearly dubious.

Nora managed to lead them up the hill to Third Avenue, where most of the finer houses had been built. She'd found one owner ready to leave the area and willing to lease his framed home to her family. Now she climbed up to the wide front porch and let Charles and Meredith into the house. She thought it might suit them. The walls were papered and hung with pictures, the heavy wood furniture covered in floral. She fancied she could already smell the perfumed powder, essence of roses, that Meredith favored.

But of course, nothing was good enough. Charles did not appreciate the view down to Puget Sound. "If I wanted to look at water, I would have moved to Boston."

Meredith was certain the house was too small for her purposes. "How am I to entertain with a single parlor? And I don't know where you think you will sleep, Nora, with only one bedchamber."

"I suppose we could put a pallet on the floor of the attic," Charles mused.

"No need," Nora said. "I have my own room at the ladies' boardinghouse."

"And do you expect us to wait for you to arrive each morning?" Meredith exclaimed. "Honestly, you are so impractical."

By the time a knock sounded on the door that afternoon, Nora was worn-out from placating them. She couldn't help beaming at the sight of Simon on the porch. He was dressed for work, bulky brown coat open at the throat to reveal a red-and-blue-plaid wool shirt over red flannels. His thick wool pants were tucked into heavy boots. At least he took the trouble to knock the worst of the mud off his feet before following her into the house.

"You are a sight for sore eyes," she told him. "Please, come meet my brother and sister-in-law."

Meredith and Charles were seated on the overstuffed chairs at opposite ends of the parlor, her brother by the multipaned window, his wife nearest the stone hearth. Charles had the *Puget Sound Weekly* Nora had left him open before him, his brows drawn down as he studied the news. Meredith had already instructed Nora in the unpacking of her things and was taking dainty stitches in the pillow cover she had been embroidering for as long as Nora could remember. Like everything else she did, Meredith put on a good show while managing to accomplish very little.

"May I have your attention?" Nora asked.

Neither looked up. "Not now, Nora," Charles said. "Shouldn't you be seeing to dinner?"

"She has no concept of time," Meredith complained. "I suppose it is too much that you would consider our needs after we took the trouble of traveling thousands of miles to care for you in this wretched wilderness, with no friends and a thorough lack of opportunity for your talented brother."

Each word felt like a nail pounding into her heart, but Nora held her ground. "I'm sorry to inconvenience you, Meredith. But you see, I got married."

She knew she should not take such delight in the way Meredith's head snapped up and her pretty pink lips gaped.

Charles lowered his paper at last, blinking at Nora and Simon as if bewildered that they'd appeared in his parlor. "Married, you say? What nonsense is this?"

"It's hardly nonsense. You can't miss him standing here beside me." Nora looked pointedly to Simon, who seemed a bit bewildered himself. She supposed Charles and Meredith might have that effect on people. Still, he stepped forward and nodded to her brother and sister-in-law.

"Mr. Underhill, ma'am. I'm Simon Wallin, and I had the honor of marrying your sister last week."

Now Charles stared, his face washing white and his hands shaking so hard the paper rattled. Whatever reaction Nora had been expecting, it was hardly that.

Meredith recovered first, rising from her chair. "I know you are given to odd fancies, Nora, but this is too much. How could you leave your brother out of what must surely be the most important day of your life?"

Her guilt rose like the tide on Puget Sound. She would not allow it to swamp her this time. "It was expedient."

"Expedient?" Meredith clutched her beribboned chest. "To ignore your family, run off with some stranger? Expedient?"

This was not going as she'd hoped. Again she glanced at Simon for help.

"We are properly wed," he assured them both. "You can ask Mr. Bagley at the Brown Church. He performed the ceremony."

Charles climbed to his feet, shoving the paper away. "You can be sure I shall, sir. No clergyman has the right to perform a marriage ceremony for an impressionable young woman without consulting her family. And I hold you responsible as well, turning her head with your promises, your flowery phrases."

The picture of the practical, stern-faced Simon Wallin swaying her with flowery words brought a giggle to her lips. She hastily clamped them together to keep it from coming out.

"Your sister is a grown woman, of age under Washington territorial law," Simon informed Charles. "She can marry whom she likes."

"Of age?" Meredith sputtered. She pointed a finger at Simon. "Oh, I see your game, sir. You think because she comes from a good family she must have a considerable dowry. Well, let me tell you—"

"Meredith." Charles's tone cut off the rest of her bile. "Please, allow me to handle this."

Meredith shut her mouth and threw herself back into her seat, sending her embroidery tumbling to the carpet. She looked daggers at Nora, as if this was all her fault.

For once, she was right.

Her brother came forward to meet Simon, raising his head in the process, which only brought him to the tip of Simon's firm chin. "You can see the trouble you've caused, sir. I demand that you annul this sham of a marriage immediately."

Fear leaped up. Could they do that? Simon had claimed that only the territorial legislature could issue a divorce. She hadn't considered what would happen if her brother pushed for an annulment. Would Simon be able to keep his claim if she was no longer his wife?

Simon, however, did not back down. He took Nora's hand, his grip sure, strong. "I will do no such thing," he told Charles. "Nora knows her mind, and so do I. I called on you as a courtesy. Whether she wishes to continue to associate with you is up to her."

Oh, but he was masterful! She'd chosen well when she'd asked him to marry her. She glanced at her brother, to find his brows once more furrowed, as if he hadn't expected an argument and wasn't sure how to deal with it.

Meredith brought both hands to her face and bowed her head. "Oh," she moaned, her voice coming out muffled. "That you would take our dear Nora away. I do not know whether I can bear it." Her shoulders shook with her sobs.

How could she be so distressed? She scarcely abided Nora. She'd been positively eager to send her off to Seattle. This had to be an act. But why?

Charles evidently thought it sincere. "See what you've done?" he said with an audible sigh. "Calm yourself, Meredith, dear. I will have words with Mr. Wallin. Kindly take Nora to the door and make your farewells."

Her farewells? He was going to let her go! Nora wanted to grab both of Simon's hands and dance around the room in pure joy, but she knew that would only give away the game. Instead, she squeezed his hand for encouragement, trusting him to withstand any of her brother's blandishments, and turned for the entryway.

The sound of a sniff behind her told her Meredith was following.

"Oh, take heart, Meredith," she said as they entered the shadowy space at the front of the house. "Think how much happier you'll be without the burden of caring for me."

Meredith sniffed again as she took down Nora's cloak from the brass hook at the side of the door. "It was a burden I gladly bore, I assure you. Right now, I can only pity you, Nora."

Nora frowned, accepting her gray cloak from Meredith's elegant fingers. "Why would you pity me? I married a good man."

"I can certainly see that you believe so," Meredith said, her hands fluttering. "I can imagine how exciting it must have been to have such a commanding fellow propose, but you must have known that it wasn't love motivating him."

Of course it wasn't love, but she wasn't about to hammer the point home. "I am satisfied with Mr. Wallin's intentions," she replied.

"How nice that you are now a better judge of character," Meredith said, her voice verging on a sneer. "I remember another young man you thought was serious, but alas he never came up to scratch."

She would bring up Mr. Winnower. Nora shook out her cloak and slipped it over her dress even as she pushed away the memory. "I will always be grateful you and Charles took me in, Meredith. But I've made my own way here, and I no longer need your help."

Meredith reached out a hand to smooth back a tendril of Nora's hair. The touch would have been tender if not for the hard look in Meredith's eyes. "You have no understanding of the world, Nora. A man says he'll marry you, take care of you, and off you go, with no thought of the consequences, no idea of the damage he could do."

Damage? Despite her hopes, a shiver went through her. She'd thought Simon Wallin a good man, had believed in him because Catherine and Rina had married his brothers and Maddie had spoken highly of him. But what did she actually know about Simon? Would he hurt her? Treat her unkindly?

"I cannot sit idly by when your very life is in danger," Meredith continued as if determined to press her case. "Did you not see the squint in his cold eyes, those brutish hands?" She lowered her voice as if suspecting Simon might be hiding just around the corner even now, waiting to pounce. "Nora, I fear for you if you go with him."

Nora squared her shoulders. "I'm not going with him. I shall live in town. He will live on his claim."

"Indeed." The sweetness of Meredith's tone warned Nora she had made a mistake, but she wasn't sure how. "What a quaint arrangement. However did you convince him to agree?"

By giving him one hundred and sixty acres.

Now she just needed to know that he would keep his part of the bargain and stop her brother from ruining her life.

"What do you want from me?" Charles asked Simon the moment the ladies left the room. "I warn you, I do not take well to blackmail."

The man was insufferable. Did he really think that Simon and Nora's marriage had anything to do with harming him?

"I want nothing from you," Simon told him. "Your

sister is of age, as am I. We married. She is mine now to protect." He met Charles's gaze head-on. The man had gray eyes, like Nora, but they were not nearly as warm and welcoming as his sister's. In fact, right now, they swam with tears.

Tears?

"Do you have a sister, Mr. Wallin?" he asked. "Would you want to learn of her marriage in this cold manner?"

Not at all. He couldn't imagine how he'd feel if Beth had walked into Wallin Landing with a stranger on her arm claiming him as her husband. But Nora wasn't Beth.

"Perhaps you should ask yourself why your sister chose to marry without informing you," he countered.

"I don't have to ask," Charles said, his voice as heavy as his look. "I know. She is simple, unaware of life's dangers. She trusts too easily. I have done all I can to shelter her."

Simon frowned. From what he could see, Nora might be a bit whimsical, with unexpected giggles and hearts embroidered on her sleeves, but she did not appear to have a diminished mental capacity. Was that how her family saw her? Was that how they treated her? Small wonder she longed to escape.

"Nora will want for nothing," Simon promised him. "I earned the patent on my original claim, and I registered another for my wife. I can provide for her, should she need it."

"Well, certainly she will need it," Charles insisted. "You didn't expect me to hand you a dowry, did you?"

Why did they both pluck on that string? Perhaps dowries were important where they came from, but not in frontier Seattle.

"I don't want your money, or hers," Simon told him.

"All I demand is that you treat her with respect and consideration. Do that, and you will have no trouble with me."

"Yes, well…" Charles smoothed back his hair with one hand. "I have some demands myself, sir. You will bring her to see us at least once a week, and you will see to it that she accepts our invitations to dinner."

"Nora can see you if she likes," Simon returned. "But I won't have time to come in weekly."

Charles's face fell. "Live that far out, do you?" He sighed. "Oh, but I cannot like it. She's never dealt with farms and animals and that sort of thing. She'll be completely out of her element, and that is never good, let me tell you. No, you must move into town, for her sake."

Simon stared at him. Was he truly so selfish he would give no thought to Simon's plans, his family's needs or Nora's hopes? He wasn't sure how to respond.

Meredith spoke for him as she sailed back into the room with Nora right behind her. He noticed she hadn't fastened her cloak. Was she uncertain as to whether she was leaving?

"No need for concern, Charles," Nora's sister-in-law announced. "Nora tells me she and Mr. Wallin do not intend to live as man and wife. She will be staying in town while he returns to his claim. We can go on as we always have." She came to her husband's side and gave his arm a squeeze. "Isn't that good news?"

Charles seemed to grow a little taller. "Excellent. Nora can stay with us, then. You can visit when you like, Mr. Wallin, but do provide a few days' notice first. Only practical considering our busy schedules."

Simon felt as if he'd turned the page in the book he'd been reading only to find his adventure novel had become a farce. "Nora?" he couldn't help asking. "Is this what you want?"

She opened her mouth, but once again Meredith spoke first. "Of course it's what she wants. We are her family. We know what she needs. We understand her."

Nora raised her head, her gray eyes solemn, then crossed to Simon's side. "No, you have never understood me. I don't need you to take care of me. I took care of myself all the way to Seattle."

"Now, now," Charles said. "I know it must have seemed that way to you, but I paid Mr. Mercer to take care of you while Meredith and I settled our affairs in Massachusetts."

Nora blanched. "What? He said nothing."

"As it should be," Meredith said with a nod. "We wanted you to have a taste of the freedom that has been denied you because of your tragic constraints."

Nora was curling in on herself again. Simon wasn't sure whether to intervene or merely pick her up and carry her away from them.

"I, for one, worried about you every moment we were parted," her brother confessed. "Now that we have been reunited, nothing will stand in the way of me doing my duty." He clapped his hands together. "There! It's all settled. Thank you for stopping by, Mr. Wallin. Safe trip home."

It was like trying to stop a falling fir. The tree was coming down, breaking everything around it as it crashed. He refused to allow Nora to be crushed under the weight of their assumptions. He owed her that at least.

"Nora?" he pressed. "Do you want to stay with them?"

She gazed up at him, her eyes stormy, then glanced

at her brother and sister-in-law, standing there with delight stamped on their faces.

"No," she said. "I want to get as far away from them as I can. I'm coming to live with you, out at Wallin Landing."

Chapter Four

Nora knew she was changing their bargain. She had made it very clear to Simon that marrying her would not affect his day-to-day life. But what else was she to do but beg to come to Wallin Landing with him? Charles and Meredith were even more determined to control her than she'd feared. Her only hope was putting distance between her and them, just as she'd done when she'd left with Asa Mercer.

But first she had to convince Simon that moving out to Wallin Landing was a good idea.

As Charles and Meredith protested her decision, she focused on her husband. Simon's eyes narrowed until she could barely see their color. His lean body was tensed, as if she had dealt him a blow and he expected another. She didn't know the words to say, the facts to offer that would ease his mind.

She simply laid her hand on his arm and said, "Please, Simon?"

After how hard she'd worked to convince him to agree to their Christmas wedding in the first place, she hardly expected instant capitulation now. But she saw the moment he reached his decision, for the green deepened as his eyes widened, and he snapped a nod.

"Fetch your things," he said. "We'll leave now."

She didn't know whether to hug him in thanks or run to do as he bid. Of course, besides her cloak, she really didn't have any of her things at the house.

"See here," Charles started, his chest puffing out.

Simon ignored him, pushing past him for the door.

"Nora, you cannot do this," Meredith cried. "You need us."

Had her sister-in-law claimed to have needed her, guilt might have halted Nora. As it was, she fled after Simon.

"You will regret this!" Charles flung after them from the doorway as they descended the front steps. "He will not treat you as we do."

"That's the truth," Simon muttered.

Nora felt it too. Whatever lay ahead for her and Simon, he would not make her feel tiny and useless. She would merely have to be careful what more she asked of him. She wanted to keep their sides of the bargain equal.

As Charles continued his threats from the safety of the porch, Simon led Nora to the wagon waiting on the street and went to untie the horses. Nora was gathering her skirts to climb up onto the bench when she felt hands on her waist. Simon lifted her effortlessly onto the seat. It was a kind gesture, convenient even. But somehow it made breathing difficult.

"I take it your clothes and other belongings are at the boardinghouse," he said after he'd climbed up and called to the horses. They were a pair of dark-coated beauties, and she was fairly sure they belonged to his brother James.

"Yes," she said. "If you wouldn't mind stopping there on the way out of town, I would appreciate it. I'll just pack a few things, and we can send for the rest later."

"You really want to move out to Wallin Landing?" he asked, directing the horses down the hill for the boarding-house. She could hear the wariness in his voice. "I thought you preferred to stay in Seattle because of your sewing."

She made a face. "Being so far out of town will make that more difficult."

"So stay at the boardinghouse," Simon said. "Refuse to have anything more to do with your brother."

Nora shuddered. "They'll find me. They did when I left for Seattle."

He cast her a glance as he eased the horses down the hill. "You stood up to me. Stand up to them."

A sigh worked its way out of her. "You don't under-stand. I stood up to you, Simon, because we have a bar-gain. We each contributed something to it. That's not the case with my brother. I owe him for taking me in, for feeding and clothing me. And he knows it."

"I would think it a brother's duty to care for his younger siblings," Simon said, his voice sharp with con-demnation for anyone who failed to live up to such an obligation. "That's what Drew did when our father died."

Nora nodded. "That's what you're doing now by working those one hundred and sixty acres. And I'm sure your family will be grateful for your efforts. I'm grateful to Charles, but oh, how I tire of having to repay him. Have I no right or expectation of a life of my own?"

She wasn't sure how Simon would answer. She wasn't even sure how she would answer. She had been raised to be a dutiful daughter. Anything less felt selfish, lazy. Yet if she had stayed with Charles and Meredith one more day, her heart would have shriveled away inside her.

"Of course you have that right," Simon said as he turned onto Second Avenue and headed for the boardinghouse. "You have won your freedom. What do you intend to do with it?"

And there lay the more important question at the moment. She could not stay in Seattle proper, yet she hated to leave the area entirely and lose the friends she'd made on the journey and the customers she'd acquired in the last six months of working. The most logical thing to do was to go out to Wallin Landing.

"I'll have to let Mr. Kellogg and his brother know where I'll be staying," she said. "I work out of their store. Perhaps people could leave commissions with them, and I could come into town when you pick up the mail to see what's needed."

"You seem to have thought this out," he said, slowing the horses as they approached the boardinghouse.

And she would have thought he would approve of that planning. Instead, he sounded rather miffed.

"I didn't realize Charles and Meredith would be this difficult," she assured him. "That is, I knew they'd be difficult. They always are. But I never thought even marriage would fail to deter them."

He shook his head as he reined in. "I never met anyone as oblivious to logic as your brother."

She ought to take umbrage on her brother's behalf. Charles was a talented accountant, after all, someone to whom business leaders turned for advice. Certainly he had managed their father's estate well, with the help of the bankers. The elderly Mr. Pomantier from the bank had come out on a regular basis to dine with them. He'd always spoken kindly to Nora but spent the bulk of his time in consultation with Charles.

Yet despite all Charles's qualities, Simon was right.

"Charles is ever focused on his own needs," she told him. "Meredith is worse. I simply couldn't bear to slave for them one more moment."

"You should be no one's slave," Simon said. "You are an independent woman of intellect and skill. You should be treated as such."

Once again, the fact that he was agreeing with her left her speechless. Back in Lowell, people had been more likely to congratulate her on having such a kind, generous brother, someone willing to take her in when their parents had passed on. After all, not every family could accommodate a spinster without prospects.

Simon climbed down from the wagon, and Nora scrambled to the ground before he could come around to help her. She felt as if she were still tingling from his touch when he'd helped her up at the house. She didn't need any distractions before she faced the boardinghouse owner. A dark-haired older woman with a narrow face and narrower opinions, Mrs. Elliott was another person who seemed to think it her duty to tell Nora what to do.

"I'll just be a minute," Nora promised as Simon stopped in front of the horses. Then she hurried inside.

The boardinghouse with its pink-papered walls and flowered carpet was much quieter these days. The piano in the dining room was silent, and no one loitered in the perfumed parlor. Most of the women who had journeyed with Asa Mercer had either found jobs elsewhere in Washington Territory or married and moved out. Only a few still lived in the boardinghouse, and they had either work or serious suitors that kept them in Seattle.

Mrs. Elliott had been advertising for more tenants to no avail. King County still boasted few unmarried women.

The boardinghouse owner caught sight of Nora as she came in the door and hurried to meet her.

"I understand your family has arrived from the East," she said, blocking Nora's route to the stairs. "I certainly hope you are not planning to leave us to live with them."

A wave of thankfulness swept over her that Simon had agreed to her request. "No," Nora said, and she darted around the woman and started up the carpeted stairs.

Mrs. Elliott followed her, her voice almost a purr. "I'm very pleased to hear that, Miss Underhill. A young lady such as yourself can never be too careful in the company she keeps. Why, I have heard of families who foisted the worst of gentlemen upon a spinster, simply to ensure she married."

That had not been her problem. Charles and Meredith seemed to prefer that she never speak to anyone but them. She nearly giggled remembering the look on Meredith's face when Nora had announced she'd married Simon.

"I can promise you my family will not be marrying me off, but I fear I will be leaving you," Nora told the woman as she opened the door to her room. Once, she'd shared the space with another Mercer Belle, but the second bed had stood empty for weeks.

Mrs. Elliott tsked as Nora went to kneel beside her iron bedstead and reach underneath. No time to fill her trunk. It would have to be the carpetbag she'd used in Olympia.

"There is no other residence for young ladies in the city," the boardinghouse owner reminded her, crossing her thin arms over her flat chest.

"I won't be moving to another boardinghouse," Nora said, swiftly folding in a nightgown, several sets of undergarments and an extra dress. "But I can no longer stay here either." The bag bulged, and she strained to clasp it shut. "You see, I got married."

As Nora rose, Mrs. Elliott's fingers flew to her lips. "Oh, my child! I wish you'd spoken to me first. Some of the men here are so wild and unkempt. You shouldn't have settled."

Nora thought of Simon, waiting for her outside—tall, strong, handsome, willing to sacrifice for family. She did not feel as if she had settled in the least.

"Oh, I didn't marry one of those fellows," she assured Mrs. Elliott, lugging her bag toward the door. "I'm Mrs. Simon Wallin."

Mrs. Elliott's astonished look was almost as gratifying as Meredith's gasp.

"I'm paid up through the month," Nora told her as the woman's mouth opened and closed wordlessly. "I would appreciate you leaving everything in the room until then. Someone will come for it shortly. Not," she hastened to add, "my brother or his wife. You are only to provide access to someone named Wallin."

Nora hurried out into the hallway, and Mrs. Elliott fluttered after her. She seemed to have recovered her voice. "Certainly," she warbled. "I will be delighted to do as you ask. Give my regards to all the gentlemen in your new family. Such fine, upstanding fellows, the Wallin men, for all you're the third of my girls they've snatched away. And if there is anything else I can do for you, Mrs. Wallin, please let me know."

Mrs. Wallin. A real bride might have felt a jolt of delight at hearing herself addressed by her new name. Yet now it sent a tremor through Nora. She'd entered into this bargain thinking nothing about her life would change save that she would rid herself of Charles's interference.

Now everything was about to change. She was heading out into the wilderness. For all that Mrs. Elliott called them fine gentlemen, Simon and his brothers were rough loggers, the sort of fellows Charles would not have allowed in his home back in Lowell. Though she knew Catherine and Rina, the rest of the group were strangers.

She had an odd feeling that she was about to learn exactly what it meant to be Mrs. Simon Wallin.

Simon drove the wagon north along the primitive road that led toward Lake Union. The rain had stopped earlier, but the firs they passed still shed a drop or two from their heavy boughs. He caught the briny scent of Puget Sound on the cool air before the trees closed around them.

He couldn't understand the woman at his side. She'd just upended her life, and his, yet she sat calm and proper beside him, her hands folded in her lap, her cloak draped about her. More, she gazed around at the forest as if it were the most amazing thing to appear in a long while. Perhaps she hadn't ventured much outside the town proper, but she wouldn't have had to go far to notice the trees, the inland sea, the mountains.

And after all that she'd been through at her brother's house, shouldn't she be a bit more upset?

"Are you all right?" he asked.

"Fine," she said with a smile.

"No regrets, concerns?" he pressed, feeling a frown forming.

"None," she said happily.

Once again, the lion had changed before him, becoming a tabby, docile and complacent.

"And you're absolutely certain you want to move out here with me?"

"Oh, yes," she said. "Thank you for agreeing. I'm sure we'll get on famously."

He felt no such assurance. "We should discuss our bargain, as you seem to have changed it."

She sighed. "I suppose so. I'm terribly sorry to inconvenience you, Simon, but I didn't know what else to do."

"It was the obvious choice," he allowed. "But it will cause a few complications." He paused, feeling suddenly guilty for not having confided the truth to his family. Right now, only John and Levi knew he had married Nora. The weather had kept him from doing more than laying out permanent stakes on the new claim, so the rest of his family was also unaware of the land. He'd been trying to find the right moment to tell them.

He knew he was not the most eloquent of men. Their father had left them a small library of adventure novels and epic poems, including *Robinson Crusoe*, *The Last of the Mohicans* and *The Courtship of Miles Standish*. Though he'd enjoyed reading them over the years, he couldn't convince himself the flowery language was necessary. If a man had an opinion on a matter, why not just say so?

Yet when he stated his opinion, he as like as not started an argument. Apparently his words were too brash, his opinions too strong. And he had never figured out a way to soften them. So, if he couldn't bring his family around to his way of thinking on something as mundane as which field to clear next, how did he expect to explain something as unorthodox as his and Nora's bargain?

At least with her he could speak his piece. Nora didn't seem to mind when he argued his point, and she was willing to listen and offer a counterpoint without claiming he was bullying her. Of course, now that he'd met her brother, he had to own that she was used to far worse than him.

"Let's start with the sleeping arrangements," he told her, drawing on the reins to guide the horses around a curve in the road.

"Sleeping arrangements," she repeated in a strained voice.

He refused to let her worry. "My cabin is small—main room on the ground floor, loft half the depth across overhead. And there's only one bed."

"Oh," she said, and he thought she hunched tighter with concern, but it might have been a reaction to the chill breeze that blew in from the water.

"You will take the bed, which is upstairs," he said. "I have a spare pallet my brothers use when they stay. I'll use it to bunk by the fire downstairs."

"I couldn't put you out that way," she protested.

Simon shook his head. "It's only logical. I rise early to work. If I'm already downstairs, it will be easier for me to slip out without disturbing you."

"Thank you." She beamed at him, and all at once the day seemed brighter, warmer.

"Then there's the eating arrangements," he said, determined to press forward. "I keep dried venison and fruit in the cabin, but everyone generally eats at the main house."

She turned to him, her face puckered. "I can't take your food without paying for it. That wouldn't be right."

Having another mouth to feed would put a strain on their supplies. But he could not accept Nora's money. They had made a bargain. It wasn't her fault her brother's behavior had forced her to change it.

"You are welcome to anything you need, Nora," he told her.

"So long as I contribute in some way," she agreed.

He smiled. There. That hadn't been so hard. Maybe he was getting better at discussing things civilly. Or maybe Nora was just easier to talk to than the rest of his family. Either way, he thought she was right—they just might make this bargain work, after all.

He reckoned without his family.

They reached Wallin Landing as the day was darkening. James was leaning against one of the supports on the back porch as if waiting for them. He strode out to meet the wagon as Simon pulled up in front of the main cabin.

"If you were going to go to the trouble of picking up my new waistcoat, Simon, you didn't have to bring the seamstress with you," he teased with a grin to Nora.

That was James. He was only two years younger than Simon, but decades apart when it came to outlook. James didn't speak—he teased, he joked. No deed was so dire, no day so dark he could not make light of it.

"How nice to see you again," Nora said as James came around to take charge of the horses, who nickered a greeting. "I haven't quite finished your commission, but I'll get to it as soon as possible."

It shouldn't surprise Simon that James knew Nora. James was the brother most likely to care about his wardrobe. Even now, his wool coat gaped to reveal a patterned waistcoat over his flannel shirt and a red silk scarf at his neck. He cut a dapper look, his short hair a shade darker than Simon's, his blue eyes deeper.

The back door opened, and Levi stepped out onto the porch as Simon climbed down from the bench.

"Hello, Nora," he said before reaching for the rifle that hung beside the door. In the act of removing it from its cradle, he froze, then turned to stare at the wagon. "Nora?"

"Good evening to you, Brother Levi," Nora said.

James chuckled. "Brother Levi? Have you joined a monastery without telling us, my lad?"

Levi colored, then turned to pull down the gun. "Maybe I should have. Things are going to get terribly interesting around here, I'm thinking."

Simon reached up to lift Nora down, feeling the warmth of her as she settled beside him. "Brace yourself," he warned her.

"Why?" she asked.

Levi fired the gun.

Nora flung herself against Simon. His arms came around her, holding her close, knowing how people generally reacted to the noise the first time. But what surprised him was that she wasn't trying to escape the danger.

She was trying to put herself between it and him.

Levi fired again, and Simon bent his head to speak in Nora's ear. "It's all right. That's just how we call everyone to dinner."

"Oh." She glanced up at him, the red rising in her cheeks. Those gray eyes held his, wise, warm, gentle. It was like looking into the early-morning mist, knowing the sun would not be far behind.

Maybe he'd learned something from the poets, after all.

"Dinner!" Levi shouted as if anyone could have missed his signal. As Simon glanced his way, the youth shrugged.

"You can't bring her out here and keep it a secret," he said, reaching for the door latch. "You'll have to tell them now."

As Nora looked up at him quizzically, Simon couldn't help his sigh. "And you sound completely delighted by that," he told his youngest brother.

"I'm truly sorry you'll get a scolding, Simon," Levi assured him. "But I'm going to enjoy eating dinner when *my* misdeeds aren't the main topic of conversation for once."

Chapter Five

Since coming to Seattle, Nora had rarely set foot outside the town. The way to Wallin Landing fascinated her. The thick forests looked cozy, and she could imagine deer and rabbits taking shelter in the thickets of fern and wild berries. Wallin Landing itself seemed nearly as welcoming, with its big two-story log cabin looking out through the trees toward Lake Union, the sturdy log barn and the schoolhouse at the back of the long clearing.

Then Levi had fired that gun, and she'd nearly jumped out of her skin. All she could think about was protecting the ones she loved from danger.

Which was silly. No one was in any danger. And Simon Wallin hardly needed her protection. Besides, she most certainly was not in love with him.

Yet she had to admit that standing in the circle of his arms felt rather nice.

"Why are you in trouble?" she asked him as he released her and started toward the house, leaving James to deal with the horses. "Are we late for dinner?"

"No," Simon said, his jaw tight. "I have to explain things to my family."

Very likely he did. They would not have been expecting Simon's convenient wife to move out to Wallin Landing. She could only hope they were better at listening than Charles and Meredith had been.

He led her up the porch and through the door. She was met with the smell of something spicy, and she spotted stew bubbling in a large kettle on a clever step stove that backed up to a stone hearth. Simon's sister, Beth, a young lady with sunny-blond hair, was taking down a jar of what looked like apple preserves from the wide shelves lining one wall. Nora could only admire the girl's simple wool gown. The blue was a good color for her clear complexion, and the scalloped neckline was a concession to style over practicality.

Beth paused when she saw Nora, then her round face broke into a smile. "Oh, Simon, how nice of you to bring us company! Are you traveling through the area, miss? Going out to meet your family?"

Nora looked to Simon, who appeared to be scowling though she could not identify the reason. "This is Nora," Simon said to his sister.

Beth bobbed a curtsy, her dark blue eyes clearly showing her curiosity. "Very pleased to meet you, Nora. I think I saw you talking to Simon at Maddie O'Rourke's wedding. I hope you brought lots of news from town. Things get a little quiet out here at times."

Unlike Simon's sister, it seemed.

"Go on in," Beth continued, reaching for Nora's cloak, which she hung by the back door next to several other brown coats like Simon's. "I'll fetch another place setting. I can't wait to become better acquainted."

What a lovely way to be welcomed to the family. Nora was smiling as Simon doffed his coat and led her through an arch beside the stove. On the other side lay the cabin's main room, a wide, warm space, with ladder-back chairs scattered here and there along the log walls and a bentwood rocker next to the rounded stone fireplace. Nora's gaze immediately lit on the small quilts, most likely the work of Simon's mother, draping the chairs.

But a noise to her left alerted her to the long table there, flanked by benches on either side. Those benches were crowded with people all gazing at her with looks ranging from eagerness to surprise.

"Simon." His mother looked up from her seat at the foot of the table. "Have you brought us a guest?"

Even as his mother's green eyes crinkled in welcome, Nora was struck by the lack of resemblance to Simon. Where he was lean, his features razor-edged, his mother was round and soft, her face more closely resembling her daughter's. Her green wool gown was clean and welltailored, for all it favored an earlier style.

"Not precisely a guest, Ma," Simon answered, and Nora was surprised to hear his voice come out stiff.

John, who had just come in the front door, stopped at the sight of Nora and raised his head heavenward as if petitioning the Lord for help.

Simon took Nora's hand in his, his grip sure, firm. "Allow me to introduce my wife, Nora."

Nora smiled at them all. Only Levi and John smiled back. The rest of them looked to be in a state of shock if the paling skin and widening eyes were any indication.

"Wife?" his mother gasped out. "Oh, Simon, what have you done?"

Simon's stomach knotted. Beside him, Nora's whole body tightened. She glanced up at him, her eyes wide, no doubt realizing for the first time that he had never told them the truth. She didn't deserve to hear their protests. He'd been the one who'd been unable to find a way to explain the situation.

Knowing he would have as difficult a time now, he slipped his arm about her shoulders and gave her a nod he hoped was encouraging, then turned to face his family.

"Nora and I introduced ourselves at Maddie O'Rourke's wedding," he said. "We discovered we share a similar philosophy."

"Family," John put in helpfully as he slipped into his seat at the table. "Sacrifice for those we love."

Nora offered his brother a tremulous smile.

"You knew about this?" Ma demanded.

John visibly swallowed. "Levi and I stood as witnesses."

Levi held up his hands as his mother's glare pinned him. "Don't look at me. It was Simon's idea. And I say he made a good choice. She can fix a sailing ship."

His mother frowned at that, but Drew rose from the head of the table. It was a point of pride that Simon was the only one who could look Drew in the eyes, for all his brother was more muscular.

"Forgive our manners, Nora," Drew said in his deep voice. "We were just surprised by Simon's news." The look in his dark blue eyes told Simon his oldest brother was merely saving his questions for later, in private. "I'm Drew, and this is my wife, Catherine."

Catherine rose as well. Dressed in a light blue wool gown, the pale-haired beauty rested a hand on her swelling middle and smiled. "Nora and I are acquainted from our time aboard the *Continental*. Welcome to the family, Nora."

Simon could feel Nora's body thawing a little.

James's wife, Rina, nodded a greeting as well. Simon had never understood what the lovely schoolteacher had seen in his brother. Even now, her golden-brown hair was elegantly confined behind her head, and her purple wool dress might have graced royalty.

"I remember Nora from our journey, and her kindness since," she said. "She is a good friend and a talented seamstress."

"A seamstress!" Beth's cry turned all gazes her way as she rushed in from the kitchen. Simon had seldom seen his sister so excited, and that was saying something, for Beth seemed to live in a giddy sense of delight.

"Oh, I knew I'd seen that dress before," she said, turning her head to gaze with obvious rapture at the back of Nora's skirts. Simon wasn't sure what was so special about the gown. Of the dresses he'd seen on Nora, this was the most severe with its gray wool and black braid trim.

"It's from the October *Godey's*, isn't it?" Beth demanded. "Only, you've changed the trim—braid instead of fringe. I thought the fringe was entirely too fussy. How would you keep it clean?"

"Beth." Ma's gentle admonition stopped her daughter in midgush. His mother stood and came to Simon's and Nora's sides.

"God blessed me with one daughter," she said with a smile to Beth, who was turning pink. "And now He's blessed me with more through my sons' wives. Please know that you are welcome here, Nora."

She opened her arms. Simon released his hold on Nora, and his mother hugged her close. Over Nora's shoulder, however, Ma's gaze was narrowed at him. If that was the worst he had to deal with, he would survive.

His family had certainly had more reasons to complain about him in the past.

Beth set a place for Nora, and everyone shifted around so Nora could sit next to Simon at his customary place on the bench facing the window. She was smiling again, her cheeks rosy with pleasure at their attentions. Whatever trouble he'd had with his family over the years, he knew they would be kinder to Nora than her brother and sister-in-law had been.

It was him they had the most trouble with.

Everyone had just settled down, with Beth and their mother bringing in the food from the kitchen, when James returned from the barn.

"What did I miss?" he asked, taking a seat beside Rina.

"Simon and Nora are married," his wife told him.

James tilted his head to one side as if shaking something out of his ear. "I must have spent too much time logging today. The crack of the ax has addled my hearing. I thought you said Simon got married."

"I did," Simon gritted out, readying himself for an endless barrage of his brother's teases. "Nora is my wife."

James rose and extended his hand across the table to her. "Welcome to the family, Nora. It's refreshing to find one of us who knows his mind when it comes to brides."

"Yes," Catherine said with a look around him to Rina. "We did have to do a bit of convincing to help you see the value of marriage."

James sat back down. "At least Levi didn't have to kidnap me a bride."

Drew flushed.

James leaned back. "Indeed, Simon always knows

what he's doing. You must be someone special, Nora, for him to ask you to marry him."

"Actually," Nora said, "I asked him."

James blinked.

"Simon," Drew put in, his voice catching on a laugh, "say the blessing so we can eat."

Normally, his brother's habit of ordering them around grated on Simon's nerves. But the honor of saying grace usually fell to Ma or Drew. That his brother had given it to him meant something.

He just wasn't sure what.

Everyone around the table bowed their heads and clasped their hands before them expectantly. He'd heard ministers recite a common prayer before a meal, but his family generally simply prayed about whatever was on their minds. They most likely wouldn't want to hear what was on his mind at that moment—relief that his confession was over, concern for the future—and he wasn't so sure his thoughts were fit for the Almighty's ears either. Then again, it wasn't as if He listened overmuch to Simon's petitions. Still, he bowed his head.

"Thank You for this food, Lord, for the seed it grew from and the land that nurtured it. Thank You for the strength to harvest it and cook it. May it be a blessing to our bodies. Amen."

Amens echoed around the table, and his family began passing the porcelain tureen of venison stew, the platter of biscuits, the pat of butter and jar of apple preserves. He could feel Nora relaxing beside him, her shoulders coming down, her head easing up.

"So," James said, digging his fork into the stew, "you asked Simon to marry you. I like a woman with gumption."

Rina smiled as she cut a piece of venison in two, knife and fork held properly.

Nora wrinkled her nose. "I don't have a lot of gumption, I fear. I'm just glad he agreed." She favored Simon with a smile that made everything taste better.

"You came with the Mercer Expedition," Drew put in. "What made you join the ladies in venturing West?"

"I wanted to live my own life," Nora replied. "Perhaps find a little adventure."

"And so you married Simon," James said triumphantly. "Excellent choice. Always the adventurer, that's our Simon."

Simon glared at him. "I'll leave the adventure to those who act first and regret it later."

Catherine passed Nora the platter. "More biscuits, Nora? You'll find that Levi has the lightest hand."

Down the table, Levi cocked a smile. "Ma taught me well."

Ma smiled too. "I taught all my children to cook." She nodded to Nora. "But that doesn't mean I wouldn't welcome new recipes or another hand in the kitchen."

"I'd be happy to help," Nora said.

Given what she'd faced with her brother, Simon wasn't about to see her forced into labor again. Not that his family was demanding in that way. They all shared the chores, and help was received gladly. But Nora found it hard to say no, and he feared she'd soon find herself overwhelmed with their requests.

"Nora plans to continue working," Simon advised them all. "She has commissions she must meet."

"Like my new waistcoat," James agreed, reaching for another biscuit.

"I'm sure I'll have time for other things," Nora said with a look to Simon.

He'd have to advise her about his family later. For now, he let the conversation veer off to other things and finished eating.

Yet he was aware of Nora beside him, the way she dug into the stew with gusto, the sigh of appreciation that escaped her when she tried his brother's biscuits. Though the bench should have felt crowded, having her next to him only made him feel warmer, more at home. How odd.

"I didn't see a trunk in the wagon," James ventured at one point. "No lady I know travels so light." He winked at his wife. "My back's still smarting from moving Rina's things."

"I left my trunk in Seattle," Nora explained with a look to Simon.

He was ready to tell her he would bring it back for her soon when Levi spoke up.

"I'll fetch it for you."

"You just want an excuse to get out of school," Beth accused him.

"We only have seven more classes until we suspend for Christmas," Rina reminded him. "And you in particular are needed to practice for our theatrical."

Levi preened. "I have the most important role."

"One of the most important roles," Beth protested.

Rina smiled. "With only five students at present, all of the roles are important."

To Simon's surprise, Nora spoke up. "I'd be happy to help if you need. Do you already have costumes?"

"Yes, we do," Beth answered for her sister-in-law and teacher. "And they are hideous."

"Elizabeth Ann Wallin," Ma scolded.

Rina held up a hand. "I fear she is correct. I have been focused on memorization and enunciation. With their other chores and Christmas preparations, Beth and the others have only been able to cobble together their costumes."

"But I know just how they should look," Beth said, eyes shining with her vision. "I'm sure you and I together could make them better, Nora."

"I'll do what I can," Nora promised.

There they went again, roping her in to more work. Yet he had to own that Nora could likely do the job quicker and with higher quality than even his ambitious sister.

"And I'll do what I can as well," John declared, rising from the bench and picking up his empty plate, cup and utensils. "I'll fetch Nora's things from town while Levi practices, so long as James lets me use Lancelot and Percival."

In typical style, James had named his horses after the knights of King Arthur's court.

"Granted," James said, his chin raised in kingly fashion. "So long as you bring back the mail and complete a commission for me while you're at it."

"Agreed," John said in his usual good-natured way. "And now I better go clean out my things." He smiled at Nora. "I've been bunking at Simon's. I'll move back to the main house with Levi."

"What!" Levi protested. "That's not fair!"

Beth, who was sitting next to him, bumped him with her shoulder. "You used to share the loft with all of them."

"Yeah, but I've grown since then," Levi told her.

"There's plenty of room in the loft, John," their mother said. "You are welcome to stay."

"Only until I can file my own claim," John assured her, "which is four months away." He glanced at Simon as if in encouragement, then hurried for the kitchen.

Simon knew what his brother expected. Here was the perfect opening to tell them about the new acreage. He raised his head. "I was afraid we couldn't wait until John files his claim for more land this spring. You know this winter will be difficult."

Drew was frowning at him. "I think you overstate the matter. We'll find a way to make it through."

And so it started. Drew only consented readily to a plan if he'd been the one to think of it. Simon had had this fight more times than he cared to remember. Of course, once he convinced Drew of the necessity, there would be no turning back. Much as he would have liked help from all his brothers, when Drew involved himself, it would be nothing but arguments over who did what and how.

"We may scrape by this year," Simon allowed. "But next year will be even harder with more mouths to feed."

Catherine put a hand to her belly, while Nora gazed up at him, her face puckering once more.

Simon pushed ahead. "John's claim can't be cleared and planted in time. So I filed for one above Drew's."

"How?" Drew demanded. "We didn't have enough money saved to buy the land."

"But a man can file for his wife," Simon reminded him.

Drew merely stared at him, but Beth gasped. "You married Nora for the land?"

She made it sound positively mercenary, as if he were

no better than Nora's brother, using her for his own gain.

"It was a fair bargain," Simon told her. "I gave her my support. She brought us land."

Nora nodded.

Ma's face crumbled, as if he'd done something beyond redemption. "But you are determined to make a marriage," she said, hope in every syllable.

Nora met Simon's gaze, and there wasn't an ounce of judgment on her round face. "I am content Simon and I will get along."

Just looking at her made it easier to breathe.

"But marriage shouldn't be about just getting along," Beth protested. "It's love and romance." She glanced among her brothers. "You all know that. You've read Pa's books."

Around the table Drew and James and even Levi were nodding. Simon squared his shoulders. "The only people to comment on a marriage should be those who entered into it."

They all started talking then. Simon let the noise wash over him. His only concern was the woman sitting at his side, the woman whose gray eyes were starting to look suspiciously bright, as if she was holding back tears.

"Wait, wait!" Beth cried, scrambling up from her seat. "I know what we should do, Simon. If you're not going to be really married to Nora, John can stay in your house and she can move in here with me. I've always wanted a sister. What do you say?"

Chapter Six

Nora could feel Simon tensing beside her at his sister's suggestion. She'd never seen a family in which the members felt so free to state their opinions. In her family, her father and later Charles spoke, and everyone else just complied.

She had a feeling Simon would have preferred that kind of order. He didn't seem to like anyone questioning his plans. But Beth had offered an excellent alternative. If Nora stayed in the main house, she wouldn't disturb Simon's peace, and he wouldn't have to pretend he cared.

"It's all right," she told him. "I'll do whatever you and your family think is best."

"As if Simon would ever agree with the rest of us," James warned.

Simon's gaze was on Nora, studying her as she might have examined a bolt of fabric to put it to best use. What did he see? A plain, sturdy woman who had offered an outrageous bargain because she couldn't muster the courage to tell off her own brother? A burden he hadn't planned on carrying? She had foisted herself on him.

She really couldn't blame him if he wanted to take the easy way out now.

He turned to his sister. "Nora and I agreed to our arrangement. We know what we're doing. Thank you for your offer, Beth, but Nora stays with me."

Something warm sizzled up inside her. Her parents had seemed a little embarrassed by her, born so late in their years when proper couples were doting grandparents. Charles and Meredith considered her a chore. No one had ever chosen to have her alongside.

His sister was not so easily swayed. "I think Nora should have a say in the matter," Beth said, crossing her arms over her chest.

Everyone was looking to Nora now. How very surprising. She managed a smile for their sakes. She knew how she'd answer, but it was tremendously gratifying to find them hanging on her words.

Beside her, she felt Simon go still. Did he doubt her answer? She wasn't going to argue with him. Until she'd reached Wallin Landing, she'd thought no one would ever argue with a fine, upstanding, logical fellow like Simon.

"I'll stay with Simon," she told Beth.

She heard Simon exhale, as if he'd been holding his breath. "Good. It's settled. Are you ready to retire, Nora?"

A few moments ago she would have liked nothing better than to stay by the cozy fire and plan costumes with Beth, but it might be best to retire, give everyone a chance to calm down. Simon had had enough trouble with his family tonight. She didn't want to cause more.

"Yes, of course, Simon," she said.

Beth's face fell. "But I was hoping you could stay for some entertainment."

"I think we've supplied enough of that tonight," Simon said, turning for the door.

James pointed a finger at the ceiling. "That's it! The end of the world has come upon us. Simon made a joke."

"Enough with you, James," his mother scolded. She turned to Simon and Nora. "Good night, my dears. I hope to see you in the morning."

Nora nodded. "Certainly. Thank you for dinner and the kind welcome. If I can help in any way, please let me know." She hurried to go fetch her cloak and Simon's coat, then followed him out the door, passing John on his way back in. His arms laden with belongings, Simon's brother raised his reddish brows in question, but Nora could only offer him a smile.

Simon did not look at her as he stalked into the woods. The moon had broken through the clouds, and just enough light flittered past the firs to show a wide path leading north.

"I'm sorry," she said, handing him his coat.

"You have no reason to apologize." He gripped the coat so tightly in one fist she thought the material might whimper in protest.

"Neither do you," she pointed out, lifting her skirts to keep up with him. "But wouldn't you feel better if you did?" She nodded her head back toward the family home.

He stopped and ran a hand through his hair, which gleamed silver in the moonlight. "Very likely, but I don't know how to talk to them. What I find logical, they resist, and what they find logical is often ridiculous. I don't understand how I could have been raised in the same family and have turned out so different."

He spoke with his usual clipped tone, yet she could feel the pain in his voice. She hurt for him. She'd grown up with no love and expected none in return. He'd grown up surrounded by love and didn't know how to return it.

"You're not so different," she assured him. "You value family, or you wouldn't have claimed the extra acreage. And your brothers seem to value family. They all stayed here at the farm when they might have staked a claim anywhere in the Territory."

"That's because of Pa," Simon said, starting to walk again. Nora fell in beside him.

"He had a dream of starting his own town out here," Simon explained. "He and Ma set their markers on the first claims, running parallel from Lake Union up over the hill toward Puget Sound. Drew and I claimed land on either side, and James's claim is beyond Drew's."

"See?" Nora said. "You do think alike."

"We agree on honoring Pa's memory," Simon allowed. "We differ on everything else."

Ahead, a log cabin loomed out of the darkness. Two stories tall at the peak, it had a cedar shake roof that dropped to a deep overhang on either side and sheltered a front porch enclosed by a rail. Windows, glittering in the darkness, flanked the plank door.

Simon went in first. John must have started a fire in the hearth when he'd come for his things, for warmth and light met Nora as she stepped through the door.

Her first impression was that Simon's cabin was nothing like his mother's. For one thing, it was much smaller, as he'd warned her, with the main room only four long strides across in either direction, and a ladder leading up into a loft over the back half of the room. It also lacked any decoration. Four chairs carved from logs squatted around a narrow plank table, with no rug or cushion to soften them. The hearth, made from smooth stones, was the only patch of color in the room, and even that was muted.

Simon nodded toward the ladder. "That leads up to the loft. Ma and Beth washed the bedding before the cold set in, so it should be fairly clean. There's a pitcher and basin upstairs as well. I'll fill the bucket down here before I leave in the morning so you'll have fresh water when you wake. The privy is around back."

So, this would be home. Nora wandered into the room, footsteps echoing on the bare floor. At least there was a crane in the fireplace for heating kettles and such. The black iron didn't look as if it had been used much. In fact, the floor was fairly clean, and she caught no sign of cobwebs along the rafters. The copper pots and tin plates piled on the sideboard were neat and orderly, any sign of his brothers' residency hidden away. Someone was a good housekeeper.

She nodded to the glass-chimneyed lamp on the table. "I'll need more light when I'm sewing. Have you plenty of oil?"

"It's stored in the root cellar to the east of the barn," he answered. "If you run low while I'm out, ask Ma or Beth to fetch it for you."

"Fine, then." There didn't seem to be anything else to discuss at the moment. He had said he rose early in the morning. She should get out of his way so he could go to sleep.

"I'll just head up to bed," she said, moving toward the ladder. It was fairly steep, the log rungs polished from frequent use. She gathered her skirts as best she could and set foot on the lowest rung. Then there was the question of pushing higher when she could use only one hand and her bunched skirts already made her lean back. She managed the second rung, feeling a bit ungainly, but her boot, damp from the ground, slipped on the third, and suddenly she was tumbling backward.

Right into Simon's arms.

Simon caught Nora as she fell, taking a step back to better hold her weight. Her head was tilted so that she looked up into his face, and he saw her gray eyes widen with obvious surprise and her rosy lips open in an O. For a moment, they merely gazed at each other.

"You're going to have to do something about the way you dress," Simon said. "Your gowns are apparently quite fashionable in some quarters, but they're impractical out here."

"Yes, of course, Simon," she said, lowering her gaze. "I'll work on that tomorrow."

He ought to put her down, show her a better way to climb the steep rungs. But she felt surprisingly good in his arms, as if the strength he'd built logging had finally been put to its best use.

Her thick black lashes fluttered. "Simon?"

"What?"

"Perhaps you should put me down."

He must have been more tired than he'd thought. It wasn't like him to stand about woolgathering. He lowered her until her feet brushed the floor, then straightened her until she could stand freely.

"Maybe I should sleep downstairs and you up," she suggested, eyeing the ladder with obvious misgivings.

He may not have been married before, but he didn't

think a husband should allow his wife to sleep on the floor while he took the bed.

"I'll go behind you as you climb the ladder," he said. "You won't fall again."

She seemed to accept that, for she approached the ladder and set her foot on the bottom rung.

Simon nodded his encouragement, giving her a little lead before sandwiching her between him and the ladder. She froze for a moment, as if accustoming herself to the feel of him right behind her, then took another step upward.

"Sorry for the trouble," she murmured, her face toward the ladder.

"No trouble," he said. "I had to do the same thing for Beth the first time she went up to change the bedding."

But he had to admit holding Beth to the ladder was nothing like holding Nora. With Nora's curves nestled against him, he felt warm and strong and needed.

What was he thinking? Of course he was needed. His family needed him to point out problems, offer solutions. They needed him to think clearly when their thoughts were muddled by emotions. That was his role.

She reached the top and scrambled onto the floor of the loft, turning to face him as he cleared the next rung. Her nose brushed his, soft as a caress.

"Thank you," she said, sounding breathless as she scuttled back. Perhaps being so sedentary in her profession made climbing ladders a strain.

He had no doubt she'd get used to it in time.

"You're welcome." He nodded to the space. "Hand me that shirt, will you? I'll need it in the morning."

The roof was so steeply pitched that he could stand upright only in the center of the loft. Being shorter, Nora had more room. She rose and fetched him the plaid flannel he had draped over the chest his father had carved for him. The carving showed a stag rearing up among trees, majestic, determined.

Alone.

"I forgot my bag," she said as she knelt in front of him again.

"I'll get it," Simon offered. "James must have left it at Ma's."

He slid down the ladder and jumped the last rungs. He could see her peering over the edge of the loft, watching him. For some reason, he thought about doing a handstand.

What was wrong with him?

He didn't need to impress Nora. They weren't courting. They had made a bargain, one she had had to change, but one he would honor nonetheless. He merely had to adjust to sharing his cabin with her. He didn't have to share his heart.

He was turning for the door, when someone rapped on the panel. Simon went and pulled on the latch.

In the moonlight, John smiled at him. "I thought Nora might need this." He held out the case.

Simon took it with a nod. "Thanks."

"Everything all right?" John asked, peering around him as if he expected to see Nora in a sobbing heap by the fire, regretting their wedding.

"Fine," Simon said. "Good night, John."

John's hand flew out to catch the door before Simon could close it.

"Wait." He drew in a breath, then spoke low, his gaze meeting Simon's. "I heard them all talking. They're worried about you."

"I'm fine," Simon snapped. "You know why I married Nora. Nothing's changed."

John nodded toward the loft. "Tell that to the woman sleeping in your cabin."

Simon glanced back in time to see Nora duck deeper into the shadows. He set down the bag, stepped outside and closed the door behind him.

"Neither of us planned to live together," he admitted to his brother. "But Nora's reasonable. We can come to terms."

"Do you hear yourself?" John shook his head, his red hair showing gray in the moonlight, as if he was wiser than his years. "I have only Drew's and James's marriages to go by, but I can't see Catherine or Rina coming to terms with them."

"Nora isn't Catherine or Rina." If she had been as strong-willed as either of his sisters-in-law, she would have found a way to stand up to her family without resorting to buying courage, as she had called it.

"No," John said, his face solemn. "She seems a great deal more fragile."

Simon pictured Nora's sturdy frame, the generous curves outlined by her dresses. He remembered the wildcat who had told him what she expected of him. No, he could not see Nora as fragile.

"She's stronger than you think," he told his brother.

"Maybe," John allowed. "And maybe all this will work out. But Ma and Beth are concerned you gave up your chance at love to make sure they were fed."

Love? What chance had he had for that? His mother and sister might be worried for him, but they were among the first to argue with him. Of his brothers, he only got along well with John, but so did everyone else.

No matter how he tried, he caused friction, dissention. Love wasn't for him.

"I'm fine, John," he repeated. "Tell Ma and Beth not to worry. I know what I'm doing."

John nodded. "You usually do. Good night, Simon. I'll see you in the morning."

Simon watched as his brother strode away through the trees. John was easy to convince, accepting things as they were presented. His other brothers and their wives would come around in time. Ma and Beth would eventually appreciate his decision, once they grew to know Nora. Like John, Simon's wife was affable, willing to listen to reason.

So why did he have the feeling that his life was about to change?

Chapter Seven

Simon was gone the next morning when Nora woke. She'd slept surprisingly well in the strange surroundings. The quilt she'd snuggled under on the bed's thick straw mattress was well stitched and done in the colors of the forest—spruce and bark and sky—that somehow reminded her of Simon. The thick cedar roof shut off all sound from outside, and heat from the chimney rising at the back of the loft kept the space comfortable.

She was glad she'd packed one of her narrower dresses, the sort she used to wear when she'd cared for her parents and Charles and Meredith. This one was of soft gray wool, because Meredith had thought the color and plain lines more seemly for a spinster. Nora had spent a week embroidering crimson roses along the hem, cuffs and simple white collar. Meredith had not been amused.

Now Nora put only one flannel petticoat under the dress so that it was easier to navigate the ladder. After all, there was no Simon waiting at the bottom to catch her if she fell this time.

The memory of his arms on either side of her, his

strong body just behind, made her blush as she stepped down the rungs, clinging to the rails. Simon Wallin was a fine figure of a man, no question. And he must be terribly smart too, to see the difficulty inherent in any situation. She was fortunate to have married such a man.

She made a face as she went to poke up the fire. Really, what did she know about the institution of marriage? After seeing how her traveling companions interacted with their beaus and husbands, she had come to realize she couldn't use her parents or Charles and Meredith as good examples. And she and Simon weren't really married for all they'd had a wedding. They merely had an agreement.

He'd certainly kept his end of it. He'd left her a bucket of fresh water, as promised, and a box full of wood for the fire. She found two thick slices of apple bread sitting on a tin plate on the table.

How considerate.

It didn't take long to heat the main room and tidy up after breakfast. There was a mirror hanging on one wall, and she used it to repin her hair, straighten her collar. If she had been in Seattle, she'd have hurried to her little corner of the Kellogg brothers' shop, with fabrics and notions piled around her like a rainbow, to work on her commissions. Mrs. Horton had burned a hole in a favorite gown, and Nora was remaking the skirt to hide the mark. Two of the sawmill operators needed new pants hemmed. And then there was that waistcoat for Brother James, a tailored affair of silver-shot satin. She tried to imagine practical Simon wearing one and smiled.

She would get her commissions soon enough. In the meantime she wasn't sure what to do with herself. She paced the little room, considering her options. Simon's cabin didn't need a lot of cleaning. And the sparse furnishings required little tending. By his own admission, the wash had been done recently. She'd never lived on a farm, but she was certain there must be a number of chores, even in winter when the fields lay empty. She simply wasn't sure what those chores would be or whether she could do them.

She had never intended to be an honored guest at Wallin Landing. If she was going to live here, she would have to find a way to contribute.

Someone rapped at the door just then, and Nora hurried to answer. Standing on the stoop, swathed in a sky blue cloak of fine wool, Catherine smiled at her, her arms full of clothing.

"Good morning," she greeted. "I fear we started out on the wrong foot last night. May I come in so we can talk?"

Nora could not imagine Simon refusing entrance to any of his family, especially one coming in the name of peace. She held the door wider, and Catherine crossed the threshold into the cabin.

She glanced around, her graceful brows arched in surprise. "Rather Spartan."

Had Simon kept her from entering? "Haven't you been here before?" Nora asked, concern rising.

"Never," Catherine said, turning to her with a smile. "Until you arrived, this was the last male bastion at Wallin Landing. Simon and John generally stayed here, with Levi joining them when he was in their good graces. Somehow, I imagined it messier."

Then she could not know Simon well. Nora was fairly sure untidiness would drive him mad.

Catherine held out the clothing. "Beth asked me to

bring you these, along with her promise to come see you as soon as school is out tomorrow. We persuaded her you might need today to settle in. These are what they were going to use for costumes for the theatrical next week."

Nora crossed to her side and accepted the clothing from her new sister-in-law. Her fingers touched worn velvet, thick wool and filmy linen. She set the bundle on the table and lifted the top piece.

"It seems a little large for children," she said as the shirt she held up to her fell past her knees.

"Well, there are no children at the Lake Union School," Catherine told her, removing her cloak and draping it over one of the log chairs. She seated herself on another and arranged her skirts. They were properly narrow, Nora noticed: good navy wool with no ornamentation around the hem, which was dotted with mud.

"But I thought Rina had five students," Nora said, folding the shirt carefully.

"She does, but Beth is by far the youngest at fourteen," Catherine explained. "Levi and his friend Scout are eighteen, and the other two are grown men who hope to better themselves by learning to read and cipher. There were others earlier, all adults, but they have graduated and moved on. It's all very progressive."

It certainly sounded that way. The school Nora had attended had been girls only, with a female teacher who brooked no nonsense. But Nora was glad her parents had sent her to school. Had they passed away when she was younger, Charles would likely have found some reason to keep her sequestered at home.

"About last night," Catherine said, her hand brushing some fir needles off her skirt, "I do apologize if anything we said offended you."

"Not at all," Nora told her. "But I think Simon was hurt by his family's comments."

Catherine started, her gaze darting to Nora's. "Simon?"

Nora took a seat opposite her at the table. "Is that so hard to imagine? He chose to marry a stranger so his family wouldn't lack for food. I find that admirable. Is it any wonder he was hurt when his family questioned him instead of thanking him for his sacrifice?"

"But marriage is about more than enlarging one's holdings, no matter the need," Catherine protested. "It is about two people becoming one, in goals, in values, in love."

Now, that was a lovely definition of marriage. A shame it would not do for her and Simon.

"Simon and I are compatible when it comes to values," she allowed, "and we are agreed to support each other's goals. As for love, I certainly never expected to find it."

Catherine frowned at her a moment, then lowered her gaze to the pile of fabric, her long fingers pleating the linen shirt. "When I came to Wallin Landing, I had no interest in finding love either. I lost my father and brother in the war, you see, and I was certain my heart would never survive another loss. But Drew changed my mind. He showed me love was worth the risk."

Nora sighed. "Oh, how romantic. I'm so glad for you."

Catherine leaned forward, her gaze rising once more, the pale blue bright and determined. "And I only wish the same for you, Nora. I will pray that you and Simon are similarly blessed in your marriage."

Nora could only smile in answer. She knew the Lord would care for her—He always had. But she had no illusions that Simon would fall in love with her. The best she could do was to earn his respect by being useful to him and his family.

And suddenly she knew just how to start. When Catherine was ready to leave, Nora threw on her cloak and followed her out the door. She had to find John before he started out to Seattle for her trunk, for she had a few more things for him to pick up.

The sun had set when Simon dragged himself home for the day. He, Drew and James had been trying to finish an order for spars, which the sawmill owner Henry Yesler wanted to have on hand for the sailing ships that stopped from time to time in Seattle's harbor. Drew was hoping for payment within the week so he could purchase something special for his bride their first Christmas together. Normally, John would have helped, but he'd gone into Seattle to fetch Nora's trunk. Until Levi passed the examination Rina and his mother had agreed on, Simon's youngest brother spent the better part of the day at school, squeezing in chores before and afterward.

With the light so dear in December, the remaining three brothers had had to work hard in relatively few hours. Simon would have thought that short duration enough to keep them quiet and focused on the work, but Drew had used the time to question him. And his brother had not appreciated Simon's answers.

"So unlike your usual habit, you made your decision based on one conversation," he said, his ax biting into the tree he and Simon were felling while James took a turn watching for trouble. John had located a stand of timber above James's cabin with several trees just the right circumference and height to serve as masts when peeled and seasoned.

"I'm not generally the one who has trouble making decisions," Simon reminded him, yanking his ax from the wood. "Nora presented her case. I evaluated it and found it worth consideration."

"But you didn't consider it," Drew said. "You just did it."

Simon paused to eye his brother. "Which concerns you more, that I married Nora or that I didn't come to you first for advice?"

Drew gave the tree a mighty whack that set it to leaning, and Simon could see his brother's tanned cheeks darkening. "You've made your point. You don't need my permission to wed. And I'm the last one to advise you on courting. If you and the others hadn't encouraged me, I might never have married Catherine."

James, who was passing on his rounds about the area, laughed. "We didn't so much encourage as threaten, cajole and harass. If you ask me, I think it's a good thing Simon didn't ask our advice first." James whistled as he continued on his way.

That was new—James agreeing with him on anything. Drew even let the matter go as they returned to their work, and Levi was just as congenial when he came by the new acreage in the twilight to help Simon clear a couple of smaller trees before dinner.

"You did a good thing by marrying Nora," Levi had commented as they had hacked at the trunk of a young cedar. Simon appreciated his willingness to work on the property, although he thought it was as much to be helpful as to escape studying.

"This land is a godsend," Simon had agreed as they repositioned their axes.

"Nora's a godsend too," Levi had said. "Beth will finally have someone who listens as much as Beth talks."

Now Simon smiled as he reached for the door latch on his cabin. Nora was unobtrusive, quiet, peaceful even. She would not cut up his life. And that was a blessing.

He opened the door, and the scent of something baking assailed him. More, colors and shapes bombarded his gaze. He blinked, thinking for a moment he'd somehow wandered onto the wrong claim.

Bright swags of fabric draped the log walls, obscured the plank table. Lacy embroidered doilies clung to the four chairs he'd carved from stumps left over from their logging. A rug patterned in roses ran from the door to the hearth, encouraging him to enter the whimsical palace.

He couldn't seem to make his feet move.

"Welcome home," Nora said from the hearth, where a cast-iron oven lay covered in coals. White dots he guessed were flour were sprinkled over her dress, and her hair was escaping her bun as if trying to flee from the grandeur around it.

"What did you do?" he asked.

She beamed at him. "I decorated."

He glanced around again, finding no words to describe the blaze of color. "So I see."

As his gaze returned to hers, he saw that her smile was fading. "You don't like it."

"Not in the slightest," he said, forcing himself into the room. "But I imagine I'll get used to it."

She seemed to accept that, for she turned to the hearth. "Dinner will be ready by the time you clean up."

She truly was cooking. He could smell ham as he moved deeper into the room, and his mouth began watering. Swallowing, he nodded to the hearth. "I thought we agreed we would eat at the main house with the others."

"Well, you didn't seem all that happy with the family dinner last night," Nora pointed out, arranging the silverware on the table. Silverware? Since when had he owned more than a few forks and a hunting knife?

"I checked with your mother," she continued, avoiding his gaze, "and she had extra ham, potatoes, carrots, flour and such, so I made dinner here."

"Inefficient," Simon said, going to the basin and splashing water into it from the pitcher. "It makes more sense for us to eat with the others. That way nothing goes to waste."

"Yes, of course," she said. "I'll speak to your mother about that tomorrow."

He scrubbed his hands, dried them on the towel that had been hung next to the stand. The white fabric had been embroidered with violets and edged in lace. Thoroughly impractical. But it left his work-roughened hands feeling surprisingly soft.

He turned to the room and glanced around again. He did his best to keep things clean and tidy. Anything messy seemed out of control. On closer inspection, he could see an order to the colors, a subtle shifting of light and shadow that was somehow appealing. And what could be seen of the floor had been swept so clean the golden patina of the cedar planks glowed through. The ash from the hearth had been cleared out, and the windows gleamed.

"There," Nora said, setting a meat pie on the table. "And there's apple preserves as well."

Simon approached her. "You didn't have to do all this, Nora."

Her chin came up. "Certainly I did. I am not one to shirk a task, sir." She bustled around the table and took her seat.

Simon sat opposite her. "You aren't a servant in this house."

She colored. "I didn't think I was. I'm very sorry you dislike everything. Let's eat."

Clasping her hands, she bowed her head. "Dear Lord, bless this food, which I wasn't supposed to make, and bless this house, which I wasn't supposed to clean and cheer. Amen."

She raised her head and reached for the serving spoon, then hesitated. "Am I allowed to serve myself dinner?"

Simon puffed out a breath. "Of course."

"Good." She dug into the pie and heaped a piece onto her plate, then offered him the spoon. "I'll tell Beth I can't help with the costumes, after all. She can likely sew the pieces herself, when she isn't studying for school, practicing for the theatrical or doing the chores I'm not supposed to do."

Simon carved out a piece of pie. "Beth does chores to prepare herself to manage her own home. You don't need the practice."

"Of course not," Nora said, though her smile felt sharp. "After all, I'll never have a home of my own."

He set down his fork. "That isn't what I meant. You gave up your life so I could claim one hundred and sixty acres. You shouldn't have to work for it."

She softened, her smile becoming the one that warmed him. "I have worked since I was twelve, Simon, first nursing my parents until their deaths, then caring for Charles and Meredith and finally at my own sewing.

I wasn't made to be a lady of leisure. If I sit around all day, I'll go mad. Besides, as your wife, I should contribute something to the family besides a tract of land covered in trees."

"What about your commissions?" Simon countered. "Won't they keep you busy?"

"Not busy enough," Nora assured him. "And I truly would like to work with Beth on the theatrical." She peered at him through her lashes. "You don't object to me helping her, do you?"

"No," Simon said.

"Good," she replied. "And tomorrow, I'll return the cabin to the way it was. John brought me my trunk today, along with some of the fabric I'd purchased at the Kelloggs' store, and I couldn't wait to use it all. It seemed such a shame for everything to stay in a trunk that could be used for more important items."

That did seem a waste. He glanced around again. "I can adjust. You don't have to take it all down."

Her smile brightened, making him feel insufferably proud of himself for having done nothing more than agree. "Wonderful. And you really must let me clean house. With you busy clearing the land, you won't have time. You wouldn't want us living in squalor."

"Of course not," Simon said.

She levered her fork at him. "And you have a button loose on that shirt. I am going to sew it back on properly. What good is being a seamstress if I cannot share my skills with family?"

When had a fork become a lethal weapon? He'd sweated less when teaching Beth to shoot for the first time. "Very well," Simon said.

She nodded, returning to her piece of pie. "Excellent. I'm so glad we could come to an agreement."

So was he, but he couldn't shake the feeling that he'd just agreed to something far more.

Chapter Eight

There. That hadn't been so hard. True, Simon hadn't reacted as enthusiastically as she'd hoped to the changes,
but he had been willing to listen to reason. And when
she showed him how she'd used fabric to soften the bedding he slept in near the fire, his eyes had lit with appreciation. That look made it easier to say good-night
and head up into the loft for bed.

And she'd even climbed the ladder all by herself. She
just wasn't sure why that made her feel disappointed
rather than pleased.

Once again, he was gone when she woke in the morning. Her only other dress with narrow skirts was a red-
and-green-plaid taffeta that Meredith had found far too
bright. Nora donned it anyway. But she had to own it
was one more blaze of color in the cabin. With winter
sunlight shafting through the windows, the room looked
a bit brighter than she'd intended. She took down some
of the draping, rearranged things on the table and decided that was much better.

Hopefully, Simon would agree.

But she wasn't going to sit around all day and wait

for him. Instead, after a breakfast of oatmeal she made from a sack of oats in the cupboard, Nora went to the schoolhouse.

The Lake Union School sat across the back of the clearing at Wallin Landing, a sturdy building of peeled logs with windows looking out toward the main house. Inside, benches dotted by slates were bracketed by a stone hearth at the back of the schoolroom and a neat teacher's desk at the front. Already a fire was crackling, warming the space, and lanterns hanging from brass hooks in the rafters gave off a golden light. Rina, in her crisp lavender gown edged in deeper purple ruching, looked right at home at the head of the class, her hair carefully combed into a bun at the top of her head.

Nora had hoped to catch the schoolteacher before her students arrived, wanting to ask about how she could help with the theatrical. Beth, however, was there before her, sweeping the schoolroom floor. She stopped to listen impatiently, shifting from foot to foot so that her gingham skirts swung like a bell, as Nora and Rina talked.

"We need nothing elaborate," Rina assured Nora with a look to Beth, who had opened her mouth most likely to protest. "The play is a simple composition based on the events surrounding the birth of our Savior."

"Only, our baby Jesus will be born in a schoolroom," Beth put in helpfully.

Nora frowned. "Why? There seems to be a perfectly good stable just across the way."

Rina stared at her, her hazel eyes widening in her creamy face.

Beth clapped her hands. "Oh, wonderful! That's absolutely perfect. I know just how to arrange it all. We can put the audience on the threshing floor and use Lancelot's stall as the manger. You're brilliant!" She threw her arms around Nora.

Nora absorbed the hug, feeling rather pleased with herself. She'd contributed, even if she wasn't entirely sure how.

Rina did not look so certain as Beth disengaged. "Is that advisable?" she asked with a frown. "We would not want to disturb the animals or damage foodstuffs needed for winter."

"Leave it to us," Beth said, turning to put an arm about Nora's shoulders. "We can arrange everything so nothing is disturbed. Right, Nora?"

Nora nodded, but she felt as if the log walls around her had suddenly grown taller and more formidable. It had seemed such a logical suggestion, but what did she know about barns and animals and winter food?

Only that Simon had changed his entire life to make sure the family did not lack. Somehow, she doubted he would be as excited about the idea as Beth. When she said as much, Beth waved Nora's concerns away.

"You let me deal with Simon. I'm sure I can bring him around to our way of thinking."

Rina shook her head. "I quite agree with Nora. Your brother, Beth, has strong opinions on a number of issues. We would be better served to ask before assuming." She turned to Nora. "Simon and his brothers are working on the hillside above our cabin, just to the south of the clearing, past the barn. Would you have time to seek them out this morning?"

The idea of seeing Simon at his work had appeal. Maybe she could spot some other way to help. "Yes, of course, Rina," Nora said with a smile. "I'll let you know what he says."

Bundling her cloak about her, she left the schoolroom and followed the heavily used path past the barn and up into the forest for James's claim.

It was not difficult to spot the differences between this claim and Simon's. The trees had been thinned around Simon's cabin, letting in light, keeping the roof clear of falling limbs. Here the firs brushed the cedar roof of James's cabin, which was even more simply built than Simon's. The two-story log home looked as if it listed a bit, and the shutters on the windows had been re-hung recently, if the little holes in the logs on either side of the windows were any indication. While Simon had tapped groundwater with a pump not too far from the front door, Nora didn't see any such apparatus nearby. Maybe James and Rina used the stream that bubbled by on the east of the cabin, likely on its way to join Lake Union below.

Of course, being younger than Simon, perhaps James needed more time to improve his claim. But Nora suspected the differences were as much about James's and Simon's personalities as the timing.

Still, it was easy to identify where they were working this morning. Glancing up the hillside to the west of the cabin, she caught the flash of crimson among the trees. A moment more brought the crack of an ax on wood. That had to be Simon and his brothers.

Rehearsing what she would say to him in her mind, she gathered her skirts to climb up through the under-growth, detouring around ferns that reached to her shoulders, blackberry vines that snaked past her boots. The ground was moist, the moss slippery underfoot. She could smell the rain in the air.

But she was so intent on finding her footing that she almost missed the cry of "There she goes!"

Air rushed past, and Nora pulled up short to see something swinging heavily through the trees toward her. She couldn't muster a cry before the fir thundered down a few yards away. The fall shook the forest floor. She staggered, sucking in a breath. Branches and leaves plummeted down in its wake, pelting her. She threw up her arms to shield her face.

"Stop, stop!" she cried. "There's someone else in the woods!"

Calls echoed all around her, concerned, searching. Before she could even lower her arms, Simon crashed through the bushes to her side.

"What are you doing here?" he cried. "You could have been killed!"

Nora lowered her arms. He sounded angry, but even in the shadows of the forest, she could see his face was white, and his hand, when he put it to her elbow, was shaking.

"Simon." Drew moved closer to them, an ax in one hand. "You're frightening her."

She wasn't frightened. Not precisely. She wasn't sure how she knew it, but she was certain Simon would never hurt her. And the danger was clearly past. She was more concerned for him.

Nora put out her free hand and touched him. "It's all right, Simon. I'm fine."

He drew in a shuddering breath. "And thank the Lord for that. A logging claim is no place for you, Nora. Why are you here?"

James and John had come down from where they had been working as well. James eyed his older brother with a frown, as if unsure what had so concerned Simon, but John moved in to put a hand to Simon's shoulder in support.

Nora managed a smile all around. "I'm sorry to trouble you. I had a question about the barn."

"The barn." Simon said the two words as if they had no meaning for him. "You risked your life to ask me a question about the barn."

"Simon." Drew's voice was firm. "No one was hurt. From what Catherine told me, Nora hasn't lived on a farm or spent time around logging. She had no way of knowing that she could have been harmed." He turned to her. "What question did you have, Nora?"

She couldn't take her eyes off Simon. He held himself stiffly, and his breath came fast and hard, but she didn't think it was because of his exertions.

"Beth and I were wondering whether we might use the barn as the backdrop for the theatrical," Nora said. "The story is set in a stable, you see, and Beth says there's room for everyone to sit and watch. I was worried it might disturb the animals."

"A play with Beth and Levi in it would be enough to disturb anyone," James quipped.

Simon spared him a glance. "I'm sure the play isn't going to be the problem. You ought to be concerned about your horses, James."

His brother waved a hand. "Lancelot and Percival will likely enjoy the show."

Simon drew in a breath as if ready to launch into a scold.

"It's all right," Nora said hurriedly. "We'll go somewhere else. It was just a suggestion."

"And a good one," Drew told her, with a look to all his

brothers. "Rina has already spoken to me and Catherine about lending a hand, so I know what she has in mind for the theatrical. I don't see any reason you can't put it on in the barn. Thank you for asking, Nora."

Nora nodded, but she couldn't help feeling she'd somehow let Simon down. "And it's all right with you, Simon?"

Her husband snapped a nod. "If Drew knows it won't disturb the animals or the grain, then I have no objections."

Some of the tension seemed to leave John's shoulders, but Simon still looked as if he wanted to eat one of the trees.

"Oh, good. Well." Nora took a step back. "I'll just be going, then. Good luck with your logging."

She turned to go and promptly tripped on a blackberry vine.

Simon's arm snapped out to catch her, and once more she found herself in his embrace. She expected to see anger in his eyes this time for sure, annoyance that she had disturbed his peace again. But what she saw in his eyes was nothing short of terror. The marked fear shut off as he averted his gaze and helped her back on her feet.

Drew reached out and put a hand on Simon's shoulder. "John, walk Nora down to the clearing. That way Simon will know she's safe."

John nodded, stepping around Simon through the brush to offer Nora his hand.

Nora glanced up at her husband. "Simon?"

He drew in a breath. "Go with John, Nora. I'll see you this evening."

She wanted to do something—touch him, stroke

the worry from his brow, tell him everything would be fine—but she doubted he wanted her to do any of those things. She wasn't really his wife, after all. Just his partner in their bargain. Still, she wished she understood why he had been so very concerned when his brothers, who must have the same experience logging as he had, could be so calm about the incident.

With a final look to her confusing husband, she took John's hand and let him lead her from the woods.

"That was quite a reaction," Drew said the moment John and Nora disappeared among the trees down the hillside.

Simon nodded. In truth, his heart was still hammering from Nora's near miss. When he'd heard her call, he'd felt as if an icicle had stabbed his heart. But he shouldn't have berated her. Drew was right; she could have no understanding of the danger posed by logging. And he hadn't thought to apprise her.

It wasn't like him to fail to think ahead. How many other dangers would Nora face because of his thoughtlessness?

"That was a bit much, especially for you," James said, cocking his head as if he could see up into Simon's mind.

"She could have been killed," Simon told him, turning for their work area. "You of all people should understand that."

He waited for the clever retort, but James shoved past him for the trees.

"I'll clean off the upper branches," he muttered, striding ahead.

"Quite an effort you're making this morning," Drew said to Simon. "You've managed to frighten your wife out of her wits and annoy the one brother impossible to discompose. Ready to take me on in a bare-knuckle brawl?"

Simon eyed his brother's bulk. "Don't push me, Drew. Not now."

Drew shook his head. "I'm not trying to push you, Simon. I'm trying to help you see that you overreacted. Admit it—you were thinking about Pa."

Their father had been killed by a falling branch while logging. Simon had watched him die. Drew was likely right that the memory had fed his reaction now. But Simon couldn't claim that was the only reason for his response.

"My concern was for Nora," he insisted. "If that tree had come down on her…" He couldn't finish the sentence, feeling that icy chill again.

"Nora is fine," Drew said. "I'm not sure she was ever in any danger. The tree missed her by yards. She was only surprised."

Simon cleared the distance between them, until he was nearly nose to nose with his older brother. "This time. What about the next time?"

Drew met him gaze for gaze. "There will be no next time. She's learned she needs to let us know when she's coming near."

There was that. By the pallor on Nora's face, the incident with the tree was not one she'd soon forget. Simon took a step back. "I'll talk to her tonight. She has to know there are a dozen ways to die out here."

Drew barked a laugh. "Now you sound like me. When Catherine first came to nurse Ma, all I could think about was how she might be hurt. I didn't want to take care of one more person. I already had enough on my hands with you all."

He started back toward the work area, and Simon followed him through the brush. "You still have a hard time remembering we're grown. We don't need you to protect us."

"And Nora might not need as much protection as you think," Drew told him. "She's obviously more sturdy than Catherine or Rina. She may not have been raised on a farm, but she seems willing to learn. You just need to be patient and teach her what she needs to know."

James, who was hacking away at the limbs on the fallen fir, glanced up at that. "Simple. Simon is known for his patience."

Simon glared at him.

Drew hefted his ax. "Simon knows how to bide his time, James. You could learn from him."

James laughed, cutting through one of the limbs in one blow. "And he could learn something from me. When Rina first came to us, she knew far less than Nora. She'd never even lit a fire."

Rina had been raised with servants at hand to care for her least need before her so-called parents had been found guilty of fraud and sentenced to years in prison. But Simon hadn't realized she'd known so little.

"Look at her now," James bragged, blissfully chopping away. "She can cook, sew, milk a goat and collect eggs from chickens without getting pecked, besides being the best teacher west of the Mississippi."

"And she's the most accurate shot out here," Drew reminded him.

James colored. "Well, I can't take any credit for that. Her father taught her to shoot in competitions. My point was that Rina has grown accustomed to living out here. So will Nora. You just have to give her time."

Easy for James to say. His wife worked in the safety of the schoolhouse. Simon had thought Nora would be content to stay inside the cabin and work on her sewing. He knew John had brought back commissions for her. If she was determined to wander about in the woods, he'd have to explain a few things to her, show her how to protect herself. If only she didn't go off on these odd tangents. Decorating the cabin. Holding a theatrical in the barn.

James and Drew advised giving her time. But did he have the time to teach her before Nora's own curiosity and whims put her in danger, a danger from which he couldn't protect her?

Chapter Nine

John saw Nora safely back to the clearing. She felt a little guilty taking him out of his way. She'd managed to find the logging claim all on her own, after all. But she was still a little shaky after the tree coming down so close to her, and Simon's strong reaction, so she kept in step with him until they reached the barn.

"And you think it's really all right to hold the theatrical inside?" she couldn't help asking as they paused beside the building. At more than two stories tall, the weathered log barn certainly looked strong enough to shelter a score of animals and a few actors.

John glanced at the barn. "It will be fine, Nora. I'm sorry Simon frightened you. He knows the dangers in the woods, better than most. He was just concerned for your safety."

And wasn't that an amazing thought in itself? "I'll try to stay closer to home for now," she promised John before sending him off with an airy wave.

She thought that would be an easy promise to keep, but after spending most of the day on her commissions, she could hardly wait to get out of the cabin and talk to

Beth. She had never considered herself the type to thrive on companionship. She and her parents had lived fairly solitary lives, entertaining a select group of longtime friends and going out only to attend church services, the theatre or the opera. The circle of acquaintances had narrowed even further when her parents had become ill. And of course Charles and Meredith had kept her closeted.

But after near-constant company on the ship from New York, at the boardinghouse and when she was working at the store, she had to admit she needed to see more than her own face in the mirror once in a while.

She met Simon's sister just as Beth was leaving the schoolhouse that afternoon.

"Simon and your brothers say it's perfectly all right to use the barn for the theatrical," she reported.

Beth beamed, broadening her round face and brightening her blue eyes. "Oh, wonderful! I already sent Scout to look at it. Let's go find him." She linked arms with Nora and tugged her toward the barn.

Sure enough, a thin boy with unruly brown hair and a forlorn expression on his narrow face was waiting for them beside the massive door, which had been rolled open just wide enough to let a person inside.

"Nora Wallin, this is Scout, that is Thomas Rankin," Beth told her.

Thomas bobbed a nod. "Nice to meet you. I always wondered who'd be brave enough to marry Simon Wallin."

"Scout!" Beth scolded.

Nora smiled at him. "I don't know how brave I am, but it's a pleasure to meet a friend of Beth's."

The lad colored, hanging his head so that the knot at

the top of his crooked nose was more evident. "I'm no friend. I've just known her since she was little."

"Yes, you are too my friend," Beth insisted. "And Levi's as well. Now, let's see what we all think about the barn."

She darted inside, and Thomas stepped back to let Nora follow her. Nora had a feeling it didn't much matter what she and Thomas thought about the space. Beth had clearly made up her mind.

"Nice and warm in here," Thomas murmured as he followed them into the barn.

He probably needed the warmth. Nora and Beth had on their cloaks, but the youth wore only a red flannel shirt and frayed-hem trousers, both of which had seen better days. A pair of good wool trousers, in a nice brown tweed, and an emerald-colored wool shirt would certainly warm the boy and brighten his demeanor. Nora knew just where to tailor them to make the most of Thomas's lean physique. But very likely he wouldn't have the money for such trappings. Perhaps she could ask Beth if there was a way she could sew for him for free without hurting his pride.

"This will be perfect," Beth said, glancing around. "I can see the angel there, the manger there, and the threshing floor has plenty of room, just as I'd hoped."

Nora followed her pointing finger. With a hazy light slipping in through the cracked door, she could just make out a wide aisle with stalls on one side and an open wood floor and a large bin on the other. The loft overhead seemed to be filled with hay if the golden straws hanging off the edges were any indication. The air was spiced with the scent of animals and earth.

Beth was tapping her chin with one finger. "Something isn't right. The picture of the Nativity in *Godey's* showed cows, a donkey and sheep in the stable. I suppose we could get by with goats instead of sheep, and of course we have Lancelot and Percival rather than donkeys, but I don't like the oxen. We really should have more animals for the background."

Nora wasn't so sure. Wouldn't more animals need more space, more food?

Thomas wiped his nose with the back of his hand. "Mr. Paul has a cow he doesn't want anymore. He told Pa he's fixing to butcher it before Christmas. I reckon he'd let us borrow it first."

Beth nodded. "Good idea, Scout. Let's ask him."

"Yes, of course," Nora said. "Let's just ask your mother first."

"Ma won't care," Beth declared, sailing toward the door with Thomas right behind her. "We can be to the Pauls' claim and back before dark if we hurry. Come along, Nora."

She seemed so sure of herself that Nora couldn't gainsay her. And she supposed it wasn't a bad thought to meet their neighbors. This Mr. Paul or his wife might need sewing done at some point. If the other claim was that close, and since Nora had company, surely Simon wouldn't worry about her going.

Beth stopped by the main house long enough to take down the rifle from the cradle by the back door.

"Do you know how to use that?" Nora couldn't help asking.

Beth broke open the barrel and nodded at the shells in the casing, then snapped the gun shut. "Everyone at Wallin Landing knows how to shoot. I'm sure Simon would teach you if you asked."

Nora eyed the sleek gray metal in Beth's grip and shuddered. All she knew about guns was that people used them to kill things. She would leave that to others with stronger constitutions.

They set off through the woods, heading south along the road. Though the clouds were heavy, no rain fell. The trees stood tall on either side of their path. Small things scampered away through the underbrush as they passed, and a gull circled overhead with a mournful cry.

Although Thomas was only a little taller than Nora, his stride was longer, and he quickly moved to the head of their group, leading them off the main road and onto a narrow, uneven path. Walking beside Nora, Beth carried the rifle carefully.

"I'm very glad you married Simon, Nora," she said as they walked.

In the act of lifting her plaid skirts out of the brush, Nora looked at her in surprise. "You are? Why?"

Beth smiled at her. "Well, it's nice having someone around who understands fashion, for one. And I know you will prove an ally. You can't imagine how I have to argue with Simon over every little thing. You'll understand."

She understood what it was like to be bowled over by a demanding brother. But Simon wasn't nearly as autocratic as Charles, and Beth didn't seem to have any trouble speaking her mind.

"Besides," the girl continued, pushing a branch out of their way with her free hand, "of all my brothers, I worried for Simon the most."

"You worried about Simon?" Nora asked. "But he has a strength of character I can only admire."

Beth slapped her hand down on her cloak. "See? That's why it's good you married him. Not many people can appreciate Simon's qualities. He's terribly dependable—if Simon says he'll do something for you, you can count on it. And he will be the first one to agree to a wise plan. But he's also the first one to tell you where you're wrong. He's hardheaded and strong willed and so very logical it makes me see double sometimes. It takes a special person to understand him. I'm glad he found you."

But he hadn't found her. Likely, he would never have noticed her if she hadn't pushed herself forward. He hadn't wanted to marry her. He just couldn't think of another way to claim those acres his family needed.

They broke out of the woods into a clearing. A wide log cabin hunkered next to a barn, with empty fields all around. An older man in a thick coat and rough trousers was chopping logs by the barn. He set down his ax as they approached.

"Mr. Paul," Thomas said with a respectful nod. "We were wondering if we could borrow your cow."

When the farmer frowned, his bushy brows heavy over a bulging nose, Beth jumped in. "It would only be for a few days, and we'd take excellent care of her. We're putting on a theatrical at the Lake Union School, you see."

Mr. Paul rubbed his hands together as if to warm them. "Don't see at all. Why'd you need a cow for a school?"

"The theatrical will be in our barn," Beth explained. "It's about the Nativity."

Nora was fairly sure the fellow had no idea what Beth meant.

"The students are putting on a play about the birth of our Lord Jesus," she told the man. "They've been working very hard. I'm sure you and your family would be welcome to watch the play Sunday next."

A smile hitched up, making him look far more approachable. "A real play? Out here? Why, that would be something to see." His smile faded. "But you don't want my cow. She's defective."

Nora frowned at the unkind term.

"Defective?" Beth asked.

"She wandered too far afield and got herself caught in a beaver trap," Mr. Paul explained. "I had to take off most of one leg to free her."

Beth cringed. So did Nora.

"Wasn't even sure she'd live," he continued. "But she's a tough old girl. She manages, but I can't leave her out anymore. Wolf or cougar might get her. And I can't afford to feed her grain all year." He waved toward the barn, where a cow had just ventured into view, walking with an odd hop every other stride. She was a pure white, with darker speckles up her legs as if she'd stepped in mud. Those big brown eyes gazed into Nora's, and the look went straight to her heart.

"She isn't defective," Nora declared. "She must have imagination to want to travel and explore."

Mr. Paul snorted. "Never knew a cow to have an imagination, but it makes no never mind. She'll be our Christmas roast."

Unthinkable! How could anyone even consider slaughtering so sweet a beast?

Nora squared her shoulders. "I think not," she told the farmer. "Mr. Paul, I want to buy your cow."

Every muscle in Simon's body protested as he hauled himself to the house after sunset. He couldn't keep working two jobs. He knew his brothers needed his help to finish bringing in the spars, and his family would need the extra money from the sale this winter to buy things they couldn't grow or make. But he had to keep clearing the new acreage. Any minute a winter storm could keep him in the house for days, and where would they be come spring? He was just glad Levi had helped him again today.

But as he approached the cabin, no light gleamed through the windows. Had Nora sewn curtains now? He was truly going to have to think of meaningful things for her to do other than change his world. He had thought giving her time to sew would be preferable to more chores, but she seemed to want to keep busy. He could only admire her for that, if he did wonder at the results sometimes.

He opened the door to darkness and silence.

He blinked. Why wasn't there a fire in the hearth, a lamp on the table? John had assured him he'd delivered Nora safely to the clearing. Had she come home and decided to go to bed early?

"Nora?" he called.

The quiet mocked him.

He shut the door and strode toward the main cabin. Even he could not believe she would be overcome walking from the barn to his cabin. He'd never taken her for the vengeful type, so she could not be punishing him for his reaction in the woods. Nor was she particularly forgetful. So why had she left the cabin?

Unless she had left him.

The thought sped his footsteps, and he burst through the front door of his mother's house. Levi looked up from setting the table, and Ma frowned from her rocking chair by the hearth.

"Where's Nora?" he demanded.

Ma set aside her sewing. "At your cabin, working on the costumes for the school theatrical with Beth."

"No. My cabin's dark." His heart was thundering in his ears again, worse than when the tree had fallen this morning. What was wrong with him? There had to be a logical reason for Nora's absence.

His mother evidently thought so, for she rose. "Then they must have gone to James and Rina's."

Of course. Simon willed his heartbeat to slow, his breath to come more evenly. Still, his mother regarded him with a frown as if she saw his agitation.

"I'll call them in," Levi offered, laying down the last piece of cutlery and heading for the back door. Simon waited for the double shot that announced dinner was ready.

It didn't come.

Levi slipped back into the room. "Pa's rifle is gone."

Their mother paled. "Why would Beth and Nora need a gun?"

Simon felt as if something squirmed inside him, pushing him toward the door. "I don't know, but I intend to find out."

"I'll come with you," Levi said, following him out the door.

On the porch, Simon shouted Nora's name while Levi called for Beth. No answer drifted on the cold night air. But it wasn't winter's breath that chilled Simon. It was the thought of Nora out in the darkness.

"Beth's smarter than this," Levi said, shaking his head. "She knows not to go out at night."

"Get Drew and James," Simon told him. "Tell them to bring their guns. I'll get John and the lanterns."

Levi dashed off toward their brothers' claims.

A short while later, they all regrouped on the porch. Rina had checked the school, Catherine the barn, and both reported no sign of Beth and Nora.

"The last I saw them," Rina said, clutching her shawl closer, "they were on their way to inspect the barn with Thomas."

The schoolteacher insisted on calling Scout by his given name as a sign of respect, but Scout Rankin was still all but a child as far as Simon was concerned. Though his sister was a fair shot, the thought of Beth being the only person to protect Nora and Scout only ratcheted his worries higher.

"Beth had some foolish notion about using the barn for the theatrical," Levi told his brothers. "She was talking about it all day in school."

"Actually, it was Nora's idea," Rina said. "I was not convinced. I understand Nora spoke to you all about it."

The reminder of their earlier meeting only fueled the fire inside Simon. "We agreed to the plan. But that doesn't matter. Something's wrong. We have to find them."

"Agreed," Drew said.

John lay a hand on Simon's arm. "Remember, Beth knows what she's doing."

But Nora didn't. They might meet a bear or a cougar. She could trip again, wander into a trap. The iron teeth were designed to hold a beaver tight, but they could easily crush human bone. Then again, the cold air made the trees brittle. She could be hit by a falling branch, like Pa.

Simon shook off his brother's grip and jumped off

the porch. "You all can stand around debating. I'm finding Nora."

"Wait!" Drew ordered. When Simon turned back, Drew handed him a lantern. "You'll need this." He didn't allow Simon to comment but turned to his other brothers. "James, with me. We'll go north along the shore. Levi, go south with Simon along the road. John, make a circuit around the Landing in case we missed them. Fire two shots if you find them. If not, report back here when the moon is risen."

For once, Simon didn't argue.

Chapter Ten

"Just. A little. Farther." Nora tugged on the halter Mr. Paul had been persuaded to include with the cow. Beth had convinced the farmer to sell the beast to Nora for a small price, which Nora would supply from her sewing money. The two of them had been walking with the beast since Scout had had to return to his father's homestead to do his chores.

Britta, as the cow was named, stopped once more on the rutted road, a sigh working its way up her heavy body. Nora knew just how she felt. What had taken them a half hour to walk to begin with had taken nearly two to return.

Now she stroked the cow's rough hide, which showed pearly in the dim light of a cloud-shrouded moon. "It's all right, Britta. We'll just rest a moment with you."

Ahead of them, Beth turned from side to side, watching for trouble. They had not seen other animals or people on their journey, but Nora had become aware of cries in the distance, the sudden movement of the bushes on either side of the road. Now the night had closed in, and mist was beginning to roll in from the lake, bringing with it a chill that went straight to Nora's bones. She hugged her cloak closer.

"How much farther, do you think?" she murmured to Beth.

Simon's sister peered ahead. "Not far. Everything looks so different in the dark, but I thought I saw a light, so we must be close. Wait—there it is again."

Nora looked in that direction as well. A golden glow bobbed through the trees.

"Someone's coming," she said.

In answer, Beth grabbed the cow's halter and tugged her to the side of the road. Before Nora could ask the reason, the girl raised the rifle and cocked it.

Nora stared at her, and then at the light. Who did the girl imagine was coming down the forest road with a lantern? Outlaws? Hostile natives? Obviously, Beth thought that the trouble she'd been looking for had found them. All Nora could do was press against Britta's warm side and put a hand around the cow's mouth to keep her quiet.

Now she could hear snaps, like footsteps on twigs, and the murmur of voices, men's voices by the timbre of them. Whoever was coming didn't care who knew it.

Lord, please protect Beth and Britta!

A moment more, and the light illuminated brown hair and a familiar angular profile.

"It's all right!" Nora cried, raising her head. "It's Simon."

Beth lowered the rifle as Simon and Levi appeared out of the darkness.

"Nora!" Lantern in one hand, Simon strode up to her. His gaze swept up and down her as if he expected to find some part missing. As Nora released her hold on Britta, the cow let out a bawl of protest.

Simon jerked back. "What is that?"

"Looks like a cow," Levi offered, his head cocked to eye Nora's acquisition.

"Nora bought it for the school theatrical," Beth explained.

Simon seemed to be having trouble following the conversation. "She bought it for the theatrical?"

That did sound rather foolish. "I actually haven't bought her yet," Nora told him. "I promised to return with the money tomorrow. And I didn't buy her for the theatrical precisely. I bought her because her owner was going to butcher her, and for no good reason."

Beth nodded, her blond hair shining in the lantern light.

Simon lowered the lamp, but not before Nora saw Levi grin.

"I say it's a great idea," Simon's youngest brother proclaimed. "Ma's always complaining the goats don't give enough milk for all her baking. Now we'll have enough to spare."

Simon stood taller, gathering his composure like a cloak about him. "Very well," he said, though his voice sounded more strained than Nora could like. "Levi, fire the gun to let everyone know we've found them."

Nora had flinched the first time she'd heard the call. How would Britta react?

"Maybe that's not a good idea," she started, but Levi was already lifting the rifle. As the first shot rang out, Britta yanked the halter out of Beth's grip and stumbled to one side. Nora hurried to hug the cow as the second shot echoed.

Simon was undeterred. "Let's get everyone home. Ma

and the others will be worried." He turned and started back the way he and Levi had come.

Nora retrieved the halter and gave it a tug. In the fading light of the lantern, Britta's big brown eyes looked up imploringly, but she didn't so much as move a hoof. Beth added her strength to the halter, and Britta dug her back hooves into the mud.

Simon must have realized they weren't following, for he stopped and glanced back at them, a tall, dark figure surrounded by light. "Well?"

"She's resting," Nora told him.

"Resting." His chin moved as if he was fighting for words.

"Yes, you see she only has three legs," Nora said. "She can't move very fast or for very long without tiring."

Levi started laughing, but Simon strode back to Nora's side, his eyes like chips of ice.

"Let me understand this," he gritted out. "You brought my sister out in the woods at night to buy a cow that can't walk."

He made her sound demented. "No," Nora said. "We started out in good daylight. We never intended to stay out this late, or to buy a cow. But we did buy a cow, and Britta can only go so fast."

"It's all right, Simon," Beth put in. "It was my idea to go look at the cow. And I have Pa's rifle." She lifted the gun as if to prove it.

"I can only be thankful you didn't have to use it," Simon said, voice as hard as his eyes. He handed the lantern to Nora. "Take this. We'll keep the light in the middle so we can all make use of it. Levi, drop back and watch for any sign of cougar. This cow is an invitation to dinner."

Nora shuddered at the thought, but Simon was turning to his sister. "Beth, go first, but keep a sharp eye out. I'll be right behind you, as soon as I get this cow moving."

Beth and Levi hurried to do as he asked.

"I'm sorry, Simon," Nora said as he circled the cow, obviously looking for the best way to persuade her to move. "I didn't mean to be so late for dinner."

"Dinner, madam, is the least of my concerns." He put his shoulder behind the cow's flank and shoved. Britta hobbled forward two steps and stopped.

"I think she's tired," Nora offered.

"I think she's useless," Simon replied, straightening. "It would be a kindness if I just shot her now."

Nora darted between him and the cow. "Don't you dare!"

From behind them came an evil-sounding howl.

Nora gasped, reaching out to clutch Simon's arm with her free hand. Britta reacted even more strongly. She once more yanked the halter out of Nora's grip and, with her hitching gait, broke into a run down the road.

"Beth!" Simon shouted. "Watch out!" He dashed after the cow with Nora on his heels.

They found Beth against a fir, where she had evidently flattened herself to keep from being run over. "She went that way," she said, pointing down the road.

Levi came jogging up behind them. "Did it work?"

Simon stared at him. "You made that howl?"

Levi preened. "Scout and I mastered the wolf howl when Rina first arrived here. We gave her a bit of trouble before James figured it out. I thought if it could scare a schoolteacher, it could scare a cow."

It certainly had. They followed Britta's trail by hoof-prints in the mud. Nora was just thankful the cow had kept to the road. At least that way she was heading toward Wallin Landing.

They reached the clearing to find that Britta had stemmed her headlong flight just short of the schoolhouse and was taking her solace by munching on the winter grass there. As Beth went to return her father's rifle to its place on the back porch, Mrs. Wallin came out, first hugging and then scolding her daughter. Nora could see Catherine and Rina peering out the windows as well. It seemed Nora had worried them all.

Even Simon.

"What were you thinking?" he asked her.

Now that they were all safe, he sounded more perplexed than angry. She had to make him understand. All her life, her father and Charles had questioned her decisions, made her feel small, stupid. She truly did know what she was doing.

"Britta is a fine cow," she told Simon. "Her previous owner, Mr. Paul, said she gave four gallons of milk a day before her injury. I saw a chance to help her and your family at the same time, so I agreed to purchase her."

"She gave that much milk before her injury," Simon pointed out, looking at the grazing cow. "She may not give at all now. And if she does, she'll have to be bred to keep up production. Besides, she'll eat the food we gathered for the oxen and James's horses."

She'd wondered about that when Beth had first suggested more animals, but the thought had escaped her head when she'd heard Britta's life threatened.

"She seems to like grass," she suggested.

"What little is left for the winter." He waved a hand. "But none of that matters at the moment. Do you know how we all felt when we found you and Beth missing?

You persist in doing things that could leave you hurt or worse."

Nora swallowed. "I didn't mean to do anything dangerous. Is it truly so bad out here, so long as I stay away from your logging?"

He ran a hand back through his hair. "Yes! We had trouble from a cougar earlier this summer. Trees fall. Ground gives way from the rain. There are rough men in those woods. I can't protect you every minute, Nora. You have to think before acting. Maybe it didn't matter when you were living in town, but out here, every moment matters. I can't lose you too."

Too? Did he mean his father or was there someone else? She was about to ask when Britta raised her head and began ambling toward the barn as if recognizing it as home now. Simon followed.

Nora could only frown after them. Once again, it seemed she'd frightened Simon. She'd understood his concern about the logging. She'd seen the size of that tree as it had veered toward her. If she hadn't been working so hard to keep Britta moving, she might have seen more dangers in the forest as well. Either way, it seemed he truly was worried about her.

Did all that mean Simon was coming to care for her?

Simon opened the barn door, as much to keep anyone from noticing that his hands were shaking as to make room for the cumbersome cow. Once again, Nora seemed to have no idea of the trouble she might have caused herself. She followed them into the barn now to stand next to the quivering beast, stroking its pale hide and crooning comfort, while he took the lantern from her and hung it from the rafter.

What was he going to do with her? Through the years, he'd watched Drew go to impossible lengths to keep them all safe. Was this what he'd felt—this fear, this terror? Simon didn't know whether to hug Nora close or lock her in the cabin for safekeeping.

As if she guessed his inner turmoil, she lay a hand on his arm as he passed.

"I'm very sorry for the trouble, Simon. If you tell me what I should do for Britta, I'll take care of her."

He could think of several things to do with the cow, all of which involved deadly weapons. And Britta, Nora had called her. Who named their animals? Well, except for James and his horses. Simon agreed with Drew: creatures on a farm served a purpose—work or food or protection. He didn't name his saw or each head of corn in the field. Britta would be their first and likely only cow. Why not simply call her *the cow*?

But Levi was right—extra milk could come in handy, if they could figure out how to keep the cow mobile.

For now, he put both the goats into a single stall and nudged Britta into the empty one. The oxen chuffed a welcome, their dark eyes glittering in the light. The cow trotted onto the straw with a grateful sigh. He could see that her udder was hanging heavily beneath her. He couldn't help a sigh of his own.

"What's wrong?" Nora asked, her arms resting on the edge of the stall, her face puckered.

Simon squared his shoulders. "She needs to be milked. I don't suppose you've ever done that before."

Nora shook her head. "Never. But I can learn."

He had to admire that about her. Ma and even Beth occasionally shied away from some of the more difficult tasks around the farm. Milking wasn't so much difficult as time-consuming, and he didn't want to add to his mother's and sister's chores. He looked around and spotted the stool Beth used to milk the goats, along with the bucket, scrubbed clean from earlier use. Bringing them over, he set them next to Britta and motioned Nora to take a seat.

"We used to have a cow in Wisconsin before we came West," he told her, moving around behind her. "The first thing you need to do is help her udder relax. Watch me."

He knelt and reached around Nora to run his hand over the heavy udder, the heat of it warming his fingers. "See? You try."

"That's a good girl, Britta," Nora said, stroking the udder. "I'm very sorry if I was so hard on you trying to get you home, but see what a nice place Simon has made for you?"

He was not going to take pride in doing as simple a job as this. "Right. Now, wrap your thumb and forefinger about there."

"Like this?" Nora asked.

Britta let out a bawl and kicked over the bucket. Nora jerked back.

"It's all right," Simon said, more to Nora than the cow. He righted the bucket. "You have to be gentle. Try again."

More hesitantly this time, Nora reached out.

"That's right," Simon encouraged her. "Now squeeze. You don't have to pull down. Gravity will do the work for you."

She must have squeezed, for a thin stream of milk shot into the bucket.

"I did it!" Nora turned her head and beamed at Simon,

and for a moment, all he could do was lose himself in the soft gray of her eyes.

Then Britta shifted, and Simon jerked upright. Why was his pulse pounding now? Nora was safe.

"Good work," he said, stepping back. "Keep going for a while, then I'll spell you."

Nora bent over the bucket, the milk shooting down in spurts that echoed in the still barn. "I think I can do it. You go eat dinner."

He was not about to leave her alone. Not at the moment. "Your hands may get tired the first time," Simon temporized, leaning back against the wall.

She shot him a smile. "You forget. I'm a seamstress. I'm used to working with my hands."

There was that. She would likely be fine. He ought to go inside, explain what had happened, talk to John about the cow. Maybe his brother could come up with some kind of splint that allowed the beast to move more easily. He'd created crutches for Levi this summer when their youngest brother had broken his leg, after all.

But there was something about watching Nora, her hands moving more surely with each stroke, her gentle voice encouraging the cow. With the animals huddled around, it was warm in the barn, and the lantern light reflected off Nora's dark hair. Simon drew in a deep breath, feeling as if a knot in his shoulders had finally loosened.

"I need you to promise me something," he said.

She nodded as she worked. "Of course, Simon."

"If you leave the cabin, tell someone where you're going," he said. "Take one of us who can shoot with you if you're going into the woods, and never stay out after dark."

That shot of milk sounded more forceful than the last. "Yes, of course, Simon. Only…"

"Only?" he challenged.

She glanced up at him, and he was surprised to see frustration looking back at him. "Only, I'm not a child, and I'm not mentally deficient."

Simon stiffened. "Of course you're not mentally deficient or a child, Nora. Forgive me if I ever gave you the impression that I consider you such."

In the lantern's light, he could see the red darkening her cheeks before she turned back to her milking. "Well, it wasn't you, precisely. My brother and father always seemed to think I wasn't very bright."

Something burned inside him. "They were mistaken. Inexperience and lack of intelligence are two different things. I'm the one who should apologize. I have to remember you aren't used to life out here. I'll do better about explaining the dangers."

"And I'll do better about thinking ahead." She stopped and eyed the bucket, then glanced up at him. "See? Milk!"

He chuckled at the foamy white in the bucket. "Milk. Congratulations. Let me finish the milking this time. But you'll need to get up with me in the morning and come out here and do this again."

Nora scrambled off the stool, her eyes widening. "That early?"

"About every twelve hours," Simon told her, straddling the stool. He bent to finish the job.

Nora hummed to herself, moving about the stall, and after a moment he realized she was tidying the straw. He hid a smile. She simply could not sit idle.

But the cow required more than milking. Already the

beast was eating part of the grain he'd reserved for the goats this winter. The pastures were close to being over-grazed by the other animals as it was. Yet Nora, Beth and Levi seemed entranced by the idea of having a cow.

Why was he the only one who saw the potential problems? Why did it always fall to him to point out the obvious?

Perhaps this time he should just let everyone find out for themselves. Perhaps he was wrong and the cow—Britta—would work out fine.

More concerning was Nora. He hadn't expected to feel this fierce protectiveness toward her. Was it only because he'd been the one to let her live out here? Her brother had warned him that she would be out of her element.

At the moment, he was the one who felt out of his element. And he didn't know what to do about it.

Chapter Eleven

Nora got up so early the next morning, she was certain she heard the sun snoring somewhere beyond the mountains. Simon lit a lantern so she could find her way about the cabin and out to the barn. He even stayed a few minutes, watching her milk. When he laid a hand on her shoulder and told her she was doing a fine job, something inside her swelled. The smile they shared before he left made the walk back to the cabin in the chilly air seem as warm and comfortable as the barn.

She had expected to find him gone, heading out to work on the new property, but when she entered the cabin, he was standing in front of the mirror, knotting his tie. Once more he wore the brown suit from their wedding, and his reflection revealed a white shirt and striped waistcoat. Nora paused on the threshold, just gazing at him a moment.

When he turned to face her, she hurried inside and closed the door. Goodness, but what would he think if he'd known she'd been admiring the breadth of his shoulders, the length of his legs, the way the lantern light gilded his hair? He'd think her positively moony!

Instead, she offered him a bright smile. "Are we going somewhere today?"

He shook his head. "No. It's Sunday. Pa always insisted that we wear our best clothes and spend the day in more quiet pursuits. We'll have to feed the stock and cook, of course. But we will all worship at the house shortly."

"Oh, I…" She glanced up at the loft. "I'd love to wear my best dress, but I can't climb the ladder in it."

"I'll help you," he said, and he didn't even sound annoyed. In fact, if she hadn't known better, she would have thought he sounded positively eager.

She scurried up the ladder, pleased with how easy the task had become, and went to her trunk, which John had hauled up for her earlier in the week. "Do you need anything from up here?" she called down to Simon.

"I'm fine, thanks," he replied.

She pulled out the lavender dress she'd worn to Maddie's wedding and laid it on the pallet, smoothing out the creases. "Your trunk is much nicer than mine," she told him as she worked the buttons on her day dress. "Where did you get it?"

"Pa made it." His voice sounded subdued. "He carved one for each of his older sons around our twelfth birthdays. After he was gone, Drew carved one for John, Levi and Beth."

She went over, traced the horns on the proud stag. How nice to have a father so dedicated to his children, so willing to work on their behalf. Her father had worked hard to build his accounting practice, employing more than a dozen men at one time. Many had been drafted into the war effort, leaving only a few for Charles to lead. But she couldn't remember her father ever going out of his way to do something for her.

"He sounds like a fine man," she said, pulling off the day dress.

"He was." Simon's voice floated up through the floorboards.

"How did he die?"

He was quiet a moment, and she wanted to call back the question. She shouldn't push him to share his past, his thoughts.

"He took Drew, James and me out logging with him," he said, his voice no more than a murmur she had to strain to hear. "None of us saw the widow-maker before the branch fell and killed him."

Reaching for the lavender dress, her fingers clenched in the fabric. That must have been what he'd referred to last night when he'd mentioned losing someone else. Small wonder the falling tree had made him react so strongly. "Oh, Simon," she murmured. "I'm so sorry."

"We all were," he said. "Pa asked Drew to lead the family, a task he's taken seriously over the years. All my brother could think about was making sure we all survived to adulthood. We had to give him every possible incentive before he'd even consider courting Catherine."

At least he was beginning to sound like his usual self again. She should encourage that. "What did you do?" Nora asked, slipping the heavy dress over her head.

She could hear the smile in his voice. "I tricked him into reading *The Courtship of Miles Standish* to her, with him taking John Alden's part."

Nora smiled as well as she settled the gown about her. She'd read her father's copy of the famous poem and knew the story of the lovers. Miles Standish had asked his good friend John Alden to plead his case to the fair Priscilla Mullins, only it turned out that Priscilla preferred John.

"The best part," Simon continued, "was when Catherine read her lines. She actually said, *Speak for yourself, Drew.* I think that slip ultimately convinced him to try."

Could it be that easy? If she said, *Speak for yourself, Simon*, would he declare his love for her? Would he take her in his arms, give her a true kiss, one that made her knees weak?

It was a lovely thought, one in which she could happily lose herself, but she knew it for the fable it was.

"Ready yet?" Simon called up.

"One more moment," Nora promised, finishing the buttons in a rush. Then she hurried to the opening in the loft and peered down. Simon was waiting at the bottom of the ladder, his head tilted back to meet her gaze. She knew he'd never let her fall, but something made her hesitate.

Simon pulled himself up the first two rungs and braced his feet. "All right. Come on down."

Swallowing, Nora turned and did as he bid. She felt his body come up behind her and pace her down the ladder, his arms bracketing her safely, offering strength on which she could lean. It was the most singular sensation, and one that left her breathless.

"I need to fix my hair," she said, dashing to the mirror. With her back turned to him, she closed her eyes and drew in a deep breath. When she opened her eyes, she found him watching her, and her cheeks heated.

She dropped her gaze, seized her hairbrush and yanked it through her thick tresses. How nice it would have been to have silky hair like Rina or golden curls like Beth. Sometimes she thought hers was as unruly as straw. She could see a frown gathering on his handsome face, as if he agreed.

"Here," he said, coming up behind her. "Let me."

Stunned, Nora let the hairbrush fall from her fingers into his outstretched hand. He ran the bristles gently over her hair, his hand skimming the dark strands.

"It's terribly coarse," she couldn't help saying in apology. "I can't do a thing with it."

"It's thick and clean and healthy," he countered. "And it likely keeps you warmer than most."

As compliments went, it wasn't at all flowery. But it was honest and true. Perhaps that was why it made her smile. She accepted the brush back from him and finished binding up her hair behind her head. A moment later, and he was slipping her cloak around her shoulders, his fingers brushing the skin at the nape of her neck. She shivered.

He frowned, stepping back. "Is that dress warm enough?"

She was warm enough. In fact, she thought she might ignite like tinder from a spark if he looked at her one more moment. "Fine," she said cheerfully. "Shall we go?"

He pulled his violin case from its place below the sideboard and led her out the door.

At least at his mother's house the presence of others took her mind off her distracting husband. As Simon unpacked the instrument, Nora greeted the rest of the family who were up. She couldn't help admiring the tiny stitches that attached the white collar to the long-sleeved green wool gown his mother wore. Beth, in her blue wool, was setting the table, and Nora could smell bacon frying in the kitchen.

All the Wallins gathered around the table a short while later, digging into the bacon and pancakes Mrs. Wallin served up.

"And dried berries with whipped cream as well," she said with a smile to Nora. "Now that we have extra milk."

"Come spring," Beth confided, leaning across the table, "I think we'll have enough we can sell it in Seattle." She looked to Simon and nodded as if to say she had foreseen as much.

"If the cow lasts that long," Simon said.

James slipped his arm around his wife. "Dreaming of steak and roast, are you, Simon? Can't say I blame you. I could use a new pair of boots."

"Britta is not about to be made into leather," Nora informed him, though she could see that he was teasing by the gleam in his deep blue eyes.

"Now behave," Beth added, "or you won't get a taste of that whipped cream."

Rina smiled at her. "I can see your sister has taken your measure, James."

James put a hand over his heart. "The quickest way to my heart is down my throat, alas." He lifted his coffee cup. "Here's to Britta. Long may she reign."

Nora inclined her head. Though Simon still looked skeptical, she was certain Britta would prove her worth, even to him, before the winter was out.

After the breakfast things had been cleared away, they all gathered near the hearth. Drew and James moved the benches and chairs away from the table to make room for everyone to sit. Nora settled on one end of a bench next to Simon. All Simon's brothers wore brown suits too, and the outfits looked as if they had seen better days. Perhaps she could do something about that. She could see John in silver gray, Levi in a bold blue, Drew in black and James in something flamboyant, perhaps burgundy. As for Simon, she would try a dark green that would bring out the depth of his eyes.

Oh! There she went dreaming again!

Drew had already stepped up to the hearth, accepting a worn, black-leather-covered Bible from John's hands. Funny. She'd grown up worshipping in a fine chapel in Lowell, but she had always felt that her parents and brother went as much to be seen as to actually praise their Creator. Aboard the *Continental*, Mr. Mercer had officiated at worship services, and she knew Catherine and her friend Allegra had felt that his lack of training as a minister and his questionable ethics had made him an unlikely candidate to instruct them on spiritual matters.

Drew Wallin certainly had never attended divinity school, yet he held the Bible with a clear reverence on his rugged face. Opening the book, he glanced up at his family. "Today, we are reading in the Book of Luke." He cleared his throat, then his deep voice intoned the words.

"'And it came to pass, that, when Elisabeth heard the salutation of Mary, the babe leaped in her womb; and Elisabeth was filled with the Holy Ghost: And she spake out with a loud voice, and said, Blessed art thou among women, and blessed is the fruit of thy womb. And whence is this to me, that the mother of my Lord should come to me? For, lo, as soon as the voice of thy salutation sounded in mine ears, the babe leaped in my womb for joy. And blessed is she that believed: for there shall be a performance of those things which were told her from the Lord.'"

Blessed is she that believed. How wonderful to know what the Lord had planned for her and simply accept it. As John rose to read from Psalms, Nora couldn't help glancing at Simon. His attention was all on his brother, his head tilted a little toward her, his eyes narrowed as if he was contemplating the praise the psalmist had written so long ago. Was this what the Lord had planned for her—to work beside him, tend his house, help his family?

Or was there more?

She dropped her gaze to her hands, folded in the lap of her dress. *Lord, is it possible Simon could come to care for me? You've always provided shelter and food and pretty fabric for clothes, ways I can contribute, Your Words to cheer. I thought Your love was sufficient for me, but I'm starting to dream, I'm starting to hope. I'm afraid I'll only be disappointed. Maybe You could just show me Your will, and I'll be blessed to believe?*

So intent had she been on her prayer, that she didn't realize John had finished reading until the first notes sounded from the violin. Around her, Drew's bass voice joined with his brothers' tenors and the ladies' altos and sopranos to blend in heartfelt song. She couldn't take her eyes off Simon, his arms cradling the instrument so tenderly. The strong lines of his face had softened as his fingers worked the bow, the strings. It was as if his own heart sang through the music.

She drew in a breath and managed to join them for the second verse, but the words stopped in her throat.

"Alleluia! not as orphans are we left in sorrow now;

"Alleluia! He is near us, faith believes, nor questions how."

Was that her answer? Could she simply believe and not question where this convenient Christmas wedding would lead her?

Simon stood while Drew gave the concluding prayer, then bent to carefully replace the violin into its case. As always, playing it touched something inside him. That he was capable of making such music never failed to humble him. It was a gift, and one he gladly shared. Yet sharing it always left him a little shaky afterward, as if he'd lost something of himself in the melody.

Perhaps that was why, as his family dispersed for various pursuits, he asked Nora to join him outside. The day was bright for a change, the pale winter sun anointing the tops of the firs surrounding the clearing. Gulls swept low, their calls echoing as they headed for the lake beyond. His breath puffed silver as he took her hand and helped her off the porch.

She seemed content to walk beside him, her gaze on the ground and her hands in her skirts. Once more he was struck by the contrast of her—small yet sturdy; quiet yet capable of making her feelings known, at least to him. He wasn't sure why he'd taken the brush from her this morning. Perhaps it had been the frustration on her face. Perhaps he'd merely wondered what that thick thatch of black hair would feel like. There had been a spring to it, as if it, like Nora, held its energy deep and only showed it on rare occasions. Touching her hair had been nearly as humbling as playing his violin.

"Britta seems to be getting on well," she said, nodding to the pasture next to the barn. John had managed to fashion a sling of sorts with a padded stick on the end. Hung over Britta's shoulder, it allowed her something to rest against when she stopped. But Simon had noticed she found it hard to lower her head into the feed trough. One more task for him to deal with, when he was done clearing the land.

The thought of the new acreage raised his gaze to the hillside behind the schoolhouse. Already fewer trees lined the horizon. So much done, so much more to do, and in such a short time.

"Come with me," he said to Nora. "I want to show you something."

He led her up the hill, careful to keep to the path he and his brothers had been using so as to prevent her skirts from snagging on the vines that crowded close.

"Those are blackberries," he informed her as they climbed. "Beth and Ma pick them for preserves."

"I saw thimbleberries too," she said.

"And we have a few apple trees behind the house, in Ma's kitchen garden. But the real produce will come from up here. Look."

They had come out on the level, and Nora sucked in a breath.

Simon smiled. Stretching out his hand, he pointed to the remaining trees. "This is the property you won for us, Nora. You can see how far we've come. There's at least three times as far yet to go to clear it all. We'll put in corn here, once the frost is gone, along with kale, potatoes and carrots."

"Perhaps Windsor beans," she suggested. "Our neighbor used to raise them. You can plant them early in the spring, and they're very good dried."

Simon nodded, pleased she understood so readily.

"Excellent choice. The Kelloggs should be able to get us the seed." He nodded toward a slight rise at the rear of the property. "I was thinking about building a house there."

She turned and set her back to it. He wondered what she was doing as she stood on her tiptoes on the muddy trampled ground and tilted her head first one way and then the other. Suddenly a smile split her face. "Yes! Once everything is cleared, you should be able to see the mountain and the lake from here." She dropped back down onto her feet with a brisk nod of obvious satisfaction.

"That's the idea," Simon admitted. "Pa always said a man should have something more to look at than his work, and something more to listen to than the sound of his ax."

She dimpled. "That's where you learned to play the violin, then, from your father."

Simon dug his boot into the good, dark earth they had uncovered. "He was the master. He could make you feel the music. I know that must sound odd, but I can't explain it any other way. I've seen people laugh and cry when he played."

"You have the same effect," Nora assured him.

She couldn't know the compliment she'd just given him. He shook his head. "I'm competent. He was a virtuoso."

She laid a hand on his arm. "So are you. I love hearing you play."

Something strong and fine rose up inside him. Why was it her praise meant more than any other's? This time he let it seep in, like water into the soil. "I thought maybe you'd want some input into the design of the house."

"No ladders," she said and added a shiver for good measure.

Simon smiled. "No ladders. If we need a second story, I'll put in good, solid stairs, like at Ma's. Anything else?"

She rubbed her hands over each other. "Well, I…" She squared her shoulders and met his gaze. "I would love to have my own sewing room."

"Done," Simon said. "We can put it on the south side so you always have good light."

"Oh, Simon," she said, her gray eyes shining, "that would be wonderful. And maybe shelves to store the fabric and notions?"

He nodded, envisioning it. "John could probably come up with some sort of system to store spools of thread by color. And we'll make room for a sewing machine. We won't be able to afford one right away, but I'd like to start putting money aside as soon as we can."

She threw out her arms and hugged him tight. "Oh, Simon! No one has ever been so nice to me!"

Stunned, Simon could only wrap his arms around her and absorb the warmth. He hadn't made the suggestion with the idea of being nice. He was thinking more practically, trying to meet her needs, allow her to ply her trade most efficiently.

But until that moment, he hadn't realized that one of his needs was seeing her smile. Could it be he was beginning to have feelings for the woman who had offered him a Christmas wedding?

Chapter Twelve

What a lovely Sunday. Nora couldn't help her sigh of pleasure as she lay back on the bed that night to sleep. Simon's entire family had been so nice to her, asking her preferences for dinner, inviting her to join them in playing chess and parlor games. She and Beth had talked and sketched out the costumes for the theatrical. She'd never felt so welcome.

And Simon. Tears gathered in her eyes as she remembered his promise to build her a sewing room. With a sewing machine! She could just imagine the gowns and linens she could create with that time-saving device. He'd even walked with her down to the Pauls' claim to pay for Britta, and he'd only grimaced a little when the farmer had asked her again why she would want such a beast. Perhaps everything would be well.

Simon's mother had offered to let Nora root through the pieces of bric-a-brac and trimmings left over from previous Wallin sewing projects to use for the costumes. So Nora ventured over to the main house the next day after milking Britta and eating breakfast. She had just unearthed a very respectable bit of blue braid when she heard the rattle of a wagon outside.

Catherine, who had joined them that morning, was sitting closest to the window, stitching at a nightgown for the baby. The nurse had explained that normally she would be out seeing to those ill in the area, but between the cold weather and her pregnancy, she was staying closer to home these days. At the sound outside, she glanced up with a frown.

"Strangers, Mother Wallin," she called, setting aside her work to rise.

Mrs. Wallin, who had been working on refilling the oil in the lamps, straightened from the table. "No one was expected."

Now Nora heard voices, querulous, complaining. Her stomach sank to her shoes as she recognized the sound.

Catherine opened the door to the knock.

"I demand to know what you've done with my sister," Charles said. "And I warn you—I will not be put off this time. The last two farms we passed assured us the next stop would be Wallin Landing."

"This is Wallin Landing, sir," Catherine replied, cool and calm. Nora imagined that she had dealt with far more confrontational people than Charles when she was nursing. "Why do you expect your sister to be here?"

"No need for concern, Catherine," Nora said, going to her side. "They're here for me."

Mrs. Wallin came around the table.

"There you are!" Meredith exclaimed, seizing Nora's arm and drawing her closer as if the Wallins had kidnapped her. "We have been looking everywhere!"

"It's only been five days," Nora reminded her, managing to free herself from her sister-in-law's clutches.

"High time we determined whether that ruffian is treating you as well as he should," Charles insisted, his hands on the lapels of his camel-colored wool coat. He glanced about. "Where is the fellow, by the way?"

"My son the ruffian," Mrs. Wallin said, her voice tight, "is working, as a good man should."

Charles colored at the implication.

Nora wasn't about to confirm that Simon was unavailable. "He and his brothers are logging not far from here. He could come through the door any moment."

Charles glanced behind him as if fearing to see Simon looming there, then returned his gaze to Nora's, straightening his tie with nervous fingers. "Yes, well, we came to speak to you in any event."

Meredith shivered in her fashionable brown coat with its fur collar, the velvet skirts peeping out beneath the hem swinging in her agitation. "Yes, and it is rather thoughtless of you to leave us standing out here in the chill when we came all this way to see you."

Guilt whispered. Survival shouted it down. "Well, you see, this isn't my house. I was just visiting."

Meredith's face fell. "You mean we have to go farther into this wretched wilderness?"

"Not very far," Nora said. She turned to Catherine and Mrs. Wallin, who were watching her with frowns. "This is my brother, Charles Underhill, and sister-in-law, Meredith. Charles and Meredith, this is Catherine Wallin. She's a nurse, and she's married to Simon's oldest brother, Drew. And this is Simon's mother, Mrs. Wallin."

"Welcome to Wallin Landing," Mrs. Wallin said, while Catherine inclined her head in greeting.

"Pleasure." The way Meredith said the word made it seem anything but.

Nora wanted to cringe. "I'll just take them over to Simon's cabin so they won't bother you."

"It's no trouble, Nora," Mrs. Wallin assured her, her gaze fixed on their unexpected visitors.

"They are," Nora replied. She gave Simon's mother a hug. "I won't inflict them on you."

"Well! I like that!" Meredith exclaimed.

"I'll be happy to accompany you," Catherine said, steel in her blue eyes.

"I can't impose," Nora told her, releasing Mrs. Wallin and turning for the door. "Besides, I'm used to them." She felt Catherine and Mrs. Wallin watching her out the door.

"Honestly, Nora, I don't know how you abide such rude people," Meredith scolded as Nora led them away from the house.

"I have a lot of practice," Nora murmured.

The comment went entirely over Meredith's head. "I imagine you have over the past five days. We told you not to go with that man."

"Say the word, and we can leave right now," Charles agreed.

Nora glanced at their conveyance. They must have rented it from the livery stable in Seattle. It was more of a cart, with a bench that would hold no more than two and a small box behind. Where exactly did they intend to put her, had she agreed to their silly scheme? As it was, she could only pity the horse that had pulled it, for the creature was already sagging in the traces, breath puffing white in the air.

"I think you're supposed to let it out to rest," Nora said with a nod toward the horse.

Meredith looked aghast at the idea. "And have it escape and be eaten by bears?"

Nora was fairly sure bears didn't eat horses. At least, Simon hadn't mentioned them as a danger to Britta, and he had seemed rather thorough in itemizing the threats. She could see the cow now, moving slowly about the pasture with James's horses. Should she let the new horse in with them, or would they all quarrel?

She was spared the decision by the opening of the schoolhouse door. Levi raced across the clearing to her side.

"I saw you from the window," he said. "Rina said it would be fine for me to help."

Nora smiled at him. "Thank you, Brother Levi. Do you know what to do with this horse?"

"I'll take care of her," he promised, then he narrowed his eyes at Charles and Meredith. "I'm more concerned about you, Nora. Simon told me and John about your family when we agreed to stand up as your witnesses."

She didn't want to know what Simon had said, if it could put such a scowl on Levi's face.

Charles drew himself up and looked down his nose at the youth. "Where I come from, young men know their place and respect their elders."

"Welcome to Wallin Landing," Levi replied. "Here we pretty much get our own say. And I say you better be nice to Nora."

"How dare you," Charles said, but Levi was turning to Nora.

"If they give you any trouble, come get me. And if they won't listen to me, I'll go and bring Simon and the others right home. They won't put up with any nonsense."

Nora's heart swelled. "Thank you, Levi."

With one last look to Charles and Meredith, he went to see to their horse.

"Barbarian," Meredith said with a sniff that wrinkled her dainty nose.

"To be expected, I fear, living this far from civilization." Charles shot his cuffs with great self-importance.

Feeling embarrassed to be related to them, Nora directed them toward the path to Simon's cabin. But as they neared the trees, Meredith balked.

"Where are you taking us?" she demanded. "I can see two houses in that clearing, rustic though they may be. Why must we venture into the woods?"

"The largest house, where you found me, was the original one for the Wallin family," Nora explained. "Mother Wallin, Simon's brothers John and Levi, and their sister, Beth, live there still. The smaller house on the edge of the clearing belongs to Simon's brother Drew and his wife, Catherine, whom you just met. His brother James and James's wife, Rina, live a ways beyond the barn. Simon and I have a cabin to the north."

Charles glanced back at the clearing. "Exactly how many people live out here?"

"Enough so I'm never alone," Nora said.

Charles turned to face her, his smile strained. "How comforting."

They lapsed into silence as she led them through the woods. She tried to see things from their point of view, but failed. She'd never been able to think the way Charles did. Like Simon, her brother and sister-in-law saw only darkness and danger out among the trees. When she gazed into the forest, she saw life brimming with purpose, promise. That point of view might put her at risk, she supposed, but she would not trade it for the dark.

They were not impressed with Simon's cabin either. "It's so small and mean," Meredith said, gazing up at the pitched roof.

Charles ran a hand over the peeled logs. "Barely more than stumps."

Nora couldn't agree with that statement either. When she looked at the cabin, she saw Simon's handiwork and foresight everywhere, from the carefully cut square corners that fit together perfectly for stability to the solid chinking that kept out the cold. But Charles and Meredith always found fault, so instead of defending Simon, Nora opened the door and ushered them inside. If she was going to have to listen to their complaints, at least she could be warm while doing so.

She went to poke up the fire, which she had left banked. Meredith came to stand beside her, rubbing her hands together before the spreading warmth as she glanced around.

"How can you abide this?" she murmured. "No pump inside the house. The two of you squeezed into so little space. It's positively primitive."

Charles shook his head from where he stood by the table. "You were meant for more than this, Nora."

Was she? Funny. She'd never felt particularly cramped in the cabin, even when Simon filled it with his presence. He was conscientious about keeping the water bucket filled, so she hadn't missed having a pump inside. And with the thick log walls and heavy cedar shake roof, the house was actually cozier than the boardinghouse in cold weather.

As Nora straightened from the hearth, Meredith took both her hands, gazing deep into her eyes, her own blue eyes sorrowful.

"We've missed you, Nora," she murmured. "Without your help, I'm simply a wreck. Please come back with us. Your family needs you."

Nora stared at her, then glanced at Charles, who inclined his head. "She's right. We are never as good alone as we are with you. We realized that the moment you left Lowell."

Meredith nodded eagerly. "I should never have encouraged you to leave, Nora. I understand that now. I merely wanted to give you an opportunity to see the world." She glanced about again. "Such as it is."

That couldn't be right. As much as they complained about her efforts, she'd thought they'd be delighted to be left without her.

"You just need to give Seattle a try," she told them. "I'm sure you'll make friends."

"Well, certainly we'll make friends," Meredith said, raising her chin as she dropped Nora's hands. "I've already had Mrs. Horton and two Denny ladies over to dinner. Their husbands are very important in the area, you know."

Nora knew Hannah Horton and Mary Ann and Louisa Denny, all of whom had been clients at one time or another since she'd arrived in Seattle, but she decided not to mention that to Meredith. Likely, her sister-in-law would see sewing for the women as far inferior to receiving them at dinner.

"There, you see?" Nora said. "You don't need me."

Meredith and Charles exchanged glances.

"Oh, but we do," Meredith assured her. "You are family, Nora. We need you there beside us."

She simply could not make herself believe what was happening. "Family without a room to sleep in," Nora reminded her. "Your house may be significantly bigger than Simon's, but you still have only one bedroom."

"We've already begun remodeling the house, making sure there's a room just for you," Charles told her.

"And you won't have to cook or clean," Meredith promised. "We'll hire someone in."

Nora stared at them. How could they be so nice to her? She'd moved out once before, coming all the way to Seattle, and only when their finances were threatened had they thought to follow. They couldn't be missing her after less than a week.

"You can have whatever you want," Charles said as if he saw her resolve wavering. "Just say you'll come back with us to Seattle, Nora. You should be where you can be appreciated."

"Which is why," Simon said, pushing through the door, "she's staying right here."

Nora's brother bristled, and her sister-in-law blanched, but Simon didn't care. He and his brothers had finished the spar work early, and he'd come home to pick up a shovel before heading out to clear the new land. John and James had offered their help, and he had hopes they could make real progress this afternoon. But then he'd seen the cart in the clearing and feared what it might mean. He'd hastened to the house only to hear Charles's ridiculous claim as Simon had opened the door.

"You have no right to hold her against her wishes," Charles blustered now. "My sister is coming with us."

"We can give her better than this," his wife agreed with a contemptuous sniff.

Perhaps they could, at least materially. But from what he'd seen of them and the way Nora feared them, they could give her nothing so far as encouragement and support.

He widened his stance and crossed his arms over his chest, effectively blocking the door. "Nora goes when she says she wants to go."

Nora smiled at him. "Thank you, Simon. I'm staying."

Just hearing the words made the day seem brighter.

Charles sagged. "But, Nora, surely you see this fellow is a bully."

He was a bully? Had the man no understanding of his own behavior?

"He is using you," Meredith insisted with a glare to Simon. "I don't know his game, but I'm certain it will end badly. We can protect you."

"Simon protects me," Nora said, crossing to his side and standing next to him. "He rescued me and Britta just the other night."

"Britta?" Charles said with a frown. "Who's Britta, another of these Wallin people?" He made it sound as if Simon and his family had somehow expanded beyond all propriety.

"A three-legged milk cow," Simon supplied. "Nora made her welcome at Wallin Landing. So I will make you welcome, as her kin. But there will be no more talk of her leaving."

"Well, I…" Charles clamped his mouth shut.

"Would you like some tea, Meredith?" Nora offered. "Perhaps something to eat?"

"Make it fast," Simon said before the woman could answer. "You'll want to start back within the hour or you could be caught in the woods after dark."

Nora scrunched her face. "Simon says it's really dangerous then."

"In that case," Charles said, putting out a hand to his wife, "we should start back straightaway. We only came to see how Nora was getting on."

"Quite nicely, thank you," Nora said. "The Wallins have made me feel like one of the family. Safe travels back to Seattle." She tugged on Simon's arm, and he stepped away from the door so Charles and Meredith could escape.

On her way out, Meredith paused next to Nora. "If you're sure you're happy, dear."

"Very," Nora assured her.

Meredith sighed as if that was the most depressing news she'd heard all week. But she managed to shuffle out after her husband.

"I'll just make sure they leave," Simon said, turning to follow them.

Nora caught his arm. "Thank you. For a moment, they almost had me."

That was what he'd feared when he'd walked in. "You have to learn to stand up to them. You can't give them control of you."

Her sigh sounded more heartfelt than Meredith's. "I know. But for now, I'm glad to lean on your courage."

He was equally glad he'd returned home when he had. Once more it seemed Nora had required his protection.

But what would happen the next time Charles and Meredith visited, and Simon wasn't there?

Chapter Thirteen

Nora was very glad to watch Charles and Meredith leave the clearing. Even though her brother and sister-in-law had offered her a better life with them in Seattle, she couldn't make herself believe their promises. Wallin Landing might not be high society, but at least Simon's family treated her with respect. And she was beginning to hope for more, from Simon.

So, she immersed herself in life at Wallin Landing. With only a week left until Christmas, there was much to be done. Teamsters from Seattle had come to haul off the spars, so Simon and his brothers focused on clearing the new land. Nora worked with the Wallin ladies at the main house, preparing for Christmas, in addition to their usual chores.

Christmas had been a simple affair back in Lowell. Her mother would put a wreath on the door, perhaps a spray of ivy on the dining table. They would go to church services and have a fine dinner. If her parents had given each other gifts, they never mentioned it in her hearing. Meredith had expected Charles to give her something elaborate—a new fur stole or a pendant with a gemstone—and she'd been very cross for days afterward if he did not come up to scratch.

Though Mrs. Wallin mentioned that she and her children generally exchanged gifts, Nora knew Catherine and Rina were working on presents for their husbands. Surely she should do something for Simon.

She had enough material left from a commission to make him a waistcoat. But measuring him without him noticing was proving challenging. She'd estimated the breadth of his shoulders by watching where he fit against the hearth, his back length by counting the logs behind him when he stood near the door. But she could think of only one way to gauge his circumference.

She rose when he did in the morning so she could milk Britta. One morning before he could put on his coat, she went up to him and wrapped her arms about his middle.

And immediately forgot her task.

He smelled cool and clean, like crisp winter air, the flannel of his shirt spiced with the tang of fir resin. His warmth seeped into her, making her want to cuddle closer. She could hear his heart beating, steadier than her own.

"Nora?" he asked. "What are you doing?"

Stop feeling and think!

Taking note of where her fingers met behind him, she stepped back. "Just giving you a proper send-off. Have a good day."

Her face was flushed as he left the cabin, a bemused smile on his lips.

And then there was the theatrical. She finished sewing the costumes and fitted them to the respective players. With so few students, Rina had enlisted several members of the family to play certain roles. Nora listened to Beth and Levi recite their lines, offering encouragement when they stumbled.

One of the afternoons, after school was out on a rainy day, Nora was helping Beth put together decorations for the main house. The girl had brought out red and green paper, which Nora was cutting into even strips that Beth pasted together, interweaving the red and green loops for a long chain to hang across the mantel. Rina was sitting by the fire, reading ahead in a book from which she was teaching, while Catherine sat across the table from Nora and Beth, squishing something into powder with a marble mortar and pestle. Nora was fairly sure it was some sort of medicine, but she hadn't wanted to pry.

Mrs. Wallin, who was tending the fire, spoke up. "And how are you and Simon getting on, Nora?"

"Oh, fine," Nora said, cutting through the red paper. "He has very precise ideas about how things should be done, but I'm learning to please him."

In the utter silence, she heard the log settle on the fire.

Nora glanced up to find them all staring at her. "I'm sorry," she said. "Should I have asked your advice?"

Catherine recovered first. "No, indeed, Nora. You are an intelligent, capable woman who needs no advice to determine what is best for her."

Nora wasn't sure how she'd given Catherine that impression, but she offered her sister-in-law a smile.

"Although, if we were to offer advice," Rina said in her polished voice, putting a marker in her book and setting it aside, "we might have encouraged you to please yourself first and Simon second."

Nora frowned. "But the Bible says to love others as

yourself. I think it would be wonderful if someone put my needs first."

Catherine opened her mouth to respond, then shut it again. She looked to Rina in obvious appeal.

Mother Wallin came to put her arm around Nora. "And that's what you deserve, my darling girl. Simon is blessed to have you as his wife."

"You are kind and considerate," Catherine added.

"Of excellent character," Rina maintained.

"We love you," Beth said.

As Mrs. Wallin pulled back, Nora stared around at them. Catherine's blue eyes were bright with her convictions. Rina's pretty face was equally determined. Mrs. Wallin nodded, setting her hair to glinting red in the firelight. And Beth positively glowed with her appreciation.

They loved her? How could they love her? She was slow to understand, clumsy. She inconvenienced people with her whimsies. She could think of more than a dozen things she'd done that her brother and Meredith had complained about in the last few years before she'd left for Seattle, and several more they'd added since they'd arrived.

Just then she heard a sound like sleigh bells jangling just outside the house. It couldn't be a sleigh. They hadn't had any snow, just a relentless rain. A moment later, boots thudded on the boardwalk that surrounded the house.

"Hi, ho, the Wallins!" called a deep voice.

Beth hopped to her feet, sending red and green links tumbling to the floor. "It's Father Christmas!"

Nora frowned as Beth ran for the hearth. Charles had never held with the custom of Father Christmas, or St. Nicholas as he was coming to be called after the publication of Mr. Moore's poem "The Night Before Christmas." Charles said it was indulgent to encourage children to believe someone would give them presents for nothing. Besides, it wasn't even Christmas yet!

As a knock sounded at the back door, Beth returned to the table carrying a tin canister that jingled as she ran.

"Oh, please, Ma, if he still has that jet trim from last time, may I purchase it?" She dropped the canister on the table with a clang. "I've enough saved up from the egg money, and I've been regretting not buying it since he called last summer."

"If it means so much to you," Mrs. Wallin said with a smile, beckoning to the others. "Rina, Nora, come meet Mr. Christopher Masters, better known in these parts as Father Christmas."

They ventured out onto the back porch to find a man heaving a massive pack from his shoulders. Copper pots and pans clanged as they bumped into each other, and something squeaked as the bag landed on the wooden porch.

"Ladies!" he declared, throwing wide his arms. "I have everything you need. Just ask."

He was an older man, with an ample girth and a bushy beard turning a silvery white. His long wool coat was nearly as white and striped in broad swaths of red and yellow. Mud speckled the hem, and rain glittered on the shoulders, salting the wool of his tasseled red hat. His brown eyes crinkled as he looked over his audience.

"Welcome back to Wallin Landing, Mr. Masters," Mother Wallin greeted him before turning to her daughters-in-law. "Mr. Masters carries his goods in a wide circuit, stopping here each summer and winter."

The man wiped his broad hand across the air. "I travel

from the gold fields of the British Columbia colony to the bounty of the Willamette Valley, and from the jagged Sawtooth to the noble Olympics. But my goods, why they come from farther still. Mysterious China with its grand palaces hidden from foreign eyes. The majesty and pageantry of France. The glittering golden halls of Egypt. No distance is too great to bring my customers what they need."

His words painted pictures, until Nora thought she could see the amazing places he described.

As if he knew it, he offered them a sweeping bow. "And I can see you have many needs, Mrs. Wallin," he said to Simon's mother as he straightened. "Why, you have more mouths to feed and another on the way by the looks of things."

"These are my sons' wives," Mrs. Wallin said with evident pride. "You met Catherine, Drew's wife, when you were here this summer."

He inclined his head. "Mrs. Wallin, the nurse. I remember."

"I hope those bunions didn't give you any more trouble," Catherine said.

"Not a bit of it," he assured her. "I only wish I could convince you to let me sell your ointment. But I brought something just for you—Dr. Furbisher's patented elixir, guaranteed to settle the sour stomach that comes with carrying a precious child."

Catherine eyed him. "Dr. Furbisher is a charlatan. I wouldn't offer his elixir to a rat. Have you any spices?"

"Oh, yes, ma'am," he said, as if she hadn't spoken harshly against one of his products. "Ginger roots fresh and snapping, cinnamon sticks imported from India and rose water right from Boston itself." He opened a section of his pack, and Catherine leaned over to examine the offerings.

"And this is Rina," Mrs. Wallin continued. "She married James this fall. She's our new schoolteacher."

"A schoolteacher," he said, bending for his pack and pulling out some books. "*Webster's Unabridged Dictionary*, perhaps? Bertam's *Cyclopedia*?"

Rina's eyes lit as she accepted the books from his hands.

"And this is Nora," Mrs. Wallin finished with a smile her way. "She married Simon earlier this month."

"Ah, a newlywed." He sidled closer and wiggled his bushy brows. "I have pots that nearly cook by themselves, real silk tassels all the way from Paris for your cloak. He won't be able to take his eyes off you."

That, she doubted. Nora shook her head with a smile.

Beth had been shifting from foot to foot as she listened to the introductions. Now it seemed she could wait no longer.

"Do you still have that jet trim you showed me last summer?" she asked the peddler.

He turned his gaze her way. "'Fraid not, Miss Beth. But jet is for old ladies stuck in their ways. What you want," he said as he bent and fished in his pack once more, "are pearls." He pulled out a paper card with a flourish.

Beth's eyes widened. "Oh! They're beautiful!"

They were indeed. Wound around the card were row upon row of tiny beads, strung together on wire, each one gleaming like a pearl.

From out in the yard came the unmistakable sound of a howl.

Nora glanced up from the pearls, expecting to see

Levi coming across the clearing. Instead, a dog was coursing toward them, nose to the ground, following some trail. She'd never seen its like. Its tail waved over its back like the plume on a lady's hat, and its fur was snowy white except over its head and upper body. The black fur there made it look as if it was wearing a hooded cape that rippled as it moved, each step confident. Britta even looked up from the pasture to watch it pass.

"Is that your dog?" Nora asked Father Christmas when he paused in his endless speech describing his goods.

He glanced back over his shoulder. "Fleet? Oh, he followed me south from Nanaimo. I can't seem to shake him no matter how hard I try." He laughed.

"He's beautiful." Nora wandered to the edge of the porch, watching as the dog zigzagged back and forth across the clearing as if searching for something. She knew the feeling. At times she felt she'd searched her whole life for a place to feel appreciated, needed.

Loved.

She turned and hurried inside. It took only a moment to fill a bowl with clean water and cut a piece off the ham she knew was being smoked in the chimney.

Father Christmas glanced up as she passed him. "Sure I can't interest you in something, newest Mrs. Wallin? Perfume from Italy? Thread from Egypt?"

Normally, she would have jumped at the chance for the exotic thread. Now all she could think about was Fleet, out in that pouring rain. She sat on the edge of the porch and waved the meat.

Fleet's head came up. He ventured closer, until Nora could see that he had eyes the shape and color of almonds.

"Now, I wouldn't do that," Father Christmas said behind her. "He's never bitten anyone, but you can't be too careful with a native dog."

"Native?" Catherine asked, coming to Nora's side. "Do you mean he was raised by Indians?"

"Them from the far north," the peddler told her. "He was trained to pull their sleds." He laughed again. "If I had half a dozen of him, I wouldn't have to walk anywhere."

Fleet was within arm's length now, his gaze on Nora as his shiny black nose twitched. She felt as if he was looking deep inside her, studying her character, her motives.

She set the ham and water down on the step. "It's all right. You don't have to like me. I just thought you might be hungry and thirsty."

Fleet cocked his head to one side and said, "Row ru."

Nora scrambled to her feet. "He talks!"

Father Christmas laughed as Fleet dived for the ham and gobbled it down. "Oh, he's a talented fellow, all right. Makes all kinds of interesting noises to get your attention, then does what he likes. But come now, Mrs. Simon Wallin, you haven't even peeked in my pack. What can I sell you that would meet your heart's desire?"

Nora turned to face the peddler. "Him. I want to buy your dog."

Simon couldn't help a sense of accomplishment as he approached his cabin that night. Though Drew had headed to Seattle for the day to pick up supplies and his present for Catherine, his other brothers had pitched in. Thanks to their help, he'd pulled up all the stumps from the last round of cutting. If they could keep going at that rate, he reckoned they'd have the property cleared by the end of January.

A shame Christmas would get in the way.

He knew the day was a celebration of the Savior's birth, but the preparations went on for far too long, in his opinion. Drew had shot a fat goose last week, and Ma and Beth were in the process of plucking it. Though they would clean and dry the feathers for use in bedding, he knew Beth had already selected a few feathers for quills and to decorate hats.

John had scouted out the tree for the Yule log. Simon would have to join his family in fetching it in on Christmas Eve, when, by his father's tradition, no other work was done. And between now and then they had to decorate the house and stage the school theatrical.

So much frivolity simply got in the way.

He opened the door of the cabin to be met with a deep growl.

His first thought was that a wolf had broken into the house. He didn't have his gun, but he raised his ax off his shoulder as his gaze lit on the creature standing before him, its fur raised and teeth bared. It had the head and ears of a wolf, but the eyes were a deep brown, and it was just a mite smaller.

"Fleet, no!" Nora ordered, hurrying to the beast's side. She bent and put an arm over the dog's shoulders. "This is Simon. We like him."

Simon stared at her. "What is this?"

Nora glanced up at him, her eyes bright. "This is Fleet. Isn't he magnificent?"

There was something majestic about the dog. Perhaps it was the big shoulders or that deep chest. Perhaps it was the look of intelligence on that black-hooded face.

"Please tell me you didn't coax a wild dog into the house," he said, eyeing the creature and fingering the handle of his ax.

"No, Simon, of course not," she said. "He came with Father Christmas."

For a moment, he thought she meant he'd been delivered by the jolly character who was supposed to leave presents for children in their stockings by the fire on Christmas Eve. Then he remembered the peddler.

"Who knows where he found that dog," Simon said. "It probably has fleas."

"Fleet was a native dog," she said, as if that would remove his concerns. "And he doesn't have fleas. I've checked him over carefully. He's perfect."

Nothing was perfect. "We can't keep him. We can't feed him."

"I'll share my food with him," Nora offered, hunkering closer to the dog and fisting her hand in his thick fur as if she thought Simon would wrest her pet away from her even now. "He's not that big. He probably doesn't eat much. And, Simon, he can talk."

Simon lowered the ax. He knew Christopher Masters could make his trinkets sound like treasure, but surely even he wouldn't claim he had a dog who could speak.

"Dogs don't talk, Nora," he said.

She nodded even more vigorously. "He does." She put her face level with the dog's. "Show him, Fleet."

The dog pulled out of Nora's grip and began scratching himself with his back paw.

Simon sighed. "Nora, you have to stop adopting strays. A wild dog has no place on a farm."

"He isn't wild," she protested, stroking the dog's thick fur as he lowered his leg. "He's been good company this afternoon, and he growled to let me know someone was coming. He's been trained to pull a sled for the natives in the north, so he could be useful."

She was clearly enamored of the beast, but Simon could only see the problems. "We don't own a sled. And even if he knows how to protect himself in the wilderness, he could be shot by the first farmer who mistakes him for a wolf."

He waited for her to beg him to relent, more than a little concerned that he might fall under her pleas. It was becoming increasingly difficult to hang on to his logic when confronted with those misty gray eyes.

But Nora straightened to her full height and glared at him. "Oh! Can you never see the good in anything, Simon Wallin?"

Simon recoiled. "Well, I…"

Nora strode forward and poked a finger in his chest, while the dog jumped back as if he thought they were playing.

"You may malign my decorating," Nora told him, her eyes now sharp as stones, "make light of my sewing and insult my cow, but don't you ever speak a word against my dog!"

Simon took a step back from her fury. "But, Nora—"

She raised a finger. "No! Fleet is my dog. I will see to his care. If you will not have him in the cabin, we will sleep in the barn with Britta."

She might just do it. He'd never seen her look so resolute, her eyes narrowed and her head high. If she'd showed this kind of spunk in front of her brother, Charles would have been cowering.

But Simon didn't like the idea of her sleeping in the

barn. She might flatten the hay they needed for the animals' feed. She'd get cold. And he'd be alone again.

Once, he would have welcomed the thought. Now the idea of his cabin empty of Nora caused something to twist inside him until it hurt.

But a dog?

He eyed the mongrel. Fleet returned the look, his gaze equally assessing. He seemed to be smiling.

But whether in welcome or perverse delight at Simon's predicament, he couldn't know.

"Very well," he said. "The dog can stay."

Nora snapped a nod. "Good. You'll see, Simon. He'll prove to be an excellent addition to the family."

Perhaps, but at the moment he was more concerned about the way this decision had come about. He'd prided himself on his logic, his ability to identify the flaw in any proposal. Would caring for Nora mean abandoning all logic? Was he willing to change that much for her?

Chapter Fourteen

Nora felt only a twinge of guilt as she called Fleet over to the hearth. In truth, she wasn't sure where that show of bravado had come from. Perhaps it was only because she found it easier to talk to Simon than anyone else. She also appreciated his insights, his logic. But, in this case, she couldn't allow him to cast off a helpless dog.

Well, not exactly helpless. With teeth that looked plenty sharp enough to defend himself, Fleet wolfed down the dried venison she'd cut up for him. He'd followed Father Christmas from the north, so he must know how to get on in the wild. Surely he'd do well here at Wallin Landing.

"You'll have to stop him from chasing the chickens," Simon said, taking a seat at the table. "Or scaring your cow."

"I already introduced him to Britta," Nora told him. "They got along famously."

He raised a brow as if he doubted that.

Leaving Fleet licking his lips, Nora stood to face Simon. Even though the day had been cold, his hair was plastered against his brow, darkened by sweat. Lines bracketed his jade-colored eyes.

"You look tired," she murmured.

He drew in a breath. "It was a long day. I'm not sure I even want to go to Ma's to eat." He closed his eyes and twisted his head from side to side as if to work out a kink in his muscles. When her father had been tired from bending over an accounting desk all day, her mother had rubbed his neck for him. The thought of touching Simon that way made her swallow.

"I'll go to the main house and fetch you some dinner," she offered, hurrying toward the door. Simon did not argue.

Fleet followed her out, pacing her as she walked to the main house. His head was up and regal, as if he defied anyone to trouble either of them.

"Simon will love you," she told him. "Just give him time."

His mouth opened as if he was laughing at her.

Why wouldn't he laugh? Who was she to promise love? The best she could do was offer it.

"Well, I love you already," she told the dog as they reached the main house. She pointed to the edge of the boardwalk. "Stay here."

Fleet sat as if fully intending to obey. But the moment she turned, she felt something brush her skirts. Looking back, she caught sight of Fleet's tail as he disappeared into the darkness.

She hated leaving him outside alone, but Simon's mother had not given Nora permission to bring the dog inside. Hoping he wouldn't get into trouble, she hurried into the house.

Simon must have taken longer than his brothers to

finish his work and return home, for it seemed dinner had already ended. Levi and Beth were studying at the table, and John was playing chess with Father Christmas by the fire. The peddler was spending the night at Wallin Landing before continuing south. Mother Wallin was in her rocking chair, knitting something with a pretty purple yarn that reminded Nora of heather. Simon's mother put the work aside when she sighted Nora.

"I was hoping to get some food for Simon," Nora said.

John glanced up. "He was still on the property when we left."

"That's Simon," Levi said, twirling his pencil. "He'll keep working long after the cows have come home."

"I thought you might be by," Mrs. Wallin said, rising. "There's stew simmering on the stove, dear. I'll fill two bowls and send along some of the biscuits."

"They're Levi's," Beth assured Nora with a smile. Her youngest brother grinned.

"Thank you," Nora told them all.

"And how did Mr. Simon take to your new pup?" Father Christmas asked Nora.

John and Levi perked up.

"Pup?" Levi asked. "Did we get a dog?"

"Nora did," Beth said. "His name is Fleet. Please say Simon saw how cute he is."

"Simon said he could stay," Nora said as Levi made a face.

Mrs. Wallin brought out the stew just then, with the biscuits in a string bag.

"You ought to hold that stew hostage," Father Christmas advised, moving his bishop to capture one of John's castles. "I for one would love to hear Mr. Simon play on that fiddle of his."

So would she. Sunday seemed a long ways back, though it was only a few days. Just watching Simon play had been a pleasure.

Mrs. Wallin cocked her head. "What do you think, Nora? Would Simon be willing to play tonight?"

He had been so tired, but she knew how much he loved music. Nora smiled, looping the bag over her arm and accepting the two bowls. "I'll ask."

Fleet was nowhere to be found when she opened the door of the main cabin. Fear nearly made her stumble off the boardwalk. She made herself keep walking as she called out, "Fleet! Fleet! Here, boy!"

Something moved in the bushes, and she nearly ran back to the safety of the house. "Fleet?"

The dog bounded out of the woods to pace her back to the cabin. The way his nose twitched in the moonlight, she thought it was as much the stew as her call that had brought him to her side.

Simon was nearly as unwilling to join her. "I've had enough company for one day, Nora," he said, digging into the stew while Fleet sat at his elbow expectantly.

"Yes, of course, Simon," she said, dipping her spoon into her bowl. "I'm sure Father Christmas can wait the six months until he passes through again."

He sighed. "Very well. Give me a few minutes to eat." He eyed Fleet. "And call your dog off. He's already had his dinner. He doesn't need mine too."

A short while later, she and Simon walked to the main cabin, his violin case in hand. He had been convinced to allow Fleet to remain in the cabin.

"Though it won't be your bedding he tears apart," he pointed out.

"If he tears apart your bedding," Nora said, "you can have mine."

Simon grunted, a thoroughly unconvinced sound.

"I never had a dog growing up," she admitted. "My parents weren't fond of them, and of course I couldn't ask Charles and Meredith to add another burden."

"You are hardly a burden," Simon said, heading toward the lights of the main cabin.

"My parents would have disagreed," Nora said, walking beside him. "They were older, you see, in their forties when I was born. They hadn't planned on supporting another child. It was very clear that I was unwanted, and a bit of an embarrassment. Sometimes, I think they were glad to go away, just to be free of me."

"Nora!" His protest was sharp. "No parent wants to leave children alone."

Too late she remembered his father's untimely passing. "Yes, of course, Simon," she said, lowering her head.

He stopped and touched her arm. "Forgive me. I have no right to comment on your family. I rarely understand my own."

"Oh, your family is easy to understand," she said, looking up at him. "They love you."

He managed a smile and went to open the door.

Nora lagged behind. Why had she told him about her parents? She was just beginning to think he liked her. She shouldn't admit that her own parents had found her unlovable. That would only put doubts in his mind.

Now she slipped into the main house behind him, watching as he crossed to the hearth, bent to set down the case and open it. Levi or John must have gone to summon the others, for all the Wallins were present. Drew and Catherine were on the bench that had been pulled away from the table, James and Rina nearby on chairs. Beth was still at the table, but Levi was lounging on the braided rug before the fire. John and Father Christmas were sitting on either side of the chessboard, but the pieces were scattered about as if they had no interest in playing now that better entertainment was here.

"What will you favor us with tonight, brother?" Drew asked, stretching out his legs.

"A love song," Beth begged, setting aside her schoolwork.

"Something soft and sweet," Mrs. Wallin agreed. She patted the chair nearest her rocker. "Come sit by me, Nora."

Honored, Nora went to perch on the chair. But she found it hard to take her eyes off Simon. Standing tall, true, he tucked the worn violin under his chin and drew the bow along the strings. Music, pure and bright, flowed from his caress. She could almost see the notes curling around the cabin, touching his family. Catherine leaned her head against Drew's shoulder, and Beth sighed.

Simon's mother bent closer to Nora. "That's called 'The Song of True Love,' dear. He must be thinking of you."

Hope lifted her head, her gaze full of her husband. Simon's eyes were closed, as if he too was carried away by the haunting melody. Was he playing for her?

She had no answer, for he didn't open his eyes until he'd finished playing. As his family applauded, his brows rose as if he were a little surprised by the enthusiasm.

"Nicely done, Mr. Simon," Father Christmas said. "You sure you don't want me to arrange for you to play at the fancy theatre down in the capital?"

Before Simon could decline, James hopped to his

feet. "Never mind the capital. How about something more lively right here? I've a hankering to dance with the prettiest gal in the room." He eyed his bride, and Rina blushed.

"The prettiest woman in the room is taken," Drew said, rising and offering his hand to his wife.

Levi heaved a sigh. "Looks like it's you and me again, Beth."

"For a few more years," Beth predicted.

They were rearranging the furniture before Nora could even wonder about a partner. Drew and James shoved chairs and benches against the log walls, and Levi and John rolled up the rug. It seemed they were all going to dance.

She'd always wanted to dance. The school she'd attended had provided lessons. She knew where to put her feet, how to hold her arms. But she'd never been invited to a dance, and Charles and Meredith had never been willing to take her with them when they'd attended balls.

She looked to Simon. He too was watching his family scurry about, violin held beside him. He was her husband, the logical one to dance with her. The only one she really wanted to dance with.

But if he was playing, she'd never get a chance.

As the others took their places, Simon lifted the violin again.

"Wait," Nora said.

Everyone looked at her, obviously surprised. She would not let that detour her.

"Brother John," she said, "would you help me?"

"Surely," John said, but she could hear the puzzlement in his voice.

She motioned him over to the bench beside the table

and struck it with one hand. A dull boom echoed around the room.

"Can you keep time like that?" she asked.

John frowned a moment, then glanced over at Simon and grinned. "I can," he promised, straddling the bench.

"And I can do better," Father Christmas promised. He joined John by the table, pulling a flat oblong metal box from his pocket. Raising it to his mouth, he blew out some notes.

A harmonica! Nora grinned in delight, but Levi raised his head. "What is that?"

Father Christmas winked at him. "Something that might find its way into your stocking if you're a good lad." He turned to Nora. "Just promise me a dance, newest Mrs. Wallin, after you've finished the one you've planned."

Nora blushed that he had guessed her intent. Turning, she looked to Simon, who was frowning at her.

"I don't need accompaniment," he told her.

Nora crossed to his side, her heart beating nearly as loud as John's makeshift drum. "Yes, you do, if you're going to put down that fiddle and dance with me."

Dance? He never danced. He played the music so others might enjoy themselves. He'd resigned himself to that fact. Now here was Nora, tugging him out of the shadows. He wasn't sure he was ready for the light.

James apparently disagreed.

"Excellent idea," his irrepressible brother declared. He released his wife's hand and strode up to Simon. "You should get a chance to dance, Simon. If you don't remember how, I'll partner you." He held up one finger. "But I lead."

Simon shook his head. "I think I can manage, James." He set down Pa's violin in the case and straightened to eye Nora. "If you're sure about this."

"Oh, yes, Simon," she said, her eyes shining bright as silver.

Simon took her hand in his. Her fingers were trembling, but he thought it was from eagerness. The smile she offered him was wide and deep. Perhaps dancing wasn't such a bad idea.

John stretched his arms, fingers interlocked. "All right, then. Let's have a waltz."

"A waltz it is," Father Christmas agreed. He brought the harmonica to his lips and began to play. John's thump-thump-thump underscored the meter.

James swept Rina into his arms and began to twirl her around the floor. Drew and Catherine fell in behind them. Levi looked to Simon and raised his brows.

Simon recognized the song—it was one of Pa's favorites. Ma had taught them all to dance to it at one point or another. He remembered following her awkwardly around the floor, tripping over his own feet until he got the hang of it. With a nod to Nora, he led her out onto the floor.

But dancing with Nora was nothing like dancing with Ma. She followed his lead effortlessly, beaming at him all the while as if he was a master of the art. Holding her as they turned, her gray skirts belling about her, he felt like a master, strong, sure, graceful. Even though it was only John pounding on the bench and Father Christmas on a wheezy harmonica, it seemed as if the finest orchestra was accompanying them.

And Nora looked so happy, her cheeks rosy and her

eyes bright, her hair coming loose to float like a veil around her face. He couldn't look away.

After one last drawn-out note, Father Christmas lowered the harmonica, and John stopped, shaking out his hands. The other dancers swung to a halt, and Simon made himself release Nora and applaud with the rest of his family.

Father Christmas grinned at them. "Who's for another round?"

James and Drew immediately chorused their interest, and Simon found himself nodding eagerly.

John stood. "Levi, come take over. There's a lady here I've never partnered, and I mean to rectify that."

Simon wasn't sure who he meant, but Levi released Beth and went to the bench to join Father Christmas.

John approached Nora and gave her a bow. "Mrs. Wallin, might I have the honor of this dance?"

Nora glanced at Simon as if unsure. He felt himself stiffen. What was wrong with him? He wasn't about to get in a fight with his brother for the right to dance with his own wife.

She must have heard something in Simon's silence, for she dropped John a curtsy. "I would be delighted, Brother John."

Levi started beating the time, and Father Christmas raised his harmonica once more.

Simon stepped back against the hearth as the others swirled past, Nora in John's arms. It was just John, Simon told himself. He was likely only being kind. After all, John was considerate to everyone. There was no reason he couldn't dance with Nora.

But did she have to look so happy about it?

"Ahem."

Beth's tone drew his gaze to his sister, who was standing beside him, her arms upraised as if ready to partner him.

"I should play," he said.

"You should not," Beth replied. "Honestly, Simon, we are trying to help you, but you don't make it easy."

Simon resigned himself to a scold and led his sister out onto the floor. At least if he danced with her, he didn't have to watch Nora and John.

"You aren't helping," he told Beth as they turned. "You're interfering."

"Which is what family is supposed to do," she insisted.

"When the other family member is confused or incapable of acting," Simon pointed out. "I am neither."

"Oh." Beth chewed on that a moment. "You're right, of course. It's not like you to be confused, and you are one of the most capable of my brothers. So why don't you marry Nora?"

Simon was glad Nora was on the opposite side of the room and likely couldn't hear his sister over the sound of the music.

"I am married to Nora, remember?" he told her.

Beth wrinkled her nose. "Maybe. But sometimes you act as if you don't particularly like the idea."

Simon dropped his hold, grabbed her hand and dragged her into the kitchen. Once he was sure they were beyond anyone else's hearing, he asked, "What are you talking about?"

Beth shook her head, clearly exasperated with him. "You order her about, disagree with most of her suggestions. A wife wants her husband to be more considerate."

Fine words for a girl still in the schoolroom. "Is this according to *Godey's*?" Simon asked her.

Beth colored. "No, it's from my observations. I don't remember much about Pa, but I do remember he always put Ma first. Drew and James are the same way with Catherine and Rina. And they have a way of looking at each other." She sighed. "So romantic."

"I don't need to romance Nora," Simon said. "That's not why we married."

Beth waved a hand. "I've heard all about your reasons. It was very noble of you, Simon, to win us the land and rescue Nora from her despicable family. But she deserves more." Beth peered closer. "And so do you. You can do it, Simon. I know you have the ability to love deeply."

He started to pull away in denial, but Beth tightened her grip.

"You do! You wouldn't have stayed here in Wallin Landing if it wasn't true. I know we all drive you mad at times. And you wouldn't have accepted Britta and Fleet."

"I accepted them under duress," Simon informed her.

"You accepted them because Nora accepted them," Beth countered. "I think you love her, but you're afraid of being hurt. You think she won't like who you are."

Said so bluntly, the fact slammed into him. But he refused to allow it to be true. "Maybe I'm just the family curmudgeon."

"Well, you certainly can be," Beth agreed. "But you don't have to be. I don't know why you don't want to try, Simon, because Nora truly is the sweetest person. And I have proof love is worth the risk. Look at Drew and James."

Something tugged at him like a rope on a log. He fought off the feeling. Nora was sweet, but it didn't follow that her sweetness would accommodate his sometimes sour nature. "I'm not Drew or James. And I have to question the experience of a fourteen-year-old."

Beth pouted. "I've read all of Pa's books, and many in Mrs. Howard's lending library. Men do great and wonderful things for love. I know you can too." She gazed up at him. "Won't you please try, for Nora's sake?"

For Nora's sake. He'd already given up his bed, had his home redecorated and provided room in his life for a three-legged cow and a native dog that was likely even now rending his clothing apart. Simon sighed. "I am doing the best I can, Beth. Leave it at that."

She sighed as well, and this time the sound was firm and unyielding. "Then you leave us no choice, Simon. We all love you and Nora, and we're going to make sure you're happy together, whether you're ready or not."

Chapter Fifteen

Nora wasn't sure what was happening with Simon. She had seen him take his sister aside, but she finished her dance with John and one with Father Christmas, Levi awkwardly tooting along with John on the bench, before Simon and Beth returned from the kitchen. They joined the other couples in thanking the musicians for their efforts. Simon looked particularly thoughtful as everyone began bidding each other good-night. His brows were drawn down, and his mouth was firmly fixed. What had Beth said to him?

"Is something troubling your sister?" Nora asked as she and Simon walked back to their house under a velvety night sky.

"No," he said, hitching the violin case closer.

Not for the first time she wished he was a bit more loquacious. "She kept you in the kitchen a long time."

"She seemed to think I required it."

She resolved to get the answer out of Beth the next day. She was just glad to find the house in good shape and Fleet sleeping curled up by the sideboard when they reached the cabin, as if patiently waiting for the next round of food to be served. Simon uttered a "Humph," which she could only hope was his way of saying the dog had done better than he'd expected. But she made sure to let Fleet out with her when she left to milk Britta the next morning.

She had to wait until Beth was done with school before asking what had happened with her and Simon the night before. Father Christmas had left for points south. Nora had been concerned Fleet might follow, but the dog seemed pleased with his new home, sniffing about the outside of her cabin and the main one.

"He thinks we're his new pack," Levi claimed, squatting to scratch the dog behind his ear. At least he seemed pleased to have the dog about. Simon's brother came into the main house with Nora, reluctantly leaving Fleet to explore the clearing.

Mrs. Wallin had told Nora earlier that she would be spending the day at Drew and Catherine's helping with baby things, and most of the men were out working on the new acreage. Levi went to study the chessboard, very likely in preparation for a match with John that evening. With the fire glowing in the hearth and something with basil baking in the oven, Beth brought greenery from the back porch and piled it in front of her on the table.

"You can help me, Nora," she said as Nora hung up her cloak. "I need three hands to bring this all together, and Levi cannot be bothered."

Levi leaned back and crossed his arms behind his head, further disheveling his curly blond hair. "That's because you're making something that will have no impact on me. You might even call it a grim reminder."

Nora wandered closer to Beth. "What are you making?"

"Something Simon will never need either, at the rate

he's going," Levi declared, and this time Beth glared at him.

Frowning, Nora slipped onto the bench beside Beth, her gray skirts brushing Beth's pink gingham, and lowered her voice. "Speaking of Simon, I was wondering what kept the two of you in the kitchen so long last night."

Beth shook her head. "It wouldn't have taken nearly so long if Simon wasn't so pigheaded." Immediately, she made a face. "I'm sorry, Nora. That wasn't very nice."

Nora smiled at her. "It's all right. I'm coming to realize your whole family has had trouble with Simon. But you needn't be so hard on him. He's very reasonable, once you give him a chance."

"Reasonable." Beth blew out a breath. "Well, that's one word for him. I was merely trying to point out to him that he could be a better husband."

Nora recoiled. "A better husband? Why, he's a marvelous husband!"

Beth raised her golden brows. "He is?"

Nora nodded. "Yes, of course. He is considerate and fastidious and asks my opinion on any number of matters."

"And then tells you where you're wrong," Beth said.

"Well, yes," Nora agreed. "But he's usually right. Except in the case of Britta and Fleet, of course. And on how I can help the family."

Beth pointed a finger at Nora. "See? That's why I took him aside. He could do better." She lowered her hand and her voice as well. "I think he's in love with you, Nora, but he's afraid to show it."

Nora must have shaken her head harder than she'd intended, for she could feel her hair slipping out of the knot at the back of her head. "You're wrong, Beth. Simon's not afraid of anything. He doesn't love me."

Beth leaned back. "Maybe. We'll see. And this just might help things along."

Nora eyed the pile of fir limbs and ivy Simon's sister had amassed on the table before them. Among the greenery she spotted pink satin ribbon and rosy apples. "What is this?"

Beth looked down and sighed. "Something I suspect I won't need either." She raised her head. "But it's a lovely, romantic gesture nonetheless. It's a kissing bough."

A kissing bough. Nora knew the tradition, though, like Beth and Levi, she had never had occasion to make use of it. A kissing bough hung in a doorway or from a chandelier. Whenever a gentleman found a lady under it, they might share a kiss. She could see the two other married couples in the family enjoying it.

But her and Simon?

Heat filled her cheeks. Would she be so bold as to stand under it? Would he kiss her, better than what he'd given on their wedding day? She could imagine those strong arms around her again, those firm lips caressing hers. Would having a kissing bough encourage Simon to confess that he had come to care for her?

Was she willing to take that chance?

Beth was watching her, likely waiting for some sign of approval or encouragement.

Nora squared her shoulders. "I think it's a perfectly lovely tradition, Beth. I would be delighted to help you craft a kissing bough."

And she would wait with trepidation to see what Simon would make of it.

Unfortunately, she and Beth did not have time to hang the bough before they had to clear the table for dinner.

Beth took their creation to the bedchambers upstairs, as if determined that Simon should not see it until the appropriate moment. Nora noticed that Beth and Levi whispered together before the others arrived, but she thought it was likely about the upcoming theatrical.

For her part, she made sure to find Fleet and take him home for his own dinner before returning for hers. Sitting beside Simon, she could barely do justice to the venison pie Mrs. Wallin had baked. She kept wondering about the kissing bough upstairs.

"Let's play a game after dinner," Beth said, looking around at her family. For some reason, her look to Nora was brightest. Simon opened his mouth as if he meant to refuse, but Beth affixed him with a stern look, and he gave her a resigned nod.

Nora helped Beth take the dishes to the tub, but when she returned to the main room, she found Simon bracketed by Drew and Levi. Seeing her standing there, Simon frowned at his youngest brother, but Levi merely smiled at him. Nora had no choice but to take the remaining seat across from Simon and next to John. Though John offered her a smile as he made room, Simon did not look amused.

While Mrs. Wallin watched from her rocker, Beth stood at the head of the table. "This is a thinking game," she announced. "It is called I Love My Love. You will be assigned a letter of the alphabet, and you must think of a name, an occupation and a quality. I will start." She clasped her hands before her and looked at her family beseechingly. "I love my love with an *A*, for his name is Adam, he is an architect and he is amiable."

Nora could see understanding dawning around the table.

"Me next," James proclaimed. He clasped his hands

together and looked out at them all wide-eyed, in a perfect mimic of Beth's manner.

"No," Beth snapped before he could speak. "It's Catherine's turn. She has the letter *B*."

Clearly surprised by her vehemence, James subsided.

Catherine sat a little taller. "I love my love with a *B*, for his name is Benjamin, he is a barber and he is quite burly."

Smiles of appreciation blossomed on the family's faces.

Before Beth could direct him, Drew gazed at his wife, his deep voice bursting forth. "I love my love with a *C*, for her name is Catherine, she is a good cook and a better nurse and she is clever."

Catherine sighed and leaned in for his kiss.

Beth beamed. "Well done, Drew. Simon, you're next."

Simon was frowning, but whether in thought or annoyance, Nora wasn't sure. "I love my love with a *D*," he said, "for her name is Delores, she is a doctor and she is far from dreary."

"Nice," Levi said before launching into his statement about his love with an *E*.

But Nora wasn't paying attention; her mind was stuck on what Simon had said. Was that what he wanted in his love—someone smart enough to be a doctor and far from dreary? She wasn't nearly that smart. Did he think she was dreary?

"Nora?" Beth asked, breaking into her thoughts. "We're up to *G*. Aren't you going to do that one?"

G? Oh, of course. John must have done *F* while she was woolgathering. "I love my love with a *G*," she said, "for his name is George, he is a grocer and he's quite good-looking."

Everyone nodded their approval.

As they progressed around the table, Simon seemed to relax, and so did Nora. It was just a game, after all. No need to apply it to their situation. She should just enjoy herself.

Catherine had just finished *K* when Levi scrambled to his feet.

"Nora, what was I thinking? You must want to sit next to Simon. Here, change seats with me. Simon, scoot over."

He was so insistent that Nora rose and came around the table, and Simon obliged by letting her slip in between him and Drew. But it wasn't until she had claimed her love as Michael the miner who was muscular that she realized what Levi had done.

Simon had the letter *N.*

Everyone was waiting around the table. She could see them all watching Simon. Would he say something sweet as Drew had done? Something romantic even? She could hardly breathe.

"I love my love with an *N*," he said. "For her name is Nancy, she is a nurse and she is neat."

Nora sagged. Even with her seated next to him, he'd managed to overlook her. She couldn't meet his family's no-doubt pitying gazes.

Across the table, Levi rose, and she couldn't help looking up at him. His deep blue eyes were narrowed, his lower lip sticking out. "Let's skip right to *S*, shall we?" he said, and no one seemed eager to argue with him. "I don't much like my brother with an *S*, for his name is Simon, he's married to a seamstress and he's rather stupid."

Everyone in his family started talking at once then. Catherine scolded Levi for his lack of tact, Rina for his poor word choice. Beth berated Simon for missing a perfectly good opportunity to praise Nora. Drew defended Simon, while James defended Levi, and John tried to calm everyone down. Simon folded his arms over his chest and refused to respond.

"It's all right," Nora murmured, and every other voice quieted. "It's just a game."

Simon lowered his arms. At least she understood. If they had something to say to each other, it should be said in private, not in front of his family. As it was, his discussion with Beth last night had troubled him most of the day, and he still wasn't sure what he felt for Nora.

His mother rose from her rocker. "Perhaps it's time we all got our rest. There's only a few more days until the theatrical, after all."

Levi and Beth exchanged glances, which Simon saw did not go unnoticed by their teacher. He could only hope his youngest siblings weren't planning something extra with their play.

After they'd taken their leave, Nora was quiet as she walked with him back to the house.

"I hope Beth's game didn't trouble you," he said as they followed the dark path.

A steady rain was falling, and she drew her cloak closer about her. "It was just a game."

She had said that earlier. It was almost as if she thought by repeating it she would make it true.

"It was just a game," Simon agreed, moving to open the door to the cabin for her. "Anything we need say to each other can be said without an audience."

She paused in the doorway, and for a moment he could almost see the hope shining in her eyes. "Yes, of course, Simon," she said, but she went straight to the ladder and climbed it with no help from him.

He eyed Fleet, who had curled up around Simon's bedding. "I have a feeling she thinks you deserve that spot more than I do right now," he told the dog.

Fleet seemed to grin at him.

Nora was gone the next morning when Simon rose. She had taken the dog with her, leaving the house surprisingly silent. Perhaps that was why his brothers' talk as they climbed to the new acreage sounded louder than usual.

Today, they were to start chopping down the next group of trees, some of the biggest on the claim. John had made the first cuts on a mammoth cedar, then pounded in boards a few feet up to use as platforms for Simon and Drew to work the big saw. While John prepared the next tree, his cap down over his red hair to fend off the drizzle that misted the cool air, James stood guard. Simon could see his middle brother strolling along the edges of the growing clearing, his head swiveling from side to side, his plaid shirt showing red over his thick coat.

"James has learned a lot since the day Pa died," Drew commented as if aware of Simon's thoughts.

"So have we all," Simon answered, positioning the center of the two-man saw into the opening John had made.

Drew chuckled. "Me more than most. This will be a more blessed Christmas than I could have dreamed, with Catherine beside me and our child on the way."

"You weren't sure of her to begin with," Simon reminded him, going to take up his spot on the other platform.

"I never thought to marry," Drew admitted, stepping

up onto the platform. "But you and the others kept pushing us together, and here we are."

Was that what he needed—his brothers' prodding? Was he not man enough to own his feelings?

Drew grabbed the handle of the saw, and Simon leaned into his handle, drawing the blade back and forth, deeper and deeper into the trunk. He'd worked beside his brother often enough that the effort took little thought. Good thing, because his mind remained on Nora.

Beth seemed to believe that Simon wasn't doing right by his wife. Was it merely a matter of perspective, or was Simon indeed failing to keep his side of the bargain? Was there something more he should do?

Or someone else he should be?

When the big tree keeled over and John moved in to start working on the branches, Simon caught Drew's arm before he could walk away. "A moment. I need your opinion."

Drew raised a brow. "I'm listening."

"You've seen Nora," Simon said. "She's happy, carefree. The exact opposite of me. How can such differences survive close proximity?"

Drew laughed. "Bringing you kicking and protesting into the light, is she, brother? That's only to the good."

"Perhaps," Simon said, and his brother laughed all the more.

Simon managed a rueful smile as he wiped mist from his cheek. "You see? I'm the cynic of the family, Drew, the one most likely to spot the flaw in any situation."

"And the one most likely to find a way to overcome it," Drew countered. "What flaw do you see now?"

Simon glanced to where the cleared trees showed the lake sparkling in the distance. "Always the flaw has been in others—their plans, their characters. This time, I fear it is in me."

Drew sobered. "Then only you can resolve the matter, Simon."

"I know." Simon shook his head. "Do you ever think that perhaps you were destined to be a certain way?"

Drew frowned. "Like what?"

Simon waved a hand to encompass his brothers. "James sees the joke in every situation. John's compassion touches us all. And you have always put family first."

"Perhaps those qualities are in our nature," Drew allowed, "but Levi has seldom thought of anyone but himself, and I refuse to believe that will be his only legacy."

Simon thought about how hard his youngest brother was working on the theatrical, how often he'd taken time to help Simon. "Levi is coming into his own. He's young."

"Whereas you are ancient and set in your ways," Drew teased.

Simon seized his end of the saw and pulled it off the stump. "Next you'll quote the Bible to me. 'Physician, heal thyself.' I don't know how, Drew. If I did, I would have changed my character long ago."

"You didn't consider your character a problem until Nora arrived," Drew pointed out. "In fact, you gave me the impression you liked being the cynic."

"And is that any better?" Simon demanded, hefting the big blade. "Is that my contribution to the family, to rant and rail about jobs not done to my satisfaction, plans ill conceived?"

Drew was unruffled as he picked up an ax to go help John. "Only you can decide that. You are an intelligent man, Simon, likely the smartest of us all. But maybe intellect isn't the issue in this case. I know what Pa would say if he was here. He'd tell you to pray about the matter."

Simon nodded, but his heart was not encouraged. If the good Lord had seen fit to make him a cynic, then it was unlikely He would change Simon when approached in prayer.

With men this is impossible; but with God all things are possible.

The remembered verse seemed to echo in the clearing, yet Simon knew he alone had heard it. It stayed on his mind as they finished their work for the day. When the time came for them to start for the house, he let his brothers go on ahead of him.

In the twilight, he gazed around at the land he hoped would feed his family. Half the trees were gone now, the rich black earth awaiting plowing and planting. In his mind he could see the house he had sketched out for Nora. Prayer came surprisingly easy.

I thought earning this land by marrying Nora was the right thing, Lord. It brought hope to our family and gave Nora safety from her brother. But she deserves more than safety. She deserves a husband who will love and honor her. How can I be that man?

For a moment, the breeze was his only answer. Then a verse popped into his mind.

Greater love hath no man than this, that a man lay down his life for his friends.

Drew had sacrificed time to be the father they had lost. How Simon had chafed as a young man under his brother's command. Was that his problem now? Was he still that boy trying to prove he was a man? Was he as self-centered as Levi?

He refused to allow that image to be himself. He had earned his patent by proving up his claim—clearing the original acreage and building a cabin. He didn't need anyone's approval.

He sighed as he started down the path toward the main clearing. Between the scarcity of ladies and his own character, he had resigned himself to being alone. He'd felt rather confident in his decision, until he'd agreed to Nora's convenient wedding.

Drew was right—Nora's presence pulled Simon into the light, made him see the good among the bad, made him dream of possibilities.

But how did a cynic go about making those dreams reality?

Chapter Sixteen

Nora passed the day in trepidation. She had lain awake a long time the night before. She'd heard Simon talk to the dog, more than once. Normally, that would have made her smile, but at that moment her heart only hurt. He could share his feelings with Fleet, but not with her?

No matter how many times she told herself the letter game last night meant nothing, she couldn't make herself believe it. His statement that he'd rather talk directly with her was endearing, only he didn't talk to her. Not about love.

She had managed to rise before he did that morning. Fleet had been waiting for her at the bottom of the ladder, hopping about as if eager to escape outside. She'd beckoned him closer and had given him a quick hug, and he'd turned and licked her face. At least her dog liked her.

Britta had been equally sweet when Nora had milked her, standing so patiently and turning her head to fix her deep brown eyes on Nora. The cow trusted her. If only Simon would trust her with his heart.

She spent the day helping Simon's mother with chores and Christmas preparations. Beth had made swags—fir boughs with ribbon entwined—to hang on the doors. She and Nora trekked around to all the houses and the school to put them up that afternoon. And then Beth insisted on hanging the kissing bough, even though Nora tried to discourage her.

"Simon just needs help," Beth told her as she dragged a chair over to the spot near the door where she'd determined the bough should hang. "We need to do everything we can to encourage him."

Nora couldn't help looking at the creation with hope. Could a collection of fir, ivy, apples and ribbons really make Simon think kindly on her? It seemed almost too good to be true.

As dinnertime neared, Nora took to pacing the floor. Mrs. Wallin had relented and allowed Fleet to come in. He followed Nora back and forth for a while, then evidently decided the game wasn't to his liking, for he went to curl up near the door to the kitchen as if to keep watch over the food inside. Soon he was asleep, his paws twitching as if he was running across the snow again.

But Nora couldn't relax. What would Simon say when he saw the kissing bough? What would he do? What should she do?

As it was, she looked up each time the door of the main cabin opened.

Levi loped through first, hurrying toward the stairs to the second story without a glance at the decoration. John came next, but at least he took the time to look around and compliment them on their work before heading toward the kitchen to help with dinner.

"He'll be here," Beth assured Nora, who managed a nod.

But Drew and Catherine and James and Rina came

through the door with no sign of Simon. Both couples took advantage of the kissing bough, their embraces so tender that Nora could only sigh with longing.

Should she worry about Simon? No, surely he was fine or one of his brothers would have reported an injury and Catherine would no doubt be rushing to tend him. Had he decided to eat at their cabin tonight?

"The house is starting to look quite festive," Rina said to Beth as she helped Mrs. Wallin bring plates to the table.

"Nora helped me," Beth said.

Nora nodded her thanks. Then she forced herself to go perch on the bench, knitting her fingers in her lap.

"Very nicely done," James agreed, looking around as if noticing the paper chains on the mantel for the first time. "You just couldn't wait until Christmas Eve, could you, Beth?"

Beth put her nose in the air. "Well, it is nearly Christmas Adam."

"Christmas what?" Catherine asked, taking her seat at the table.

"Christmas Adam," Levi said, coming down the stairs. "Today's the twenty-second. The twenty-third is the day before Christmas Eve, and Adam came before Eve so tomorrow is Christmas Adam."

Nora tried to smile like everyone else. It was rather clever. But all she could think about was that kissing bough hanging near the front door. She rose and moved closer to it again.

James sidled up to her and glanced at it. "I cannot let that hang there without a second try, you know."

For a moment, she thought he meant to kiss her, and she couldn't help taking a step back. The only kiss she wanted was Simon's. But James turned to the table, where the other ladies were gathered.

"Mrs. Wallin," he called.

His mother, Catherine and Rina all looked up.

James laughed, then crooked his finger at his wife. "Rina, would you come here a moment?"

Rina smiled, her gaze going to the bough above him, before dropping to his face as she approached. "Yes, James?" she asked, all innocence.

"Happy almost Christmas Adam," he said, then he bent his head and kissed her.

Oh, that Simon would look at her that way, would hold her so gently, as if she were precious. Another sigh escaped her as James released his bride, who gave him a rather wobbly smile.

"Perhaps you could find a quiet corner," Simon suggested from the doorway, "so a man can enter his family's home?"

Nora's heart leaped in her chest. He was here. She brushed her palms against her skirt, stood straighter and offered him a bright smile.

"Quiet corner?" James returned with an upraised brow. "In this house?" He took Rina's hand and made way for his brother.

And Simon strode past before Nora could intercept him.

"The spring pool had ice on top," he reported to Drew, who was standing by the fire, absently scratching Fleet behind the ears. "I broke it up, but we'll have to keep an eye on the situation. If that pool freezes solid, we'll have to go a lot farther to water the animals."

"Duly noted," Drew said. "Thanks."

Nora wandered over and plopped down on a chair.

She'd missed the perfect opportunity. Simon wouldn't pass below the bough again until it was time to leave. Her nerves would never last that long.

Beth must have realized the problem as well, for she hurried up to her brother. "Did you notice our decorations, Simon?"

Simon glanced around. He must have stopped by their cabin first, for his face was clean, his red-and-green-plaid shirt and rough trousers brushed free of the dirt he might otherwise have tracked in. Now he nodded slowly as if satisfied with the effort.

"Very nice, Beth," he said. "You might want to straighten that paper chain on the mantel."

Beth flushed. "Thank you so much for pointing that out. I'll be sure to fix it. I just wanted you to know that Nora put a great deal of effort into the decorations too."

Nora stood as Simon's gaze swung her way.

"Thank you, Nora," he said.

He didn't even look at the bough. She felt as if she'd pinned all her hopes on air.

"It was no trouble," she murmured.

But Beth wasn't finished. "She worked particularly hard on the one by the door," she said, her voice overly loud as if she wanted to make sure she had Simon's attention.

Nora watched as Simon looked toward the kissing bough. Did he understand its significance? Would he make use of it? Had her chance come at last?

Nearby, James elbowed John, who had just come out from the kitchen. John nodded, and he wandered to the bough, head cocked as he considered it.

"Excellent work," he pronounced. "Come see for yourself, Simon."

"I'm sure it's fine," Simon said. "Like everything Nora turns her hand to."

He thought she did good work? Warmth began to spread through her limbs.

"I don't know," James said, going to stand by John and staring up at the bough. "I think I spotted something loose, just there. See what I mean, Nora?"

Had she and Beth neglected to tie in an apple? She certainly wouldn't want it to fall on anyone's head!

Frowning, Nora went to join James. "Where?"

"There." He bent to put his head next to hers and pointed upward, as if to lead her gaze. Then he winked at her.

Oh, the darlings! Simon's brothers were trying to get him under the bough for her.

"I'm not quite certain what you mean, Brother James," she said, afraid to look at him or she'd give away the game.

John shook his head. "I see the problem, James. But she's too short to reach it. No offense meant, Nora."

Nora could barely nod in agreement.

"So are we," James pointed out. "Simon, why don't you come over and see if you can fix it?"

She heard Simon's sigh as he came to join them.

"Where?" he demanded, looking up.

James seized Simon's shoulders and pivoted him until he was directly under the bough and facing Nora. "Just about there," he said, releasing Simon and stepping back. "And really, brother, don't you have better things to do under a kissing bough than look for problems?"

Simon's head came down so fast she wondered that he didn't get dizzy. But when his gaze met Nora's, she was the one who felt as if she might swoon.

John cleared his throat. "If you like, I could show you how it's done."

"Go away, John," Simon said. Then he bent his head and kissed her.

Nora melted in Simon's arms, her lips soft beneath his. The room, his meddling brothers, everything faded away until there was only her. He felt as if his heart had been as frozen as the spring pool and was now thawing inch by inch. Once again, he didn't want to let her go.

But somewhere, far beyond his embrace, he heard a yip. Raising his head, he found Fleet dancing around, just beyond Nora, as if he thought it all a great game.

Nora's eyes had been closed. Now they opened wide, brimming with tears.

"Oh, Simon," she murmured.

Had the kiss been that bad? Or that good? Was he a fool for even wondering?

"Levi, you may need to fire that rifle," John said with a smile. "I think Simon forgot there are people waiting for dinner."

"I think Simon forgot there was such a thing as dinner," James agreed. He clapped Simon on the shoulder. "Come along, brother. You've done your duty, and right manfully too."

Nora was turning red, and Simon could have wished his brother to the moon at that moment, but he knew James and John were right. It was time for dinner.

He waited as Nora led Fleet to the rug and settled him down again. But as she started toward the table, he offered her his arm. "May I?"

Nora glanced at his arm, then up at him as if surprised by the gesture. Perhaps Beth was right. Perhaps he hadn't treated her with the respect and honor she deserved. That ended now.

As if she saw the determination in his gaze, Nora put her hand on his arm. "Yes, of course, Simon."

He led her to the table, and Levi made room for them on the bench.

"Nicely done," his youngest brother murmured, and Simon wasn't sure whether Levi meant escorting Nora to the table or finding the courage to kiss her.

James went so far as to wink at him as he took his seat next to his wife. Normally, his brother's jokes failed to amuse Simon, but he had to admit James and John had done him a favor this time. Without their goading, he might never have met Nora under the kissing bough.

She sat next to him now, her cheeks still pink and her generous mouth turned up in a smile. Everything and everyone seemed to please her, but that was nothing new. Nora had mastered the art of contentment. He wasn't sure how his kiss had affected her or what to do next.

His family had no such trouble. They engaged in lively conversation as soon as they sat down.

"We made excellent progress on the new acreage today," Drew said as they passed the smoked salmon and a bowl of potatoes in cheese sauce. "Simon has a vision for it. Tell them."

All gazes swung to him, Nora waiting expectantly. Simon swallowed the sip of water he'd taken. "I'm hoping to put in corn and beans," he explained. "Nora knows a type that can be planted early, so we'll have fresh produce all year."

Nora beamed at him.

His mother nodded. "Very wise. Your father always hoped we'd get to this point on the claims."

The salmon in his mouth seemed to taste sweeter.

"Always planning ahead, that's our Simon," John said. "Tell Nora about the town."

Simon swallowed again. "Pa had a dream of a town along the lake, a place where people could come together in fellowship, helping each other. James is planning to claim the land along the lake that will give us the necessary space for the town proper while we use the better land for farming."

James raised his wife's hand to his lips and pressed a kiss against the back. "I'm claiming it in Rina's name."

Rina smiled. "And that's why you built the schoolhouse so large, for all the children you hope will one day live here."

"That was Simon's idea," Drew said. "Of course, he wanted to build the hospital first, but we talked him out of it."

"I think it was the other way around," Simon reminded him. "You promised Catherine a place to ply her much-needed nursing skills. She had to convince you that a school should come first."

Catherine smiled at him. "And then you went and found the perfect place for the dispensary."

"Where?" Nora asked as if she hung on every word.

"There's a shelf of land above the lake," Simon said, "on James's claim. It's easy walking distance from Drew's cabin, and closest to the road from town so those needing help can reach it quickly by land or by water."

"An excellent location," Catherine said. "I can always count on you, Simon, to think things through."

Simon nodded, but he felt a frown forming. Why were they all going to such trouble to praise him? They were generally more likely to argue with him on every little matter.

"No doubt about it," John said, digging into his mashed potatoes. "This is going to be a Christmas to remember."

Ma beamed. "They all are, if you ask me."

Beth giggled. "What about the year everyone found rocks in their stockings?"

Ma laughed. "That was James, always the tease."

"He'd heard about how St. Nicholas is supposed to leave bad children coal instead of presents," Simon explained to Nora.

Nora gazed up at him. "But you couldn't have been bad, Simon."

His face felt hot, and he realized he was blushing. Blushing!

James shrugged. "None of us was really bad. That was the joke. I couldn't find coal, so I used basalt. Nearly tore a hole through Beth's stocking."

The others laughed.

"I remember Drew this one Christmas," Ma put in as she smiled fondly. "He was four when your father started the custom of presents in the stockings, and he was big for his age even then. He nearly ripped the stocking in half trying to get to the ball that was inside."

Drew chuckled.

"John, now," Ma said, warming to her theme, "was always one to share. James would gobble down the sweets, knowing John would give him some of his."

John grinned. "What are brothers for?"

"Wait until this Christmas Eve," James said, "and I'll remind you."

Beside him, Nora stirred. "What about Simon?"

Simon stiffened, waiting for Ma or one of the others to complain about his behavior. Had he criticized a gift? Rehung a stocking in a more orderly fashion?

"Ah, Simon," Ma said, favoring him with a smile. "I never had to worry about Simon. Whatever we managed to put in his stocking, he was always grateful for it, even in the lean years. He was a blessing to me and to his father."

His eyes burned, and Simon had to look away. Was that really how his mother saw him—as a blessing?

"Yes, dear Simon," James rhapsodized. "Such a treasure. It was only later that he began to resemble Mr. Dickens's Scrooge."

"James Tiberius Wallin!" Ma protested.

Simon knew who his brother meant. Beth had received a copy of *A Christmas Carol* last year in her stocking, and she had read it aloud to the family. Ebenezer Scrooge had struck Simon as a shrewd businessman who had allowed circumstances to bend his character. But surely that wasn't Simon's fate. Despite Ma's claim about him being a sweet child, he thought he'd always been the cynic. His character hadn't changed. That was precisely the problem. He didn't know if he could change it now.

All throughout dinner and afterward, his family continued their crusade to make him appear the most perfect of men. They either played games they knew he excelled at, like matching composers to tunes, or let him win. Finally, Ma wished them all good-night and went up to her bedchamber, and everyone made their goodbyes. Drew and Catherine, then James and Rina, took a turn under the kissing bough, and he could feel Beth watching him as he and Nora moved toward the door.

He paused for a moment, but Nora's face turned red, and she called Fleet and all but ran with the dog out the door. Simon followed them.

Lanterns bobbed across the clearing as Drew and Catherine, and James and Rina, headed for their homes. Nora walked beside Simon, her head turning as she kept an eye on Fleet, who was coursing along with his nose to the ground. "I liked hearing stories about your family."

So had he. "I'd heard most of them before," Simon admitted. "Except the one where Ma thought me a blessing. That surprised me."

Nora cast him a glance. "Why? You're very good to your family, and to me. I'm sure we're all grateful."

Perhaps they were. Perhaps he simply hadn't looked for the smiles or let the praise in before. He felt as if he'd been living in a shell that was gradually cracking open.

But what would he find when he emerged? And would that man have any more right to call himself Nora's husband?

Chapter Seventeen

Had the kissing bough worked? There was a subtle difference in the way Simon talked, the way he looked at her. But Nora was afraid to hope. Wishing for Simon's love was a little like wishing for the moon. Wouldn't it always remain out of reach?

Yet when she woke the next morning, she could still feel the sweet pressure of his lips against hers, the warmth of his embrace. At last she understood why her friends seemed so delighted to be kissed by the men they loved. That had truly been a momentous kiss. She'd wanted to press herself closer, inhale the clean scent of him, give herself over to the feeling of being wanted.

Perhaps he was falling in love with her. It was nearly Christmas, after all. A time when anything was possible.

She couldn't help the anticipation that was building that day—Christmas Adam, she recalled. And she wasn't the only one who felt it. Though the twenty-third was a Sunday, and she enjoyed another worship service with Simon and his family in the morning, the afternoon was spent in fevered preparation for the theatrical that evening. Some proper theatres refused to allow performances on the Lord's Day, Nora knew, but since the Savior's birth was the centerpiece of Rina's play, the schoolteacher had allowed the show to go on.

Those who were performing spent a great deal of time in the barn, and Simon had taken Fleet up to the new acreage to keep him out of the way. Her husband had seemed a little disappointed when she had refused his offer to join him and Fleet, but she needed time to finish his waistcoat. Mrs. Wallin had pitched in to hem the back piece while Nora sewed on the buttons—emerald-colored glass from the notions she had amassed over the years. The color would draw attention to his eyes and go with the suit she hoped to sew him next.

Mrs. Wallin had risen to fetch them each a cup of tea when she frowned out the window. "Someone's coming into the clearing. I believe it's your brother, Nora."

Nora joined her in peering out. A familiar cart rattled over the frozen ground and came to a stop, the horse's breath fogging the air. Her spirits plummeted. "I'll just go see what he wants."

Mrs. Wallin caught her arm. "It will be all right, Nora. He must care to have come out on such a cold day as this and a Sunday. Invite him inside before he's chilled clean through."

Charles certainly looked chilled when Nora ran out to greet him. He was shivering in his brown wool coat, and the fur hat that sat on his chestnut hair did not seem to be warming his blue-tinged skin.

"Charles," Nora greeted him with a nod. "What brings you out in this weather?"

He did not climb down. "Meredith insisted that I bring you your Christmas present." He waved a hand to the box in the back of the cart.

Nora stared at it, then at him. "You brought me a present?"

Charles drew himself up. "Certainly I brought you a present. You are my sister, my only living kin. It is bad enough we must be separated on the most holy of days, but I wasn't about to let you think we had forgotten you as easily as you've forgotten all we've done for you."

Guilt slithered across the stiff brown grass, drawing closer. She refused to look at it. "I haven't forgotten you or what you did for me, Charles. I simply have my own life now. Won't you come in and get warm?"

Charles glanced longingly at the main house. "Where is your husband?"

Nora bit back a smile. "Simon is out at the moment. His mother has tea ready."

That moved him to descend. One of the men in the play, a Mr. Borden, came out of the barn just then. Seeing Nora, he hurried to help with the horse. He wore the gold paper crown Beth had made for him, and Charles frowned at him before Nora led her brother into the cabin, her present in her arms.

Mrs. Wallin welcomed him, took his coat, wrapped him in a quilt by the fire and brought him a cup of tea.

"Thank you," he said before blowing steam off the brew. "I grew up where it snowed a great deal, but this cold cuts to the bone." He took a sip and seemed to melt a little in the chair.

"It doesn't snow every year here," Mrs. Wallin acknowledged. "But I remember the winter of 1860. Drifts as high as the eaves and Seattle down to its last barrel of flour."

Charles stared at her. "My word. Do you think it will get that bad this year?"

"Not if the good Lord wills," Mrs. Wallin said. She turned to Nora. "Do you want to open your brother's present before he leaves, dear?"

She had to admit to some curiosity. The most she'd ever received from Charles had been a packet of needles, and those were only so she could finish sewing up a shirt he'd needed. Going to the box, she removed the string that held it shut and pulled off the lid.

What she saw inside momentarily stilled her hands. Then she reached in and drew out a hat. It was tall, black brushed velvet, with a black satin band and a black net veil, and two ravens clung to the crown. Their glittering black eyes seemed to gaze back at her, surrounded by shiny black feathers.

"Did someone die?" Mrs. Wallin asked, her hand flying to the bodice of her green wool gown.

Charles drew himself up. "Meredith says black is considered quite sophisticated."

Nora slipped the hideous hat back in the box. "Very kind of you both, Charles. I'm sure I'll find an occasion to wear it."

Mrs. Wallin did not look nearly so certain.

Charles was watching Nora. "You are determined to stay out here in the wilderness, then?"

Simon's mother bristled, but Nora nodded. "Yes, Charles. I like it here."

As Mrs. Wallin's smile reappeared, Charles slumped. "A shame. Meredith was hoping I could persuade you to come for Christmas dinner at least. You could bring your husband if you feel you must."

"I hoped to spend Christmas here," Nora said. "I'm sure you and Meredith will get on fine without me."

Charles sighed. "She cries every day you are gone. It is most discouraging."

Meredith cried? Nora couldn't believe that. "Perhaps you should hire her a maid."

"We have brought on a housekeeper and a maid," Charles told her. "But no one can replace your company, Nora." He glanced up, his face as tight as the day he'd come to tell her she must move in with him and Meredith. "Please, won't you come home?"

She felt his pain, his bewilderment. It seemed he did long for her company. How extraordinary! If she went with him, and he truly was determined to treat her like a sister and not a servant, she might sleep as late as she wanted, have as many pretty gowns as she pleased, give Meredith's ugly hat to the poor, if she could find one desperate enough to wear it.

Yet she had a chance for something more here, and she could not convince herself to give it up. She had Britta and Fleet, Beth and Mrs. Wallin, John and Levi, Simon's other brothers and their wives. And maybe, just maybe, she might have Simon as a true husband.

"Why don't you stay tonight, Charles?" she suggested. "The school is hosting a theatrical. You could go back to Seattle on Christmas Eve."

He shook his head. "No, no, I must return, or Meredith will worry. Are you certain you can't join me?"

The guilt was rearing up again, reaching for her. She dodged it. "After Christmas, Charles," she promised. "I'll come to visit the day after Christmas. You will have to be contented with that."

Charles smiled, as if she had given him a pardon from prison. "Wonderful. I know Meredith will be delighted to have you with us again. You must promise to stay for dinner. We'll have a friend over. Nothing fancy, just something to let you know you are always welcome."

A dinner party seemed a bit excessive, but she agreed, and he left shortly thereafter.

"What will you do with that?" Mrs. Wallin asked, eyeing the hatbox.

Nora scooped it up. "I'll take it to the cabin so it doesn't sour anyone's appetite. I'll be right back."

The rest of the day sped by, and before Nora knew it, others began arriving at Wallin Landing. Mr. and Mrs. Paul came first, their heads down and glances darting as if they somehow expected to be evicted. They relaxed when they saw Nora and asked after Britta. Knowing the role the cow must play in the theatrical, Nora promised to reintroduce them later.

Thomas came next. He'd managed to find shoes for his long feet, but the way he kept grimacing as he walked told Nora they didn't fit him well. Mrs. Wallin fed him stew and biscuits and set him and Mr. Paul to work with John ferrying the chairs and benches from the house to the barn as Nora slipped away to her cabin to change.

As costume designer, she'd been privy to more scenes than the other members of the family who were not involved, but she had to own she was excited to see the entire production. "But you cannot come," she told Fleet. "I never had a chance to see how you'd fit in the script."

Fleet turned and gave her his back as if thoroughly put out with her.

Simon came in just as she was fastening her mother's pearls about her neck in front of the mirror. She could see the frown on his handsome face as he looked her way.

"What are you wearing?" he asked.

Nora spread her satin skirts. It was her favorite dress, for all someone else had sewn it for her. The scoop neck and puffed sleeves graced the fitted bodice, and the full skirts swung as she walked. What made the simple style elegant was the material—matte silver satin printed with pink, rose and purple butterflies.

"It's a dinner dress," she told Simon. "My parents always dressed before going to the theatre."

He shook his head with a smile. "It's a school play in a barn, Nora."

"And no acting troupe ever worked harder," she insisted. "I think we should honor them with our best too."

He nodded. "Very well. I'll meet you at the main house shortly."

Disappointment bit at her. How fine it would have been to stroll through the moonlight on Simon's arm. Warmer too. As Christmas approached, the nights had dipped below freezing. But she offered him a smile before throwing her cloak about her shoulders and leaving.

A portly man, a sheen of perspiration on his balding head, was waiting with Mrs. Wallin on the boardwalk in front of the main cabin. His red flannel shirt and tweed trousers were of good material, but stains marred them. He looked Nora up and down and tipped his double chins in her direction.

"We getting a new schoolmarm now that Miss Fosgrave went and married one of your brood?" he asked Mrs. Wallin.

Simon's mother took a step away from him. "Rina is perfectly capable of being a teacher and a wife too. Nora, dear, this is Mr. Rankin, Scout's father. Nora is Simon's wife."

He raised bushy brows. "Simon got married? You either have more patience than anyone I know, little lady, or a whale of a dowry." He laughed at his own joke.

"He's Thomas's father?" Nora murmured to Mrs. Wallin.

"Yes," she said, "as improbable as that might sound. Pay him no mind, dear. He's more bluster than bite."

John came out of the house then, dressed in his brown suit, and offered his mother his arm. "May I have the honor of escorting the loveliest lady in our family to the theatre?"

His mother laughed as she took his arm. "You scamp."

Mr. Rankin advanced on Nora. "I'll walk you over, new Mrs. Wallin."

Everything in her recoiled. "I'll wait for Simon."

"As you should." Mrs. Wallin affixed Mr. Rankin with such a stern look he shifted on his feet a moment before following her and John away from the house.

Nora stood on the boardwalk, alone.

The night felt colder, darker. Why? She'd been alone since she'd left Lowell nearly a year ago. In truth, she'd been alone even with her parents and Charles and Meredith. She should be used to it by now.

A movement on the edge of the woods caught her eye. Simon strode toward her. He'd put on his wedding suit, the white shirt gleaming in the lights from the house. His only concession to the weather was a pair of heavy-soled boots that clumped on the planks as he came to her side.

He bowed. "Worthy of escorting you, Mrs. Wallin?"

"Yes, of course, Simon," Nora said, clasping her hands together to keep them from trembling. "I am the one honored."

He drew her away from the house, walking with her to the barn.

"Your dog wanted out," Simon said.

Nora nodded. "He'll stay close to the clearing. He always does."

Simon chuckled. "I'd say he was well trained, but I doubt that's the case."

She didn't think it was so much training as feeling. The way Fleet behaved around Simon, the dog had evidently decided her husband was the leader of the pack and therefore must be followed.

Still, she caught no sign of Fleet as they crossed the clearing. The clouds scudded out of the way to reveal stars across the deep expanse of sky. Nora sighed, feeling as if she floated among them.

"Remember," Simon said, opening the door for her, "it's just a school play in a barn."

But Nora knew he was wrong.

Her hand in his, she went to sit behind Mrs. Wallin and John. The chairs and the benches from the house crowded so close on the threshing floor that her shoulder brushed Simon's chest. Mr. Paul and his wife were in the front row, and Mr. Rankin had seated himself next to Rina, who was none too pleased with his presence if the tap of her slipper under her lavender skirts was any indication.

"Should there be more lights?" Simon murmured to Nora, glancing up at the lantern hanging near the door. Positioned as it was, it left most of the barn in shadow. The presence of so many people made the space toasty, encouraging Nora to slip the cloak off her shoulders.

"Shh," she cautioned Simon as a glow sprang to life from the haymow. The lantern brightened to reveal Beth standing on the top rung of the ladder, her golden hair cascading over her white linen gown. The blue braid around the neck made her eyes shine.

"I am Gabriel, Angel to the Lord Most High," she announced, her clear voice ringing to the rafters. "I have come to tell you of things revealed long ago. Listen to me, and marvel."

Marvel, his sister said. Beside him, Nora seemed ready to do just that. Though the audience was largely in darkness, Simon could see her craning her neck to watch Beth up on the ladder. It was a nice perch for an angel, he had to admit, but had no one considered what would happen if a spark from that lamp fell on the hay? They could lose the bulk of their animals' food for winter.

"There was a man named Joseph, pledged to be married to a virgin named Mary," Beth recited, oblivious to the danger. Another light appeared, this one at the back of the barn, where the rear door gave out into the forest. Drew and Catherine came forward, dressed in long robes with scarves on their heads. Drew had a staff in one hand, his other arm about Catherine's shoulders, each step careful and kind as they walked farther into the barn.

"She was with child through the Holy Spirit," Beth continued. "When the time came for her to give birth, she wrapped her son in swaddling clothes and laid him in the manger, for there was no room for them at the inn."

Catherine and Drew stopped below Beth and settled onto the straw of one of the stalls, where Beth's old doll lay in the manger, glass eyes gleaming in the light. Britta put her head over the stall and let out a soft "Moo." From beyond her, the oxen lowed in response.

"They're singing to the baby," Nora murmured, her own eyes shining.

It did indeed seem that way. Then the cow pulled back to go down on her only knee as if genuflecting to the babe in the manger. How had they managed to train her to do that? Or could it be she too felt the weight of the moment?

Simon shook his head. It was just a play and a makeshift one at that. Despite Nora's clever work with a needle, he recognized Drew's robe as his mother's favorite tablecloth, Catherine's headdress as the doily Beth had sewn for her dressing table. There was nothing amazing about any of it.

So why did he feel awed?

Drew dimmed his light, putting the focus back on Beth.

"But there were others who needed to hear the news of the baby's birth," she said.

In the center of the barn, a light blossomed, low and dancing, as if coming from a campfire. Levi and James stood looking at each other. They too wore long robes, simple, well-used. Lancelot and Percival watched from their stalls as if fascinated.

"We are but poor shepherds," Levi said, a little woodenly, his gaze darting about as if he tried to see the audience beyond the light. "Watching our flocks by night. We are the lowest of the low, the ones forgotten, left behind. There is no call to include such as we in the blessing of Israel."

At the words, Simon heard Nora suck in a breath. Sometimes she sounded as if she had been made to feel the lowest of the low. Was she thinking of her brother and sister-in-law? Her parents?

Suddenly, James clutched his chest with one hand and pointed a trembling finger to Beth with the other.

Levi looked up, arrested. "What's that?" His voice trembled.

"Fear not," Beth told them, "for I bring you glad tidings of great joy, which shall be to all people, great and small. Today in the City of David your Savior has been born. You will find him lying in a manger."

Levi looked at James. "We must go and see what has been told to us."

Above them, Beth raised her hands until the light brightened the whole barn. "Glory to God in the highest, and on earth peace to those on whom His favor rests."

Levi and James crossed to Drew and Catherine's sides and knelt with their heads bowed in honor of the babe.

"Led by the Light that had come into the world," Beth continued, "wise men traveled far to see the Holy child."

The door behind them opened, sending an icy blast whipping through the barn. Straw whirled like spun gold as three kings moved past with stately tread.

"From my great wealth I bring gold for His crown," said the first, and Simon recognized the towering figure as Mr. Hennessy, the oldest, largest and most determined student at the Lake Union School.

"From my deep wisdom, I bring frankincense to perfume His path," said the second with a decidedly Irish accent, and Simon knew it must be Mr. Borden, who had recently joined the school.

The last king came forward and knelt humbly beside the shepherds. "From my heart," Scout said, his voice heavy with emotion, "I bring myrrh for the wounds we will inflict upon Him. And I ask His mercy on all who call upon His name."

His words hung in the air a moment, and Simon heard the animals shifting in their stalls, as if even they were listening. *I ask mercy...* Mercy for mistakes, flaws, problems. Mercy for things undone, words unsaid. Was such mercy available to him?

Another movement caught his eye. The three kings must have left the door open just enough, for Fleet entered the barn. Undeterred by the audience, he moved with steps as firm as any great actor, approaching the manger. Seeing the baby there, he lowered himself to the straw, the king of dogs acknowledging One greater than he.

Nora caught her breath again.

Then Beth's voice rang out. "And He shall be called King of Kings and Prince of Peace, and of His kingdom there will be no end."

"Amen and amen," chorused the kings and the shepherds.

Fleet raised his head to howl, the sound echoing through the barn. Gooseflesh rose on Simon's arms.

Above him, Beth smiled. "Everyone join me in praise." She lifted her head as if gazing up into the sky.

"Silent night, holy night..."

Beside him, Nora lifted her voice, soft and sweet.

"All is calm, all is bright."

Now the others joined in as well, voices blending.

"Round yon virgin mother and child

"Holy infant so tender and mild

"Sleep in heavenly peace

"Sleep in heavenly peace."

Something inside him swelled with the sound. Was peace possible for someone like him?

Was love?

He glanced at Nora, whose face, turned up toward the angel, was rapturous in the light. She saw a vision from the past, a Savior come as a child. With her beside him, he saw it too, felt it deep down.

How could he not love her? She was gentle, kind, endlessly cheerful. She was all he'd need.

And he knew he had to find a way to prove it to her.

Chapter Eighteen

Mind and heart full, Simon followed his family back to the main house after the play. Sleet was pelting the clearing, and most of the cast members lifted their finery out of the icy puddles as they scampered across the ground. Mr. Paul, Drew, James and John were busy carrying the chairs and benches back to the house. Beside Simon, Nora hummed the last few bars of "Silent Night," her silvery skirts swaying below her cloak.

The house certainly wasn't silent. Rina and John were praising the actors while Ma served up generous slices of her famous apple bread and spiced apple cider she'd kept simmering on the stove. Beth, still dressed in her flowing white robe, beamed at them all, and even Mr. Hennessy was flushed with happiness.

Nora sat beside Simon at the table and leaned her head against his shoulder. "What a lovely evening."

Simon's arm slipped around her waist. He told himself it was only for stability. With her leaning so close, they might easily topple the old wood bench. But there was something right and good about holding her this way.

"You made a marvelous Mary," John was telling Catherine, who was sitting next to Drew across from them.

She smiled at his older brother. "That's because I was paired with a magnificent Joseph."

Drew snorted, then popped a piece of apple bread into his mouth.

Standing near the head of the table, Rina clapped her hands. "Attention! May I have everyone's attention, please?"

Voices quieted. Gazes turned her way. Though she was a schoolteacher, Simon knew that at least some of her considerable presence came from being brought up to believe she would one day rule a small European nation.

As Nora snuggled closer, Rina nodded to them all. "Thank you. I just wanted to say how proud I am of our thespians this evening. You recited your lines accurately and with great feeling. You brought your audience with you into the scene. No seasoned actor or actress could have done better. I give each of you a grade of excellent for your work."

"Huzzah!" Mr. Borden cried, raising a fist into the air.

"Huzzah!" James and John chorused.

Rina smiled. "Congratulations on your accomplishments. Enjoy your time off for Christmas. Class will resume the first Monday after New Year's. Merry Christmas to you all."

"Merry Christmas, ma'am," Mr. Borden declared.

Mr. Hennessy went one further. He lumbered up to Rina and enfolded her in a hug that lifted her off her feet.

James strolled over and tapped him on the shoulder. "My turn," he said as Mr. Hennessy lowered her to the floor. The giant smiled and hurried back to his cider.

Simon watched as James murmured something to

Rina, and she blushed and smiled. Across the table, Drew and Catherine likewise had their heads together. Ma and Mrs. Paul were discussing how she kept the apples so moist in her bread. Levi, John and Scout were arguing over sleeping arrangements, for the boy and his father, like the rest of their guests, would be spending the night. Mr. Paul and Mr. Rankin were joking with each other, Scout's usually quarrelsome father looking decidedly happy for a change.

Everyone seemed so contented. Simon let the feeling bathe him, lifting his spirits. But his enjoyment of the moment was nothing compared to the feeling of holding Nora. He shifted her closer, and she glanced up, looking surprised. All he could do was smile at her. As if she understood things were changing between them, her smile blossomed.

She was right. It was a lovely night.

The party broke up an hour later. Levi asked for his help to rearrange the pallets in the loft for him, Scout and Mr. Rankin. Mr. and Mrs. Paul would be sleeping in Ma's bed while she bunked with Beth. When Simon came back downstairs, Nora was nowhere in sight. Disappointment threatened his good mood, but he shook it off. Likely, she'd been worried about the dog and gone to check on him. He'd find them both warming themselves before the fire in the cabin.

His mother and Beth were putting away the last of the bread as he strode for the door.

"Good night, Simon," his mother called.

"Sweet dreams," Beth added.

"You too," Simon said before leaving.

And he thought he might just have sweet dreams that night. Always before, he had struggled to find the joy his family so easily grasped. Sometimes he felt as if he lived at the bottom of a well, with only glimmers of light reaching down into the dark shaft.

Then he'd met Nora. When she was near, it was easier to relax, to think of possibilities, to see the light. Beth might have played the angel tonight, but Nora was the star in his Christmas. He could only be thankful she had chosen him to wed.

When he opened the door of the cabin, the fire was glowing in the hearth. Fleet raised his head from his blanket on the floor, his tail waving in welcome. Simon glanced up at the loft and smiled.

"Already in bed?" he called up.

Mr. Hennessy's head popped into the opening. "Just about."

Simon shoved the door shut behind him and strode into the house. "What are you doing here?"

Hennessy's meaty grin faded. "Mrs. Nora said I could stay here. There wasn't room for me at the big house."

Nor at Drew and Catherine's, Simon realized. And Mr. Borden was staying with James and Rina. "Where's Nora?"

Hennessy frowned. "I thought she was with you. She's your wife, isn't she?"

Not in the ways that mattered. But Hennessy had no way of knowing that.

Simon turned for the door. "Gather your things. There's a better place for you to sleep. I'll be back for you shortly."

With a yip, Fleet leaped to his feet to follow.

Simon's pulse was unnaturally rapid as he stalked back to the main house, Fleet running along beside him. One of the things everyone loved about Nora was her kindness, her willingness to put others first. But by putting them first, she put herself last. She seemed to think that was her lot, but he was no longer willing to see her treated so shabbily.

"She deserves better," he told Fleet, who bobbed his head as if agreeing wholeheartedly.

Ma was just heading for the stairs when Simon poked his head in the door.

"Tell Nora to come home," he called.

His mother paused to look back at him. "Nora isn't here. She left with Drew and Catherine."

Simon thanked her and headed across the clearing. Fleet ran ahead, stopping expectantly at the door of the barn, but Simon called him to follow to the edge of the clearing, where Drew's cabin lay. He couldn't imagine where they'd put Nora in his older brother's cozy cabin. Drew already had plans to enlarge the house next spring after the baby was born.

But when Drew answered Simon's rap on the door, his brother assured him they had not seen Nora.

Worry sat like an itch on his skin, but he made himself trek to James's cabin, only to receive the same answer.

"Are you certain she did not stay with your mother and Beth?" Rina asked, peering over James's shoulder, her hair down for the night.

"Positive," Simon said, Fleet sniffing about his feet.

James hitched up the suspender that had been hanging over one shoulder. "I'll come with you."

"No," Simon said. "If I don't find her, I'll come back for help."

He set off through the forest once more. Fleet crowded close, as if he thought Simon needed his support. Strange to say, but he did. Where could she be? How had she fared in the sleet? The icy drops felt like darts against his face, chilling him even in his wool suit.

Please, Lord, keep her safe.

A peace slipped over him, a surety, completely out of place with the circumstances. Nora was clever, and she knew the area now. He just had to find her and bring her home. Funny how the Lord seemed closer now that Simon had opened himself up to listen.

He tried the schoolhouse next, but the classroom and teacher's quarters beyond were dark and empty. That left one other building on the property. Once again, Fleet ran ahead of him to the barn door and sat, waiting for him to catch up.

"Sorry I was so slow," he told the dog, and he didn't just mean his footsteps.

Britta mooed a welcome as he slid open the door. With the theatrical over, the barn had been returned to its normal configuration, and he took a few steps into the pitch blackness. Chickens clucked a scold at being interrupted. The goats, horses and oxen shifted in their stalls.

"Nora?" he called, afraid to hear silence in answer.

"Yes, Simon?"

Something moved in the loft. Going to the wall, where he knew a lantern and flint were stored, he lit the light and raised it.

Nora peered down at him from the haymow.

Simon shook his head. "What are you doing up there?"

She blinked. With her hair tumbled about her and straw sticking in the tresses like feathers, she looked a bit like an owl awakened from its sleep.

"Well," she said, "Mr. Hennessy needed a place to sleep."

"And you had to give him your place." How could he not admire her kindness?

She nodded. "Yes, of course, Simon. I knew you were concerned about the hay, and I am certainly smaller than Mr. Hennessy, so I would likely do it less damage."

She had a point. As usual. Simon lowered the lantern. "Very considerate of you. But there was no need. Hennessy can sleep in the schoolroom—there's a teacher's quarters behind. Rina hasn't used it since she married James."

"Oh," she said. "Well, I suppose that will do. I'm sorry if I inconvenienced you."

Indeed she inconvenienced him. As well as shook him up, frustrated him and made him see that the world could be a brighter place. "No need to apologize. I'm just glad you're all right. Come back to the cabin, and I'll send Hennessy to the school."

But Nora didn't move.

Simon sighed. "What is it, Nora? Aren't the teacher's quarters good enough for Hennessy? You don't have to be given the worst portion because that's all your family would allow. You deserve better."

"That's not it." Her head came up, making the straw in her dark tresses stand at attention. "I was very proud of myself for climbing the ladder in my dinner dress, but I haven't changed out of it yet, and I'm not entirely sure I can get down."

"Let me help you." He hung the lantern from a hook, then climbed the ladder until his face drew level with hers. Those eyes brushed his soul, drew him in, made him feel entirely unworthy.

"Thank you, Simon," she said.

Any lingering frustration melted away. He reached

out a hand and touched her cheek, her skin like satin under his fingers.

"I should thank you," he said. "I don't think like you do, Nora, but I find myself wishing I did. You see so much wonder in the world."

"Because there is so much wonder to see." Her smile was as soft as a caress. "Can you count the number of stars in the sky? Have you heard a baby laugh? It's simply amazing!"

Gazing at her, he wanted so badly to agree. "You are amazing."

The red rose in her cheeks. "Thank you, Simon."

It was the work of a moment to take the last step, lean in and kiss her. And in that kiss he knew they might have a chance at a true marriage, if only he could open his heart all the way and let her in.

Oh, that kiss held so much—hope, joy, wonder. Nora was still trembling from it when she woke the next morning.

Please, oh please, Lord! Keep working Your will!

There she went again, praying for herself. Yet she knew the prayer was for more than her own happiness. It was for Simon's as well. Surely the Lord would honor that.

Christmas Eve had dawned to a cold fog that chilled Nora through her cloak as she trudged down the path of frozen mud to the barn, Fleet trotting at her heels. Simon had left earlier, as usual. Nora pulled the barn door open and spotted Beth gathering eggs.

"You'll have to wait outside," Nora told Fleet, knowing the dog's presence might frighten the chickens. She fluttered her fingers at him, and he happily dashed off across the clearing.

"Thanks," Beth said, coming out of the chicken roost, basket on one arm. Her blue eyes twinkled. "Well? Are you ready for Christmas?"

Nora nodded as she sat to milk Britta. The cow's udder was warm under her hand. "I just need a little time to stitch the two pieces of Simon's waistcoat together."

"I don't know how much time you'll have today," Beth confided, twitching her gingham skirts so her pink flannel petticoat peeked out beneath. "We have to bring in the Yule log."

Nora was about to ask her to explain the custom when the door opened and Simon strode in.

"I'll finish for you, Nora. Go and have some breakfast."

Nora would have preferred to stay with him, but Beth skipped to the door. "Oh, good. Come on, Nora. You wanted some time to yourself."

Nora hurried after Beth before he could ask her why she wanted to be alone.

She managed to finish his waistcoat and return to the main house to be met by the tantalizing smell of spiced cider, thick with cinnamon, drifting from the kitchen. Their guests, Levi, Beth and John crowded around the table. Nora helped Mrs. Wallin finish serving them breakfast. Simon stopped by only long enough to leave the milk bucket before slipping out again.

A little while later Nora stood with his mother and siblings on the porch to wave goodbye as the Pauls and the Rankins set off for their respective homes.

Mr. Hennessy pumped her hand. "You're a fine lady,

Mrs. Simon. You made me look like a king in that costume."

"Me too," Mr. Borden put in, smiling to reveal his crooked teeth. "If that lad gives you any trouble, you just send him to me, and I'll be the making of him."

"Simon is a fine husband," Nora assured him as they took their leave.

"Are things going a little better, then?" Mrs. Wallin asked her as they went back into the house.

"Yes," Nora said, then hid a smile as she realized she was being as economical in her word choice as Simon.

"Good," his mother said, heading for the kitchen, where Nora knew a pile of dishes waited. "I thought Simon just needed the right encouragement. Where did he head off to, by the way?"

Nora made sure Fleet was settled in his favorite spot looking into the kitchen, then followed Mrs. Wallin to the washtub, where John was even now pouring in steaming water from the kettle.

"Simon is busy for the moment," she told them. "I'm sure he'll be along shortly."

John frowned, lowering the empty kettle as his mother began slipping the dishes in to soak. "Busy? Why would he be busy? We never work alone at logging or clearing, and it's Christmas Eve."

Mrs. Wallin nodded. "Go fetch him, John. We should be going for the Yule log shortly."

John started past, but Nora caught his arm. "I wish you wouldn't. He must have something very important to do to leave us today."

John's eyes, green like his mother's, were kind as he looked at her. "There is nothing more important than family on Christmas Eve, Nora. I'll bring him back for you."

She released him, but she couldn't help following him to the door. Neither could Fleet. John also collected Levi and Beth, who had been playing chess by the fire, and they put on their winter coats and swept out into the clearing, calling Simon's name. Drew and Catherine and James and Rina were coming into the clearing from their cabins, and they joined in as well, with Fleet howling an accompaniment. Levi was just heading for the rifle when Simon poked his head out the barn door.

"There you are," his mother called. "We're ready to go for the Yule log."

"Hurry or *Yule* miss out," John called.

Beth groaned at the pun.

James smacked his younger brother on the shoulder. "*Yule* have to do better than that if you want to keep up with me."

"Enough," Drew ordered. "*Yule* have everyone in stitches."

Despite herself, Nora giggled.

"You don't need me," Simon said, but he took a step out of the barn and shut the door carefully behind him. "I have work to do here."

Beth wagged a finger at him. "Oh, no, you don't. You know the rules. No extra work on Christmas Eve or Christmas Day."

Nora could see the struggle in him, one foot forward as if he longed to be part of the fun, the other back as if his tasks called to him even now. Perhaps all he needed was encouragement, like his mother had said.

"I'd love for you to join us, Simon," Nora called.

Something softened in his face. "Give me a moment,"

he said, and he turned and slipped into the barn once more. Levi went to fetch the big saw, while James and John each took up an ax.

"Thank you, Nora," Mrs. Wallin murmured, giving her arm a squeeze. "You are good for him."

Oh, how she hoped that was true!

Simon came out a moment later, shrugging into his coat, and they all joined together to troop through the woods. The fog was lifting, leaving the trees limed with frost. Their voices echoed in the stillness.

Simon and Nora fell in step behind the family and Fleet.

"Thank you," she said.

He started, then shook himself. "It was no trouble," he assured her.

It might not have been trouble, but for a moment she had a feeling he'd expected her to thank him for something else. What was he up to in the barn?

As if he saw questions in her eyes he didn't want to answer, he hurried on. "Did Ma or Beth explain about the Yule log?"

"I hadn't had a chance," his mother said. "You tell the tale, Simon."

He nodded. "We've gone to bring in the Yule log for as long as I can remember. Part of Ma's family came from England. They always brought in the Yule log on Christmas Eve, so she wanted to continue the tradition in her family."

"John has been searching for the perfect tree," Mrs. Wallin added. "We need a log that's small enough to fit in the fireplace but big enough to burn from Christmas to New Year's."

Ahead, John called out to the family, and everyone

joined him around a thick fir. Two deep V's had been cut near the base, one on either side, and wedges were stuck in one of the openings. Now Levi jogged forward, a long saw bouncing over one shoulder.

Drew stepped up and took one of the handles. "Simon?" he called. "Lend a hand."

Once more Simon started, glancing around as if he thought someone else might carry the same name. Then pink stained the ridge of his cheeks.

"Go on," Nora urged. "I'll be fine."

"Watch Fleet," he said, then went to take up the other side of the saw.

Mrs. Wallin moved up next to Nora. "It's an honor to be the one to chop down the tree. Simon generally lets his younger brothers have a turn, but I'm glad Drew insisted on him this year."

So was Nora. Simon's head was high, his grip firm. A light shone in his eyes, as if he knew this was his right. She could scarcely take her eyes off him.

"Let's bring her down," Drew said.

Nora knelt and wrapped her arms around Fleet's big chest, her gloved hands deep in his fur. He shifted as if annoyed by her grip, but she wasn't about to let him go until that tree was down.

The blade bit into the thick trunk as Simon shoved and Drew pulled. Back and forth, back and forth they went, every cut inching deeper. There was a rhythm to it, as if each brother knew what to expect of the other and relied on his skill to keep the big saw moving. Muscles bulged under Simon's coat. Sweat beaded his brow. The scent of sap tickled Nora's nose as the song of the saw echoed through the woods.

Then Simon and Drew stopped.

"She's coming down!" John cried.

Nora flinched, but this time, the tree toppled away from her, bouncing as it hit the ground. The earth trembled.

All the Wallin ladies applauded. Nora released Fleet to rise and join them, her eyes on Simon. He was strong and sure and so very capable. She pressed her fingers to her lips as he looked her way. She wanted to hold him, tell him how magnificent he was.

Her husband.

Could it really be? Could Christmas finally break through the last of his reserve and allow them to forge a true marriage?

Chapter Nineteen

John and James moved in, axes swinging, to chop the branches from the trunk. Simon had to force himself to take his eyes off Nora to help. Her look was so bright, her gaze so appreciative, that he wanted to puff his chest out with pride and crow like a rooster.

He'd spent part of the night silently laying out his plan to show her how much he had come to admire her. It seemed odd to be courting a woman he'd already married, yet he could think of his plan in no other way. And when it came to courting, he hadn't had a lot of experience.

Until Asa Mercer had brought brides to Seattle, there had been precious few women to woo, even if Simon had had the time or interest. He'd seen Drew's and James's courtships, of course, but he was fairly sure neither could be counted as traditional. Levi had kidnapped Catherine to bring a nurse to help Ma and a bride for Drew. Rina and James had come together after being forced to survive in the wilderness alone.

He knew Beth looked to his father's books for examples of romance. But the romances in *The Last of the*

Mohicans and *The Courtship of Miles Standish* had not turned out particularly well. So, when it came to showing Nora he wanted to make theirs a true marriage, he had remarkably little to go by.

Still, in the weeks they had been married, he felt as if he had come to know her fairly well. She was kind, loyal, sweet and optimistic. She shared her love with everyone and anyone, from a lost dog to a man seeking shelter for the night. Surely that sort of kindness was what she might hope for in someone who loved her.

So he had laid out a set of tasks designed to please her. He'd been hard at work at them in the barn that morning when his family had interrupted. And her beseeching look had told him it was better to capitulate and please her now than hold her off until later.

But that didn't mean he was going to abandon his plan. He'd simply have to bide his time.

Now Nora joined his mother, Beth and his sisters-in-law in clearing away the broken branches around the tree trunk. John and Levi would come out later to hack the branches into firewood. For the moment, his youngest brothers were busy wrapping ropes about the trunk, securing it to a harness that John had made and brought out earlier.

Drew stepped back and eyed their handiwork.

"Time to bring it home," he declared.

Nora looked up with a puzzled frown. "Shouldn't we have brought the oxen?"

"We don't use oxen to bring in the Yule log," his mother explained. "We bring it in by our own hands."

Nora's eyes widened.

Drew started. Taking the thickest rope over his shoulder, he gripped it with both hands and leaned against it. Simon heard someone, likely Catherine, suck in a breath as his muscles bunched. Like a gladiator of old, his brother dragged the log forward on the wet ground.

"Clear the path for him," Ma ordered, bending to push aside the brush. Beth rolled stones out of the way, and Catherine and Rina helped.

Aware of Nora's eyes on him, Simon took up the rope behind his brother.

"Together," he said, digging in his toes.

The log moved faster.

Nora applauded.

Oh, but he could get used to her attentions. She made him feel as if he were the most clever, the strongest, the best of his brothers, when he knew he was anything but. For her, though, he wanted to be that perfect man, that example she could look at with pride. He put his back into the rope and pulled harder.

One by one, James, John and Levi joined in, until the five of them were walking at an almost normal pace. The massive log followed behind, like a cow on a lead. Nora's eyes were shining as Simon passed her, her hands clasped together as if she could scarcely contain her delight in him.

That was the look he craved. Her acceptance, joy.

As they came out into the clearing, his mother and sister hurried ahead to open the door to the house. Drew and Simon climbed the steps, then bent to lift the head of the log. His other brothers shoved until the log was flat on the boardwalk, pointing toward the open door.

His mother and Beth came out of the house then, bearing cups of hot cider.

"God rest ye merry, gentlemen," Ma began to sing in her warm alto.

Beth took up the song as she helped distribute the cups. Then the family joined in.

"O tidings of comfort and joy," Simon sang, "comfort and joy. O tidings of comfort and joy."

Until he'd met Nora, he'd never known true comfort or joy. Now he felt as if anything were possible. He raised his cup in toast, his gaze brushing Nora's as he did so. Her smile was warmer than the heated tin in his hand.

His family raised their cups as well before drinking deep.

But Simon's gaze remained on Nora, and once again hope gathered in his heart.

Nora helped the Wallins get the log the rest of the way into the house and hearth, where it filled the stone opening. Her heart felt just as full. With everything he'd done, Simon had looked to her, as if determined to make her feel part of the family. It was almost as if her acceptance was important to him. He made her want to hope.

Yet hope was dangerous. What if she'd misunderstood as she'd misunderstood Mr. Winnower's attentions back in Lowell? What if it was only the spirit of Christmas that motivated him, not a particular appreciation for her? She'd never inspired such looks before. Could she believe them now?

"I have the brand," Beth announced, hurrying to bring a porcelain box to the hearth. She opened the lid to reveal a partly blackened shard of wood. Pulling out the stump, she held it in the lamp's flame until it glowed red and fire danced on the tip.

"Nora?" she asked, offering her the tiny torch. "Would you like to light the log?"

Nora's gaze darted from one smiling face to the other. "Me?" She looked to Simon, who nodded agreement.

Beth's smile deepened. "You. Simon can show you how."

Fingers trembling, Nora accepted the flaming stump.

"It's the remaining piece from last year," John explained as Nora turned to the Yule log.

The whole thing looked so huge. How could one little flame ignite it?

Simon came up behind her, put his arms around her, his hands cupping hers. "You just need to find a bit of dry bark," he murmured in her ear. "That should start it burning."

Having him so close, she was the one feeling warm. It was hard to concentrate, but she hunted over the log until she found a patch of bark that must have been sheltered by a branch, for it was dry and rougher than usual. With Simon's hands holding hers, she laid the brand against the bark and watched as the spark ignited and spread.

Was that what it would be like if Simon loved her? Would the spark of love spread, bringing light and warmth to her and anyone around her?

"Huzzah!" John cried, and the others took up the cheer.

"Well done, Nora," Simon said.

She closed her eyes a moment, leaned back into the circle of his arms, until she felt his chin brushing her hair.

Oh, Heavenly Father, could this feeling last? Could Simon really come to love me?

Simon's arms fell away, and she opened her eyes to find him already moving toward the door. "If you'll excuse me, I have work to finish in the barn."

She wanted to cry out, rush after him, but what could she say? She couldn't beg, and she didn't want to embarrass him in front of his family.

Beth had no such worries, for she darted in front of him. "Simon, no! The house is still a mess after all our visitors. I need you here. And there are apples to peel for the pie and stuffing to make for dinner tomorrow."

James strode up to him and clapped him on the shoulder. "Might as well bid your bride goodbye, Simon. You have been conscripted into the Christmas army."

"And so have you," Beth scolded. "Now hop to it."

James saluted smartly, laughing all the while.

Simon glanced around, his gaze crossing Nora's. "You have plenty of help. I'll be back to do my part shortly." With a nod to Nora, he pushed past his sister for the door, Fleet following him.

Nora puffed out a breath.

Beth stomped her foot. "Oh! Boys! When I'm grown, I won't have another in my house."

"Aren't you the one always talking about love and romance?" her mother reminded her with a smile.

"For other people," Beth assured her. She glanced after Simon. "Though I'm beginning to think that brother is a lost cause."

A shiver went through Nora despite the warmth from the fire. For, deep down, she feared the same thing.

Despite Nora's concerns, it was a merry afternoon, with Simon's family hurrying about between the cabins, and some furtive scurrying between the loft and the main room. Surprises seemed as sure as the spice in Mrs. Wallin's cider. Beth was the prime director, ordering this person here, that task done there.

"You have to go back to Simon's cabin," she informed Nora at one point, "and get your stocking and Simon's."

Nora glanced to the hearth, where Levi was already pounding a nail through the top of a purple wool sock that must have been his. The dainty one next to it, patterned pink and blue, was surely Beth's.

Nora slipped on her cloak and ventured out into the cold. She couldn't help casting a glance toward the barn, but there was no sign of Simon. She thought she caught the sound of pounding, but that might have been one of the other Wallins hanging a stocking by the fire.

Something white danced in the air when she entered the cabin, and for a moment she had the odd thought that it had somehow snowed inside. Then she realized the snowflakes were actually goose feathers. Fleet stood by the hearth, his mouth still full of Simon's pallet, which lay like a flattened balloon at the dog's feet. Simon must have returned him to the house instead of taking him to the barn.

"Oh, Fleet! What have you done?" Nora shut the door behind her and rushed into the room.

Fleet leaped back, dragging the nearly empty pallet around the table. Nora finally jumped on the thing to get him to stop pulling. Then she rose and looked around.

Feathers flecked every surface, from the mantel to the floor. The pallet was ripped wide-open in at least three places, as if the dog had clawed and chewed his way into the bag. And the quilt was rent in two.

Nora dropped down on the floor. What could she say to Simon? She'd brought Fleet into the house, insisted upon it in fact, and he had all but destroyed Simon's bed.

"This is not acceptable!" she scolded Fleet, shaking the quilt in his face.

In answer, Fleet bit into the material once again and tugged it out of her grip.

Nora rose. "No! Put that down. Now!"

She thought it was surprise more than obedience that made the dog open his mouth.

Nora drew in a breath. "We'll have to clean this up. And I can see I'll have to find something more useful for you to do than stay in the house. I do understand being bored, truly I do. But I cannot allow you to harm our things. It isn't right."

Fleet sat down and said, "Noooooo."

Nora pointed her finger at him. "That's entirely enough from you, sir. If I could teach you to sew, I'd put you to work right now. As it is, you're going outside until I clean up this mess."

It took quite a while to set the cabin to rights. The best she could do for the moment was to slip stitch the bag partway shut, shove in as many feathers as she could gather, and then stitch it the rest of the way. The quilt would take more work. She managed to carry it up to the loft and tossed hers down. Then she located a spare stocking.

Where would Simon's be? Likely in the trunk.

Nora lifted the carved lid and peered inside. She wasn't surprised to find everything folded neatly and arranged by color. What did surprise her was that the only colors were brown and gray, and many of his stockings were worn. Did he not know how to darn, or had he been busy and refused to ask his mother for help? Well, she could certainly help. That would be her next project.

As it was, she dropped her and Simon's stockings off at the house for Levi to hang and barely made it to the barn with Fleet in time to milk Britta. Simon looked up from the manger when she opened the door, then strode to meet her before she could set a foot inside.

"I'm sorry, Nora," he said. "I'm not quite finished. I'll milk Britta for you tonight, and I'll see you at dinner. Fleet can stay with me."

But she couldn't? Well!

Perhaps he truly did have work to do. Perhaps her short sojourn in the hayloft had disturbed something he felt must be fixed. Perhaps he was working on a present.

In the barn?

She entered the main cabin feeling unsettled. The table was ready for dinner, and everyone else was lounging about. No, not lounging. Excitement hung in the air, and glances zipped from person to person.

"We were just waiting for you and Simon," Mrs. Wallin said, coming to take Nora's cloak. "But I think I see something in your stocking."

She couldn't help the tingle of anticipation as she looked to the hearth. Sure enough, her stocking bulged. She glanced at Mrs. Wallin, who nodded toward the fire. "Go ahead, dear. See what Father Christmas left for you."

Nora ventured to the hearth, even as Levi and Beth pounced on their stockings, and the others moved closer to inspect theirs as well. Nora pulled the stocking from the nail and reached inside to find a tangerine, a handkerchief embroidered with her initial, a knit scarf of a familiar-looking purple heather yarn and a book of poetry.

Simon's stocking, hanging next to hers, looked significantly less thick.

Glancing around to make sure no one was looking,

she slipped her hand in his stocking. Her fingers met the rough edge of a rock.

Oh, no. She would not stand for Simon getting coal. She pulled out the rock and tucked it in her pocket. Then she put in her tangerine. She couldn't very well give him the handkerchief or the scarf, but after a moment's thought, she slipped in the poetry book as well.

The door opened just then for Simon, a bucket of milk in hand, and Nora scampered back from the hearth. Fleet bounded in on his heels, going from person to person and saying hello. The others were examining their gifts and exclaiming over the thoughtfulness. Mrs. Wallin had a new comb for her hair, edged with pearl beads that looked suspiciously like the ones Beth had purchased from Father Christmas. Beth had received the latest issue of *Godey's* and was already curled up in her mother's rocker scanning the pages of the famous ladies' magazine. John was fingering a fishing lure. A loud metallic hum proved that Levi had indeed found a harmonica in his stocking and was trying it out.

Nora could hardly wait for Simon to peer into his stocking. But he didn't go near the hearth even after he left the milk in the kitchen. Instead, he came up to her with a smile.

"And did Father Christmas reward you for your kindness?"

"Yes," she said, holding up her handkerchief and scarf. "Aren't they lovely?"

"Not as lovely as you," he murmured.

Nora caught her breath.

"Go on, Simon," James called. "You haven't looked in your stocking yet."

Simon turned and looked to the stocking. Then he frowned and wandered closer.

Nora let out her breath. He was only being kind. She knew she wasn't lovely. But the words had sounded so sweet.

His mother looked over as Simon scrutinized the book of poetry. "It seems Father Christmas was a bit mixed up this year," she said with a look to James.

"I'll say," James agreed, tossing his tangerine in the air and catching it. "First time in years Simon hasn't gotten coal. But I'm not sure love poems are any more use to him."

Love poems? She should have paid more attention to the title!

Simon pocketed the book. "I can assure you, James, that I'll find a use for them." He looked to Nora.

Oh, my!

Simon's promise was only the start to a delightful evening, with songs and good food and laughter. When they walked home together, Simon took Nora's hand, and she couldn't help her sigh of happiness.

Fleet bounded ahead to stop and sit before the door, and too late she remembered their earlier difficulties.

"Simon," she said as he opened the door, "I need to tell you something."

She had left the lantern burning, so she saw his brows go up. "Is something wrong?"

"Not exactly. That is, I fixed it as well as I could." She let Fleet in and shut the door behind them. "There was an accident with your bed."

"My bed." He looked toward the pallet, which she had to admit seemed a trifle lumpy from this vantage point.

"Fleet must have grown tired of waiting for us," she

hurried to explain. "Truly, it was my fault. I should have thought ahead."

"Nora," he said.

She scurried around the table. "It's not that bad, really, and I can get some of the new goose feathers from Beth and stitch it up more firmly. The quilt will take a little more work, but I'm sure I can fix it so you'd never know it had been ripped."

"Nora," he said, advancing on her.

"It's no trouble, really. I'm just so sorry that I—"

He took her in his arms and kissed her. And she felt as light as a feather drifting in the air.

Yet she sensed something in his embrace, a tenderness that hadn't been there before. Could it be Simon's heart was changing, after all?

Chapter Twenty

Nora woke on Christmas morning to the sound of voices calling. She poked her head out of the loft to see Beth and Levi in the doorway. Simon, already dressed, stood beside them, with Fleet dancing about them all.

"It snowed last night!" Beth cried. "Come out and welcome Christmas with us!"

Nora eagerly reached for her clothes. The rock from Simon's stocking tumbled out of her pocket and skittered across the floor of the loft to slide out the opening. She heard it clatter as it hit the floor. She'd have to find it later, if Fleet didn't find it first. For now, she couldn't wait another minute to give Simon his present. She dressed hurriedly, then wrapped the new waistcoat in the ripped quilt she'd slept under and went to navigate the ladder.

Levi and Beth were back outside, but Simon bent to peck her cheek. "Merry Christmas, Nora."

The tentative touch was so unlike the kiss they'd shared last night that she could only frown up at him as he drew back.

"Merry Christmas," she told him. "I have something for you."

Simon cocked his head. "For me?"

Was she mad to hear eagerness behind the question? She nodded, unwrapping the quilt to hand him the waist-coat. "For Christmas."

He took the garment, turned it in his strong hands, the buttons winking in the light. "You made this."

He sounded awed. Nora's mouth felt dry. "Yes. I think it will fit, but I can tailor it if it's too wide." She swallowed. "You could try it on, if you like."

He set it on the table. "Later. When I change into my suit."

"Yes, of course, Simon," she said, feeling tears behind her eyes. She would not let him see them. It wasn't his fault she was disappointed. He was only being practical.

"Will you come out and enjoy the snow with us?" she asked.

He shook his head. "Snow is hardly something to enjoy. We'll have to feed the stock in the barn until it thaws. The weight could snap branches on the trees, making the woods dangerous. If it gets too thick, it may break through the roof. And if it thaws too fast, we could see flooding."

Perhaps it was her disappointment over the reception of her gift. Perhaps it was the fact that it was Christmas. But for whatever reason, she couldn't bear hearing him enumerate the risks.

Nora put a hand on his arm. "It's just snow, Simon. Can't we enjoy it without worrying what will come?"

He drew in a breath. "Yes, of course, Nora. Only, I have work to finish in the barn."

On Christmas? Could she never get through to him?

"But you'll come to the house later?" she pressed. "For Christmas dinner?"

He laid his hand over hers. "Wouldn't miss it. I've already milked Britta for you, and I'll take Fleet with me."

Her work was done, it seemed, so she ventured outside.

Snow covered the path to the main house, blanketed the bushes. It glittered from the needles on the firs and clung in white tufts to the trunks, as if someone had pasted balls of cotton here and there. Despite what Simon had said, she could only see it as beautiful.

A snowball sailed past her as she stepped off the porch.

"Sorry," Levi said, his head popping up from behind the white hump of a rhododendron. "I was hoping to hit Simon."

"He has work to do," Nora reported, moving onto the path.

Beth materialized from behind a tree, a snowball in her mittened hand. "On Christmas?"

"Simon works hard every day," Nora said, her head high as she started for the clearing.

"No wonder James called him Scrooge," Levi muttered, falling in beside her.

The clearing was a sheet of white, though even now she saw footprints leading from cabin to cabin and cabin to barn. Snow capped each fence post, covered the main cabin's roof, which looked in no danger of caving in. Why couldn't Simon just see things for what they were, let in the light and not seek the darkness?

Mrs. Wallin beckoned from the porch. "Merry Christmas, Nora. Come in for some cocoa."

Now, that sounded like a delightful way to start

Christmas Day. Nora left Beth and Levi to pummel each other with snowballs and went into the house.

The goose Drew had shot had been stuffed and trussed and was cooking by the fire, the savory scent permeating the room. Mother Wallin had hot cocoa and shortbread on the table, and Nora helped herself to some of each.

One by one, Simon's other brothers and their wives arrived, and Beth and Levi were persuaded to leave off their war and join them. Everyone admired the new bag Drew had purchased for Catherine to hold all her nursing supplies now and baby things later. It was a merry gathering, but Nora kept watching the door.

"Do you want me to fetch him?" Levi asked her as if he'd noticed her darting glances.

Nora shook her head. "Simon will come when he's ready."

But half the morning had passed before Simon appeared in the doorway, and then he came bearing his father's violin in his arms. Fleet arrived with him, shaking snow off his fur. But what drew Nora's gaze were the green glass buttons shining on Simon's chest. The waistcoat fit him perfectly.

Of course, James noticed. "I will not have it, Simon," he proclaimed, pointing a finger at him. "I'm supposed to be the brother with style in this family. I demand to know the name of your tailor."

Simon looked to Nora with a smile that warmed her. "She's too good for you, James. Now, shouldn't there be carols?" He went to the hearth and anchored the fiddle under his chin.

Beth clapped her hands. "Yes, please, Simon!"

He played then, and they all joined in singing carols and hymns, from "While Shepherds Watched Their Flocks" to "Joy to the World." Once again, though, Nora realized, Simon kept himself apart. By playing, he made himself different from the rest of his family, and though he seemed to lose himself in the music as usual, she couldn't help wondering if he felt the distance.

At least he joined in with helping bring the feast to the table. Besides the goose, they had mashed potatoes and rich gravy, rolls that had been sent out from Maddie Haggerty's bakery, blackberry preserves, parsnips with onions and, finally, apple pie for dessert. Nora felt more stuffed than the goose by the time they were finished.

As soon as the table had been cleared, Beth looked ready to organize another game, but Simon took Nora's hand. "Will you walk with me?"

He looked so serious, as if everything depended on her answer. Nora nodded. "Yes, of course, Simon." She went to fetch her cloak, asking John to keep an eye on Fleet.

Simon led her out into the clearing, where a fitful sun made patches of snow radiant. Helping her across the uneven ground and drifts, he drew her toward the barn.

"I know I'm not the best at expressing how I feel," he said, his gaze on his gloved hand holding hers. "But I want you to know you've made a difference in my life. You help me see the good. Thank you, Nora."

She felt as if her heart was swelling. "If I have truly helped, you are welcome, Simon."

"I wanted to give you something for Christmas," he said. "It's in the barn."

In the barn? So that was what had kept him. She couldn't imagine what she could need in the barn, but whatever he had done would be nothing short of magnificent, she was sure.

Simon did not seem nearly as confident as he rolled open the door. His face was set, his lean body stiff beside hers.

"It was very thoughtful of you," Nora said with an encouraging smile.

She thought she saw him swallow.

Sunlight speared inside, anointing the wooden floor where she and Simon had watched the play and the stalls holding the goats, oxen and horses. Britta looked up from her manger at the light.

Nora blinked. Something was different about the manger. Wandering closer, she saw that it had been lifted from the floor and redesigned to be flatter. Already Britta was happily eating the grains in it.

"You did this?" she asked Simon, who had come up beside her.

He nodded. "She was having a hard time balancing when she leaned over to eat. This will make her more comfortable."

Tears gathered in her eyes. "It's wonderful."

"There's more." He went to the back of the barn and brought out a low sled with a high bar at the back. "This is for Fleet. I saw an Indian using one once with his dogs. Fleet can pull it about the farm, helping us carry things. I'll work with John to add wheels to it for the summer."

"Father Christmas said he was born to pull a sled." She looked at the clean lines, the polished wood of the rails. "Oh, Simon, it's perfect. I don't know how to thank you!"

He came around the sled to her side. "The smile on your face is thanks enough. Just know that I admire you,

Nora, beyond measure. Thank you for showing me that life can hold joy."

Joy, he said. She felt it bubbling up inside her even now, filling her heart to overflowing. He had had little use for Britta in the beginning, yet he helped Nora milk her and now he'd gone out of his way to make the cow more comfortable. He'd been concerned about how Fleet would get on at the farm, but he talked to the dog, made light of his mistakes and created a way for Fleet to contribute to the farm.

"You bring me joy," she told Simon. "You make me want to hope for a future."

He took her hands, eyes as bright as the buttons on his new waistcoat. "And what do you hope for the future, Nora?"

Could she say it aloud? If he didn't answer the way she dreamed, she knew her heart would shatter. She had fallen in love with her husband. Worse, despite all her experiences, she had dared to hope Simon might love her in return, that they might have the tender, happy marriage she saw with his brothers and their wives. Christmas had made her believe it was a possibility. But what if she was wrong?

Something white shot through the door and landed on the wood floor. Simon frowned down at the snowball.

"Hey in there!" Levi's voice was demanding. "It's Christmas! No more work! It's time to play."

Simon started shaking his head, pulling back from her, but suddenly Nora knew what she wanted. Just once, Simon needed to play.

"He's right, Simon," she told her husband. "It's time to have fun. Let's go play in the snow."

* * *

He was playing in the snow.

Simon ducked behind the side of the barn to escape Levi's barrage of snowballs. Nora handed him another missile.

"Try for Drew," she said. "He makes a bigger target."

Simon laughed. Laughed! Poking his head out around the corner, he sighted his older brother near the schoolhouse. Beth, Rina and James had rolled snowballs big enough to build a fort of sorts around the schoolhouse door and were using the bell stand like a tower at the corner. Levi had commandeered the wagon and was hunkered behind it. Ma and Catherine were watching from the porch, with John on guard in front of them to prevent any stray balls from finding home.

But Nora was right—Drew was big enough he simply could not hide. Simon took aim and fired.

Drew shook the snow off his head and glared around. "Who threw that?"

"Simon!" Levi claimed, pointing toward the barn.

"Very funny," Drew said, scooping up a pile of snow and packing it in his fists. Levi frantically began scraping snow together.

Of course Drew didn't think Simon would join them in a snowball fight, for all Nora had been the one to rally the rest of his family out into the clearing. Simon was the serious one, Simon was the hard worker.

"Give me another one," he told Nora, and she filled his palm with two more snowballs.

This time he aimed for Levi, dropping a ball neatly down his youngest brother's back.

"Hey!" Levi leaped up, ducked his head and fished down the neck of his coat.

Nora giggled.

Drew was frowning toward the barn. "That really did come from Simon." A smile worked its way onto his brother's face.

James leaped from behind the fort, his arm raised. "In that case, charge!"

Drew and James raced toward the barn, Fleet barking at their heels. Simon seized Nora's hand and pulled her around the back and into the rear door, slamming it ahead of his brothers. He heard the thuds as the balls hit the wood.

"That's not fair," Nora said, but he could see her eyes twinkling.

"That's survival," Simon countered. "Now quick— they'll be coming around to the front any minute."

They hurried through the barn and up to the front door. Cautiously, Simon cracked it open. All seemed quiet. In fact, he couldn't see any of his siblings, their wives or Fleet, only Ma and Catherine smiling on the porch. Hand on Nora's, he opened the door wider and took a step out.

Snow rained from the roof, covering him and Nora. She gasped in a breath and then started laughing. He shook the snow off his head, his shoulders.

"Got you!" Levi shouted from the roof of the barn.

"Get down here before you slide off and break your other leg," Simon shouted at him.

Nora was still laughing, her whole body trembling next to his. He couldn't help it. He gave it up and laughed as well.

James came up and slipped an arm about Nora's shoulders. "I always knew you were an amazing seamstress. It seems you've sewed me up a whole new brother."

Simon almost felt that way, as if he were a different person, a better person. He nudged James aside and took Nora's hand to lead her back to the house.

The rest of the day flew by. He didn't recall half the games Beth encouraged them to try, only that when he played with Nora at his side, the parlor pastimes were more enjoyable than he could remember. Nor could he remember a more joyful Christmas. The only drawback to the day was that the question he'd asked her in the barn that morning hadn't been answered. *And what do you hope for the future, Nora?* Walking home with her in the moonlight, he wanted to ask her again. But something held him back.

He was beginning to hope for a life together as husband and wife. Was she? She'd found the courage to ask him to marry her. Why couldn't he find the courage to ask her to truly be his wife?

Perhaps because it meant so much to him. Asking risked everything—his peace, his heart.

The matter kept him awake much of the night, but her statement the next morning made him stop in his tracks by the door.

"You promised your brother what?" he asked as she came down the ladder.

"That I would come to visit the day after Christmas and stay for dinner," she explained, setting down her carpetbag long enough to pat Fleet on the head. "And I can check for any new commissions while I am in town."

"I'll take you, then," Simon said, going for his coat. He hadn't intended to let his frustration show, but she must have sensed it, for she followed him and laid a hand on his arm.

"John said he was going in for the mail. I can accompany him. You can drive in for me tomorrow. I know you want to continue clearing the land today."

"The land can wait," he said, and she looked as surprised as he felt to hear the words coming out of his mouth. "I'm more concerned about you and your brother."

She raised her head. "Charles and Meredith won't sway me this time, Simon. I promise."

He didn't like it, but he knew he had to take her at her word. Perhaps he wasn't the only one who had changed over Christmas. Perhaps Nora was ready to have her say in her family.

He kept Fleet inside the house in case the dog tried to follow her, walked her to the wagon and lifted her onto the bench. She offered him a bright smile.

"Don't look so worried, Simon," John said behind the reins. "I'll take good care of her."

"See that you do," Simon said, stepping back. "Keep an eye out for cougar. Remember that the roads will be in bad shape with the melting snow. Don't go through any puddles that look too deep—you could lose an axle. And watch the horses on that turn below the lake. They always want to take it too fast."

John looked at Nora and then grinned at his brother. "Yes, Simon. Now, if you don't stop talking, we won't get to Seattle until after dark, and you know how dangerous it is *then*."

Simon stepped back and let them go.

There he went again, he thought as he headed back to the house for Fleet. Seeing the darkness instead of the light. But how could he not think things through? He didn't want anything to happen to Nora.

He came into the cabin to find Fleet nosing about at

the foot of the ladder. Something dark flashed against the wood.

"What have you got there?" Simon asked, squatting beside the dog and picking up a black rock. It looked a lot like the one James usually slipped into Simon's stocking at Christmas, only this stone had cracked, opening a V at the top and making a point at the bottom.

It almost looked like a heart.

Simon sat back, absently rubbing Fleet's fur as he fingered the rock with his other hand. The basalt was warm in his grip, the surface smooth. Was this what had happened to him? Being around Nora had opened his heart, warmed it, smoothed the rough edges. She made him better, made his life better.

Small wonder he had fallen in love with her.

It had crept up on him, little by little, but he could not deny it any more than he could deny the trees growing on the hillside, the mountain rising in the distance. He loved his kind, gentle, whimsical wife, the woman who made him see that there was more to life than work, the lady who brought him beauty in the form of a three-legged cow and a talking dog.

And as soon as she was home, he was going to tell her. It was a dangerous undertaking. He would be letting down his guard all the way. Yet how could he not take the risk, when the result was Nora as his wife?

Christmas may have been yesterday, but the best present would be Nora, sweet Nora, returning his love.

Tomorrow seemed a long ways away.

Chapter Twenty-One

Nora settled into her seat as John drove the wagon down the forest road. The snow was melting, leaving white piles here and there like scattered pillows. Heavy clouds threatened rain. She pulled her cloak closer.

She wanted to be good company to John as he drove, so she kept up her end of the conversation. Still, her mind kept going to Simon.

Yesterday his gifts had been so thoughtful, his mood so joyful, that she'd hoped she might hear a declaration of love. Yet no such words had come from his mouth. And she hadn't had the courage to ask.

She knew why the question was so hard for her. She couldn't bear to hear him confirm that admiration was all he could muster. Her whole life she'd waited to be loved—by her parents, by her brother and his wife, by a suitor. She didn't know if she had it in her to keep waiting any longer. Simon and his family had given her something she'd never expected—kindness, appreciation. They had made her realize it was possible to feel loved. Could she settle for less from Simon?

She must have grown silent, for John glanced in her

direction. "Don't worry. Simon will be fine for a night without you."

Were her thoughts so obvious? "Of course he will." Nora smiled at her brother-in-law. "But I'd appreciate it if you would check on him and Fleet. The two of them sometimes disagree. And perhaps help him with Britta. She likes someone to talk to her while she's being milked, and Simon might be too quiet and in a hurry to get the job done. And do remind him to eat dinner. He gets so busy working he forgets."

John chuckled. "I think Simon is starting to wear off on you. You sound just like him, looking for problems."

Nora blushed. "Perhaps everyone worries about those they love."

There—she'd said it aloud, admitted it to Simon's brother. She was in love with Simon. She felt the rightness of it deep inside her. She could hardly wait to get back to him.

For a moment, it seemed as if John had sensed her thoughts, for he called to the horses to pick up their pace.

"I'm very happy to hear you say love in connection with Simon, Nora," he said. "My brother needs someone who loves him."

"But he has all of you," Nora protested. "I'm not sure why he doesn't realize he's loved. Your mother called him a blessing."

"He is, Nora," John insisted. "Make no mistake. Drew can be bullheaded. Simon keeps him from doing anything stupid. James can't take the world seriously. Simon helps him see the dangers he might miss. I can get lost in my own thoughts. Simon brings me back to reality. And he's a steadying influence on Levi and Beth."

He was a steadying influence on her as well. Sometimes her enthusiasm led her down paths before she thought. Simon helped her see problems, even when she didn't want to think about them.

John glanced ahead to where the trees gave way to stumps surrounding Seattle. "Listen, do you mind coming to the post office with me before we go to your brother's? We can stop at the Kelloggs' store as well. I'd like to give Lancelot and Percival a rest before making them climb that hill."

"I could walk from the post office," Nora offered, but John would hear none of it, so she agreed to his plan.

He picked up the mail and a newspaper, then took Nora by the Kellogg brothers' store to see if she had any commissions. The mercantile was crowded with shoppers—burly miners and sawyers, ladies wrapped in warm cloaks, bonnets on their heads. A few of the customers glanced her way as she passed, and more than one frowned.

"So it's true," the shorter Kellogg brother said when she asked after her customers. He handed her a sheaf of notes left for her and shook his head. "You have no interest in farming."

Nora frowned at the dapper, mustached man who had given her space to ply her trade from his store. "We are farming. Simon and his brothers have cleared most of the land. They intend to plant this spring."

"Not if he isn't married to you," Kellogg warned.

Not married to her? Even if Simon found he could never love her, they would still be married.

"I don't understand," Nora said.

Kellogg waved a hand, and several more of his customers glanced their way from among the piles of food tins, saw blades and bolts of cloth. "It was in the last two issues of the *Puget Sound Weekly*. Simon and Nora Wallin are not living together as husband and wife. He has to forfeit the claim."

Nora's stomach sank. Clutching the notes Kellogg had given her, she ran out to the wagon and John.

"Look in the paper," she begged him before he could come around to hand her up. "See if there's anything about me and Simon."

John frowned, but he reached for the paper he'd tucked behind the seat. "Why would there be anything about you or Simon in the newspaper?"

Nora shifted from foot to foot, her green skirts swinging in the chill air. "Mr. Kellogg said there was. He said Simon's going to lose the claim."

"What?" John snapped open the paper and scanned the pages. Then he gasped. "There it is, a legal notice. 'To Whom It May Concern—It has been brought to the attention of the Land Office that Simon Wallin of Seattle is not living as a husband. The one hundred and sixty acres claimed for his wife, Nora Underhill, will be forfeit unless they make an appearance before the registrar by five in the afternoon on December 27, 1866, to prove they are husband and wife.'"

Nora caught the sideboard, feeling faint. "That's tomorrow."

John nodded, lowering the paper. "Who told them?"

Nora shook her head. "It doesn't matter. I won't let Simon lose that acreage. He's worked too hard for it. You all have." She looked to John. "Go back to Wallin Landing, John. Show Simon that article. Tell him I'll find us a passage on a southbound ship tomorrow, if I can. I'll wait for him in Seattle."

"Right." John jumped up on the bench and gathered the reins.

"And, John," Nora said.

Her brother-in-law met her gaze.

Nora did not hesitate. "Tell Simon I love him, and I won't let him down. Ever."

Simon took Fleet with him up the hill to the new acreage. He and James were going to see about one of the bigger trees. He helped his brother hack away at the trunk to make a groove for the big saw. Then James pounded in the wedges.

Simon knew he should be helping, but he couldn't seem to keep Nora off his mind. The glow on her face when she'd seen his presents, the joy when she'd instigated that family snowball fight and the warmth of her in his embrace all combined to make him dream of a future together, in a true marriage.

He never would have thought such a thing possible. Most likely it wouldn't have been possible with anyone but Nora. She accepted him as no one else ever had, yet helped him be the best man possible. It seemed to him he felt a hand on his shoulder, a presence encouraging him.

Your ways are higher than ours, Lord. You knew what I needed in a wife. Help me be what Nora needs in a husband.

"Ahem."

James's cough made Simon meet his brother's gaze. As usual, laughter danced in James's deep blue eyes. "A little help here, brother?"

James had positioned the big saw and stood waiting at one end. Simon moved to take up the other. Before he could give it the first shove, Fleet started barking.

Turning, Simon saw the dog hopping about near the path to the main clearing.

"Someone must be coming," James said, leaning on the handle.

"Simon!" John loped out of the trees. His face was nearly as red as his hair as he veered around the stumps to reach his brothers' sides, Fleet bounding along beside him.

"There's trouble," he said as he came abreast of them.

Simon dropped the saw's handle and grabbed John by the shoulders. "Nora? Is she all right? What happened?"

Fleet came to pace around Simon as John put a hand to Simon's chest and gasped in a breath. "Nora's fine. We're the ones in trouble. According to the Land Office, you and Nora are not husband and wife."

Simon frowned in confusion, and John went on to explain what he and Nora had read in the newspaper.

"We could lose it all," he concluded with a wave of his hand that took in the cleared field and the woods beyond, "if you can't convince the registrar your marriage is real."

Simon shook his head. "First I have to convince Nora."

James chuckled. "Oh, I don't think that will be much of a problem. When we set our minds to it, Wallin men are irresistible. Even you, Simon."

"That's not the issue, James," Simon informed him, his mind whirling.

John opened his mouth, but James spoke first.

"Will you quote me the problems, then? Let me guess. You look at Nora and see the potential for heartache and loss. But I can tell you that love is worth the risk. And Drew would say the same thing."

"Actually—" John began.

Simon ignored him, more focused on James. He could not let his brother's comment stand. "You're looking at it the wrong way. What if I disappoint her? What if living with me doesn't make her happy? What if I fail her?"

James clapped him on the shoulder. "I hate to be the one to tell you, Simon, but you're human. You're going to fail at some point. And then you ask her pardon and work to make things better. That's what the rest of us imperfect mortals do."

Simon pulled away from him. "You make it sound so simple."

James laughed. "There's nothing simple about it."

Fleet opened his mouth and said, "Noooo-ra!"

James stumbled back. "He talks!"

Simon stared at the dog. "Nora always claimed he did. I never believed her, until now." He bent and rubbed the dog's dark head. "Good boy, Fleet. You know what's important, don't you? It's Nora."

"You can't actually be talking to a dog," James said, collecting himself. "Not the ever-logical Simon Wallin."

Simon straightened. "Right now, the only person I need to talk to is Nora."

"And she wants to talk to you!" John stepped between his brothers rather forcefully. "Simon, I've been trying to tell you something. Nora said she loves you. She wanted me to make sure you know it."

And just like that, light pierced his heart. He laughed, and both his brothers frowned at him as if suddenly worried for his sanity. But Fleet wagged his tail and gave a happy yip.

"Don't you see, John?" Simon said. "The land doesn't matter. Nothing else matters. Nora loves me."

John grinned. "Congratulations, Simon. So, are we headed for Seattle?"

"I am," Simon said, turning for the path down the hill.

"I pushed Lancelot and Percival pretty hard to make it home in time to tell you," John warned him, following him to the path. "They'll have to rest before they can make another trip."

"Then I'll take the oxen," Simon said, lengthening his stride as he started down the hill. Fleet ran through the bushes beside him, his bushy tail waving overhead like a victory flag.

"They won't make it before nightfall," James called from behind John.

"Then I'll bring a lantern to light the way," Simon replied.

"You'll need someone to hold the lantern, and someone to bring them back to Wallin Landing if you head for Olympia," John said as they detoured around a stump.

"I'll hold the lantern and walk beside them if it gets too dark," Simon said, his boots slipping on the muddy path in his hurry. "And you can fetch them back from the livery stable."

"Drew's not going to like it," James predicted.

"Drew has enough to worry about with you all." Simon looked back to scowl at his brothers. "I have to get to Seattle and Nora. You know that. Why do you find every flaw?"

John and James shared a glance, then grinned at him.

"Now I know you're in love, Simon," John said. "You overlooked every problem. You just have to tell Nora and get to Olympia before the Land Office closes tomorrow."

Nora climbed the hill to her brother's house, reasonably pleased with herself. A lumber schooner was heading south on the morning tide tomorrow, and the captain had agreed to carry her and Simon. So long as Simon arrived in Seattle before eight in the morning, they could reach Olympia in time. She could sleep on the sofa at Charles's house and be ready to go when Simon arrived to take her up.

But Charles had other ideas.

"Nora!" he cried when the severely gowned housekeeper answered her knock and escorted her to the parlor as if Nora would not know the way. "Meredith, dear, come see! Nora has returned to us."

Meredith, who had been busy arranging place settings in the dining room, hurried in and enfolded Nora in a hug. "Nora, dear, I'm so glad you're back. It's been so long."

She smiled at the housekeeper. "Mrs. Yearly, this is Charles's sister, Nora. She lives with us. Will you make sure her room is just as she left it?"

A thin whippet of a woman, Mrs. Yearly frowned. She had a long nose in a longer face, and her black hair was drawn back so tightly that Nora wondered her brown eyes didn't cross. "Room, madam?"

As Nora had chosen this house for her brother in part because it had only one formal bedchamber, she wasn't surprised by the housekeeper's confusion.

"It's all right, Mrs. Yearly," Nora told her. "I'll just be spending the night."

Meredith's face fell. "One night? That's not nearly long enough."

"No indeed," Charles agreed. "You must stay a fortnight at least. I won't hear no. After all, we are responsible for you. We cannot have you gadding about where you might endanger yourself."

A fortnight? What was he thinking? She had to go to Olympia with Simon and then return to Wallin Landing. And even if that hadn't been true, she had no intentions of living with Charles and Meredith, servants notwithstanding.

But she already had enough on her mind without starting a fight with her brother. "Simon might have something to say about that," she replied, laying her trump card on the table.

Neither Charles nor Meredith quailed this time. Meredith went so far as to wave a hand. "Simon, Rupert, Everest, Henry—I cannot keep up with your beaus."

Nora frowned. "I have no beaus, only a husband. You remember—Simon Wallin."

Charles laughed. "Always a tease, my dear sister." He turned to the housekeeper, who was watching them with a frown. "Mrs. Yearly, might I hope we still have some of that excellent salmon for dinner tonight? It's Nora's favorite."

Nora doubted he had any idea of her preference in food. He had never asked nor paid the least attention to her while they ate.

"I'll go down to the market and fetch some myself, sir," his housekeeper promised him, standing taller as if proud of her ability to serve. With a nod of respect to the ladies, she hurried from the room.

The moment she was out of earshot, Meredith turned to Nora. "Really, Nora, you would do well not to mention that man's name in front of your brother. You know how it upsets him."

That was precisely the point, but Nora decided not to mention that either. "If it's too much trouble to sleep on the sofa, I can check at the boardinghouse."

"You will not be sleeping on the sofa," Charles informed her. "Meredith and I refitted the attic. Our room is there. You will be sleeping in the master bedchamber."

That was a concession. "You needn't have done that, Charles," she said. "I only came to visit. Simon will be expecting me home."

Meredith frowned. "Why, when you clearly cost him the land he cared so much about?"

Nora stared at her. Meredith had seldom read the paper back in Lowell. Had Charles seen the odious complaint against Simon and then told her?

As if sensing an argument coming, Charles stepped between them. "Now, then, we shouldn't quarrel. We're expecting company for dinner."

Meredith's face lit, and she clasped her hands together. "Yes, of course! That delightful young Mr. Pomantier from the bank." She sobered as she turned to Nora. "You likely remember his father, dear."

Certainly she remembered her father's elderly banker. It sounded as if the son had taken over.

"I remember Mr. Pomantier," Nora said. "But why has his son come all the way West? Is the bank moving to Seattle?"

"No, no," Charles assured her. "He had dealings in San Francisco and made the trip north to consult with me. It's all a matter of business. Nothing that need concern you."

"No indeed," Meredith agreed. "In fact, he can be a bit intimidating, dear, so I'm sure no one will mind if you let me and your brother do all the talking."

"Capital idea," Charles proclaimed. "In the meantime, come see your room."

She allowed Charles and Meredith to lead her to the

main bedchamber, which looked considerably different. The wide bed had been replaced with a smaller one, and the coverings and curtains were now made from a dainty red chintz.

She wandered in, touched the tortoiseshell brush on the dressing table, the ivory combs waiting for her hair. What a shame they'd gone to such trouble, for she had no intention of using the room beyond tonight.

"Very nice," she told the two of them.

Charles and Meredith had been watching her avidly, as if eager for her approval. Now Meredith let out a breath.

"Oh, good," her sister-in-law said. "Then you'll stay."

"Only for tonight," Nora insisted.

Meredith's look leaped to Charles. "Will that be sufficient to satisfy Mr. Pomantier?"

Her brother frowned as if considering the matter.

Nora glanced between them. "Satisfy? Charles, what is all this about?"

Meredith fluttered her fingers before her face as if feeling faint. "Why must you question your brother after all he's done for you? Is one dinner too much to ask?"

Nora refused to let the guilt catch hold of her this time. "What is going on? Why is it so important that Mr. Pomantier meet me?"

Charles sighed. "I had hoped to spare you this, Nora. It is a matter of Father's last wishes."

"Father's wishes?" Nora shook her head. "Father has been dead for eight years."

"But he impressed upon me the importance of caring for you," Charles insisted. "He had grave concerns about your future, so he left money in trust for you."

Nora frowned. "In trust? His solicitor said nothing to me."

"Well, of course he wouldn't have," Meredith scolded. "You are your brother's ward."

Nora glanced between them again. "Father left me money, and you were managing it?"

She must have sounded skeptical, for Meredith drew herself up. "Your brother managed it brilliantly. It's not his fault that wretched war wreaked havoc with the stock exchange."

"So you lost it," Nora said with a sigh.

Charles took a step back, but he didn't deny it. "I fear you will remain dependent on me even after you reach your majority, Nora. Mr. Pomantier of the bank wants to confirm we are treating you well. Just smile and be pleasant, and then you can go about your business."

Meredith took a step closer, her eyes narrowing. "But give him the impression you are unhappy with us, and I can promise you will never leave this house again."

Nora started forward, but Charles pulled Meredith out the door and shut it. Nora heard a lock snap into place. She ran to the door, pulled on the handle. "Charles! Let me out this minute!"

"It will all be fine, Nora," her brother said through the panel. "Just play your part, and you will be free to go back to your wild mountain man in a few days."

A few days? Simon didn't have that long.

She turned and glanced around, her gaze lighting on the curtains. She rushed to the window and yanked the pretty material aside to find a wrought-iron screen like lace covering the glass. She would never be able to force her way through that.

Lord, please help me!

The prayer came easily, guilt free. She'd always believed the Lord looked out for her. She knew now why she had hesitated to bring her concerns to Him before. Charles and Meredith had made her feel worthless. Simon and his family had made her see the lie in those feelings. Now she could only pray for wisdom to thwart her brother.

But had she found her courage too late?

Chapter Twenty-Two

The sun had long set by the time Simon reached Seattle. Leaving Fleet in James's care, Simon had stopped at the cabin only long enough to collect his and Nora's marriage certificate. John had insisted on coming with him while James explained the situation to the rest of the family. Now John took charge of the oxen while Simon climbed the hill to the Underhills' home.

The house was ablaze with lights as he approached the front porch. Count on Nora's brother to make a show, not bothering to consider frugality or practicality. But Charles was a minor inconvenience next to the anticipation of seeing Nora. Simon couldn't wait to talk to her, take her in his arms and confess his feelings. All he wanted was to see her smile, hear her say she did indeed return his love.

He was a little surprised when an older woman in a tailored black dress answered his knock.

"Mr. Underhill is entertaining," she informed Simon. "He cannot be disturbed. Come back tomorrow."

Simon refused. He'd go mad waiting.

"If you tell Nora her husband is here, I'm sure she'll want to see me," he told the woman, who he assumed must be a new housekeeper.

She put her long nose in the air. "Miss Underhill has no husband. Be gone with you, fellow, before I send for the sheriff." She shut the door in Simon's face.

No husband? Simon's stomach sank. Had John got it wrong? Had Nora decided against Simon? Had he made her wait too long?

No, he refused to give up. He stepped back from the door and glanced through the window overlooking the porch. The Underhills had yet to shutter the glass, and he had a clear view through the parlor to the dining room beyond. Charles sat at the head of a table that sparkled with crystal and silver; his wife perched at his right.

For a moment, he didn't see Nora, then the gentleman on the left side of the table leaned back, and Simon spotted her at her brother's left, still gowned in the dress she'd been wearing that morning, the spring green one in which she'd married him. The newcomer, a dark-haired man in a fancy suit, was speaking intently to her, and Nora was smiling as she answered. It all looked very proper except for one thing.

Charles's shoulders were hunched, and Meredith kept fidgeting in her chair. What was going on?

Simon strode back, grabbed the handle and pushed the door open. The woman must have assumed he'd heed her warning, for she hadn't set the lock against him. Simon walked into the house.

He could hear the guest now, speaking in a pleasant voice.

"I had hoped to meet you sooner, Miss Underhill.

My father served as your father's banker for some years before passing the account on to me. He was most concerned about you and made me promise on his deathbed that I would make sure your father's wishes had been honored."

Simon eased around the entry and peered into the dining room in time to see Charles shift forward on his chair.

"As you can see, Mr. Pomantier, Nora is well cared for, just as our father intended," he insisted. "She remains under my protection. There was no need for you to travel all the way from San Francisco to check on her."

"Or to suspend our monthly stipend," Meredith put in. "It is difficult to see to Nora's needs when funds are low."

"And nothing is more important to me than my sister," Charles said, laying a hand on Nora's. Though his touch seemed kind, the look he leveled at Nora promised retribution if she should gainsay him.

Simon tensed, waiting to see how she would respond.

Nora pulled away. "That is not at all the case, Mr. Pomantier." Her quiet voice rang with conviction. "Even now, my brother is attempting to silence me and hide me from the world. I won't stand for it another minute."

Neither would Simon.

"And that is why she offered to wed a stranger at Christmas to escape his domination," Simon said, moving into the room.

Nora's head snapped up. Her smile to Simon lit the room. Whatever her brother had planned, Simon knew he and Nora would triumph.

Charles surged to his feet. "Who are you, sir? How did you get into my home?"

The woman who had told Simon to leave came through the door to what must be the kitchen. "I'm so sorry, sir," she said to Charles. "I told him to leave. He claims to be married to your sister."

"Rubbish," Charles said, but Simon could see sweat beading on his noble forehead. "Nora, you know I have always been the only one who cared for you. I took you in when you had nowhere to go, gave you a home. Tell Mr. Pomantier that you have no husband."

Nora glanced at Simon. Once again her brother had reminded her of the debt she felt she owed. Would she have the strength to gainsay him at last?

"No, Charles," she said. "That would be a lie. I gave Simon Wallin my hand in marriage nearly a month ago, and I've given him my heart every day since."

Joy leaped up inside Simon, and he took a step closer, ignoring the outcry from Charles and Meredith. "To my shame, I found it harder to give my heart, Nora. I suppose I had grown used to everyone arguing with me, being the cynic in the family. But from the first, you treated me with admiration and kindness, which is far more than I deserved. I want only to be a good husband to you."

Nora rose, her gaze on his. "But, Simon, are you sure you didn't come to this conclusion to protect the land?"

"No!" Meredith scrambled to her feet before Simon could answer. "Don't you see? He's after your dowry! Why else would he marry you?"

Simon met Nora's gaze. "Because she is good and kind. Because she makes me believe that love and laughter are possible, every day of my life. You see, I love my love with an *N*. Her name is Nora, she is a needleworker and she is all I will ever need."

With a cry, Nora ran around the table and threw herself into his arms.

Simon cradled her close, pressed kisses against her upturned face. Laughter rose inside him, mingled with her precious giggles. He would love and honor her all the days of his life. He would never let her go.

Nora cuddled against Simon, her heart so full she could scarcely speak. He loved her! She could see it in his tender smile, feel it in his gentle touch. This was what she'd longed for all her life. This was where she belonged, at his side and in his heart.

"It's a joke!" Meredith shrieked from the table. "It's a lie! Look at her! No one would marry her. She needs us to take care of her."

Nora turned in Simon's arms, determination blazing inside her like a torch. "No, Meredith. I don't need you. I will always be grateful you and Charles gave me a home, but my place now is with Simon."

Mr. Pomantier rose. "Miss Underhill— That is, Mrs. Wallin, you seem to be laboring under a misperception." He glanced at Charles. "And I begin to suspect why."

Charles bristled. "Now, see here, my good man…"

Mr. Pomantier ignored him, turning his gaze to Nora once more. "The fact of the matter is that your brother had no choice but to take you in. Your father's will makes it a condition of his inheritance. Further, your father set aside a portion of his estate to be kept in trust until your twenty-fifth birthday, longer if you do not marry. You were to be given a monthly allowance for your upkeep until that time. The amount was paid to your brother. Am I right to assume you have seen none of it?"

Nora stared at Charles. "Not one penny."

Charles shriveled.

"Ah." Mr. Pomantier straightened. "It appears my father was right to bring this situation to my attention. I called at the house in Lowell some months ago now but was told you were unavailable. The next time I called, the house was empty, and a neighbor said your family had moved to Seattle. A letter requesting the forwarding of your allowance arrived shortly thereafter. It seems your brother felt it necessary to hide his omissions."

Charles adjusted his bow tie. "I sought only to care for my sister. I will say no more on the matter."

"Just as well," Mr. Pomantier said. "With your permission, Mrs. Wallin, I will draw up the papers to have the allowance sent directly to you instead of your brother. And of course, you will have the entire fortune at your disposal at your next birthday when you turn five and twenty."

"But she is my responsibility," Charles protested, albeit weakly.

Nora held up her hand to silence her brother. "How much money are we discussing, Mr. Pomantier?"

He named a figure. If she hadn't been standing in Simon's arms, she would likely have fallen over.

"And I may spend that however I like?" she asked.

Mr. Pomantier smiled. "It is entirely at your discretion, yes. Once you reach your majority, of course."

Nora cocked her head. "Does my brother have a similar amount?"

The banker's face hardened. "I regret to report that, though your brother's portion was significantly larger, he has already spent the lot."

"Of course he has!" Meredith exclaimed. "Do you think living in society comes cheaply, sir? We have a reputation to maintain. And to be held responsible for such a nonentity. Is it any wonder I encouraged her to leave?"

"That's enough, Meredith," Charles murmured.

"Quite enough, Mr. Underhill," Mr. Pomantier said. "By all rights, I could have you brought up on charges of fraud."

Charles cringed.

How very sad. They simply had no concept of family. But Nora did.

"Mr. Pomantier," she said, "I will not press charges against my brother. Please arrange the paperwork so that he and his wife receive an allowance each month from my share of the estate, but—" she held up a hand as her brother brightened "—they must learn to live within their means."

Meredith slumped.

"And," Nora concluded, "if they cause me or anyone associated with me the least bit of trouble, they are to be cut off without a cent."

Charles blanched, but Mr. Pomantier nodded. "I'll start on it tonight, Mrs. Wallin."

"I plan to travel to Olympia tomorrow," Nora told him with a look toward Simon, "but I'll be back on the twenty-eighth. For now, we have a land claim to save."

They left for Olympia at eight the next morning. John had stayed at the livery stable with the oxen, and Nora and Simon had stayed with Maddie and Michael, each taking one of Maddie's siblings' beds while Ciara and Aiden camped under the dining table. Maddie had made them all a hearty breakfast and sent Simon and Nora off with cinnamon rolls wrapped in paper for later.

"So my father thought of me, after all," Nora mused aloud to Simon as they stood at the rail of the lumber schooner. On either side, the mountains rose beyond the blue-gray waters and the clouds crowded close. "He provided for me even if he put Charles in charge. I can't believe Charles lied to me all those years."

"I can," Simon said darkly.

Nora rubbed a hand along his arm. "It doesn't matter now. Mr. Pomantier will make the arrangements. And when I have my fortune, I am buying Thomas Rankin new clothes and picking out the perfect material to make you and your brothers new suits."

"Of course you will," Simon said. "You always think of others. Have you nothing you want for yourself?"

With him beside her, her wants were few. She grinned at him. "A sewing machine. And a new hat, something in purple, I think, with roses. Meredith can wear that awful black one."

She laughed as he shook his head with a smile.

"All we have to do now is convince the registrar we deserve those acres," she reminded him.

Simon wrapped his arms about her. "That doesn't matter either. I meant what I said last night, Nora. I love you. With you beside me, I know we will succeed."

"Whatever happened to my cynical husband?" Nora marveled. "The one who saw problems everywhere?"

"He realized what was truly important," he said, resting his head against hers. "And what was worth the risk."

So had she. Nora did not leave his embrace until they docked at the capital.

The registrar eyed them when Simon stated the reason they had come. Then he pushed his hair out of his eyes and pulled out his record book.

"We had a formal complaint lodged by a Charles Underhill," he told them. "He said you had fabricated a marriage for the purposes of filing a land claim."

"Charles Underhill is my brother," Nora explained. "He was perpetrating his own fraud, and he needed it on record that I had never married. He is the one lying." She handed the registrar the marriage certificate that Simon had brought with him from Wallin Landing. "As you can see, Simon and I are legally wed."

The registrar scanned the certificate, then glanced up. "There's married, and there's married." He looked to Simon. "Mr. Wallin, did you marry this woman for the sole purpose of claiming land in her name?"

Nora looked to Simon as well. His head was high, his eyes were narrowed and the clerk could have cut himself on those sharp cheekbones.

"Yes," Simon said. "I did."

Oh, no! She should have known Simon wouldn't lie, and she wouldn't have asked him to do so. But as the clerk stiffened, Simon went down on one knee and took Nora's hands in his. Those jade eyes gazed solemnly up at her. "But I would marry her now if she could offer me nothing but her smile."

"Oh, Simon." Nora bent to press her lips to his. In his

kiss was all the surety, all the hope and all the love she could have dreamed.

Behind her came a thump. Startled, she looked up to see that the clerk had slammed shut his record book.

"Case closed," he said. "Go home and enjoy your land. And happy New Year to you both."

"Happy New Year," Nora answered as Simon rose, seized her hand and pulled her out of the narrow office.

Nora hugged him close. "We did it! You won!"

"*We* won," Simon assured her. "And I'm going to keep my promise to you, Nora. I'll be the best husband you could want."

Nora pulled back to smile up at him. "You already are."

"I haven't been," he argued. "I admit there were times I wasn't sure what you were doing. But you saw what was true and right, and I'll do my best to believe you in the future. You and your talking dog."

Nora brightened. "Fleet talked to you? What did he say?"

Simon drew her close once more. "He said the most important word I'll ever hear. He said *Nora*."

She giggled. "Oh, I hope he says it again in my hearing."

"I'm sure he will," Simon said. "And as soon as the land is cleared, I'm going to build you that house I promised, Nora, with your own sewing room and a view of the lake and mountain."

Perhaps it was the fact that she knew Simon loved her. Perhaps it was her triumph over her brother at last. But Nora asked the second bravest, boldest question a lady could utter.

"Could it have more than one bedroom?"

Simon's smile dimmed. "Certainly, if that's what you want. But I was hoping we could have a true marriage, Nora, sharing everything."

Nora blushed. "Oh, I was hoping that as well. I just want extra rooms for our friends and family. And children."

"Children." He looked stunned a moment, then he smiled so brightly Nora was certain she could hear his violin playing. "You have a bargain, Nora. As many rooms as you want. For the first time in my life, I can't wait to be part of a family."

* * * * *

Don't miss these other FRONTIER BACHELORS
stories from Regina Scott:

THE BRIDE SHIP
WOULD-BE WILDERNESS WIFE
FRONTIER ENGAGEMENT
INSTANT FRONTIER FAMILY

Find more great reads at www.LoveInspired.com

Dear Reader,

Thank you for choosing Simon and Nora's story. I hope their Christmas love reminds you of special times.

Every family has its own customs for the season. One of ours is maple sugar candy. My father was raised in a little town on the border between New York and Vermont, and even when times were tough his parents tried to purchase some of the sweet treats for their ten children. I carry the tradition on in my own family, putting a box of maple leaves under the tree in my father's memory.

If you'd like to learn more about how Christmas was celebrated in the nineteenth century, visit my website at www.reginascott.com, where you can also sign up for a free email alert to hear when my next book is out.

May all your Christmases be merry and bright!

Regina Scott

COMING NEXT MONTH FROM
Love Inspired® Historical
Available December 6, 2016

PONY EXPRESS CHRISTMAS BRIDE
Saddles and Spurs • by Rhonda Gibson

Finding a husband is the only way Josephine Dooly can protect herself against her scheming uncle, so she answers a mail-order-bride ad. But when she arrives and discovers her groom-to-be didn't place the ad himself, can she convince Thomas Young to marry her in name only?

COWGIRL UNDER THE MISTLETOE
Four Stones Ranch • by Louise M. Gouge

Preacher Micah Thomas is set on finding himself a "ladylike" wife. But as he works to catch a group of outlaws with Deputy Sheriff Grace Eberly—a woman who can outshoot and outride every man in town—he can't help but fall for her.

A FAMILY ARRANGEMENT
Little Falls Legacy • by Gabrielle Meyer

Widower Abram Cooper has ten months to build a vibrant town in the wilds of Minnesota Territory—or his sister-in-law, Charlotte Lee, will take his three motherless boys back to Iowa to raise. Can they possibly build a family by her deadline, as well?

WED ON THE WAGON TRAIN
by Tracy Blalock

Matilda Prescott disguises herself as a boy so that she and her sister can join the wagon train to Oregon. But when her secret is revealed, she must temporarily marry Josiah Dawson to save her reputation.

LIHCNM1116

REQUEST YOUR FREE BOOKS!

2 FREE INSPIRATIONAL NOVELS
PLUS 2 *FREE* MYSTERY GIFTS

Love Inspired HISTORICAL

SPECIAL EXCERPT FROM

Love Inspired **HISTORICAL**

*Finding a husband is the only way Josephine Dooly
can protect herself against her scheming uncle,
so she answers a mail-order-bride ad.
But when she arrives and discovers her groom-to-be
didn't place the ad himself, can she convince
Thomas Young to marry her in name only?*

Read on for a sneak preview of
PONY EXPRESS CHRISTMAS BRIDE
*by Rhonda Gibson, available December 2016
from Love Inspired Historical!*

"You have spunk, Josephine Dooly. I've never heard of a woman riding the Pony Express. And now here I find you outside when you know it could be dangerous."

Josephine turned her gaze back on him. Had she misheard him a few moments ago? The warmth in his laugh drew her like a kitten to fresh milk. Was she so used to her uncle treating her like a child that she expected Thomas to treat her the same way? She searched his face. "You aren't angry with me."

"No, I'm not. I am concerned that you take risks but I am not your keeper. You can come and go as you wish." He pushed away from the well. "I came by to tell you that tomorrow we'll go into town and get married, if you still wish to do so."

Josephine exhaled. "I do."

He nodded. "Can I walk you back inside?"

A longing to stay out in the fresh air battled with wanting to please him and go inside. The cold air nipped at her cheeks, helping her to make the decision. Josephine nodded and led the short distance back to the house.

His boots crunched through the snow as he followed her to the kitchen door. She stepped up on the porch but then turned to face him. He deserved an apology. "I'm sorry. I should have done as you asked and stayed inside."

He reached up and brushed a wayward curl from her face. "I understand your need to come outside. I'm not sure I could stay inside for three whole days, either."

The light touch of his fingers against her cheek surprised Josephine. Her gaze met his. She felt the urge to lean her face into his warm palm. He smiled and pulled his hand away. "I best be heading back to the house. I'll see you tomorrow."

As he turned to leave Josephine called out, "Thomas."

He stopped and searched her face.

"I'm glad you are home." She smiled as her mind went blank. She could think of no more words to retain him.

His lips twitched into a grin. "Good night, Josephine." And he walked into the shadows.

She stepped into the kitchen but turned to watch Thomas climb onto his horse and head into the darkness that now enveloped the world. It seemed she was forever watching him leave.

Tomorrow they'd be married. Would they be compatible? Or would he soon tire of her and want to go on with his life, without her? She didn't know why, but the last thought troubled her.

Don't miss
PONY EXPRESS CHRISTMAS BRIDE
by Rhonda Gibson, available December 2016 wherever
Love Inspired® Historical books and ebooks are sold.

www.LoveInspired.com

Turn your love of reading into rewards you'll love with

Harlequin My Rewards

**Join for FREE today at
www.HarlequinMyRewards.com**

Earn **FREE BOOKS** of your choice.

Experience **EXCLUSIVE OFFERS** and contests.

Enjoy **BOOK RECOMMENDATIONS**
selected just for you.

PLUS! Sign up now
and get **500** points
right away!

Earn **FREE REWARDS** Join Today! HarlequinMyRewards.com

MYR16R